The Unlikely Adventures of Alex and Nan

To order additional copies of this book, contact:
Xlibris
1-888-795-4274
www.Xlibris.com
Orders@Xlibris.com
797973

ALSO BY MARTHA HORTON

Faun

An Older Eye:
Poems and Commentary

ALSO BY ALAN DE WOLFE

Rugs

Gems

South of Manila

Attack of the Koto Maru

The Unlikely Adventures of Alex and Nan

Adventure One: Reappearing Persons

Horton-De Wolfe

1

DAMN THAT MAN!
Nan didn't know whether she'd said it aloud or just thought it.

Alex Rayburn had just passed by her without the slightest acknowledgment and jostled her hand - the one holding a glass of wine. A few drops of Bully Hill red sloshed over the rim and landed on her saffron silk dress. The dress was not new, but one of her best and very elegant with the opera-length strand of pearls.

It wasn't as if they were strangers. They had been introduced at least three times over the past year, and although Alex had nodded and said, "Ms. Holloway, a pleasure," she could tell he wasn't experiencing anything really pleasurable.

She had noticed his arrival this evening at Hill House, the Huffton's family mansion. It was annual symphony fund-raiser and all of local society was there. Of course, Alex was in attendance, very much the silver fox in a dark suit and dove gray tie. He was escorting Dorothy Vandencamp, a lively widow in her eighties and a symphony board member. He had deposited Dorothy with her peers at the punchbowl and began working the room (as did

Nan herself), and she had seen him stop cold and peer intently at something or someone over her shoulder –perhaps one of the lovely young violinists or the tall, hunky trombone player? Then he had set out in purposeful pursuit.

Thoroughly annoyed at being both ignored and practically run down, she speculated aloud to her companion, "Is Alex Rayburn gay?" She dabbed at her dress with a cocktail napkin.

"I wish!" replied Stephen Smithfield, who definitely *was*, rolling his eyes heavenward. Stephen was a big, good-looking guy, a successful realtor, patron of the arts, and a fellow opera buff. Nan and he had teamed up for a number of cultural events, but she really couldn't call it dating. She hadn't dated since turning sixty-five, seven years ago. Good Lord!

Alex Rayburn was one of the few unattached men in her general age range. She had encountered him at several events where he had squired a beautiful young redhead who clung to his arm and laughed up at him with delight. It turned out she was his niece - grand-niece, rather. Then there had been a woman about his own age, quietly stunning, the wife of an out-of-town friend. And a variety of attractive male companions of varying ages.

Not that she cared. Nan was making peace with no longer being a star, no longer having admiring glances cast her way when she entered a room, or seeing people's eyes light up when she spoke with them.

After earning her master's degree in communications from Columbia, and a few on-air moments with network TV, she was looking forward to a brilliant career. She began receiving better and better assignments, including some overseas. Her work was noticed and rewarded, and she became a regular correspondent with a cable news network. The brilliant career was launched! And to add to the bonanza, love walked in - real love - and she married Tom, who was making a name for himself on Wall Street. There was talk of giving Nan her own show when, as fickle fate would have it, she got pregnant. Tom surprised her and said that he wanted to return Upstate to the family law practice and "raise the kid in a better environment." She had gone along with that, albeit somewhat grudgingly.

A year after Tom, Junior's birth, Nan went back to work, quickly landing an anchor position on a local station. She loved it. She could use all her skills in reporting and presenting a story, human interest and hard news alike, and still maintain a normal home life. She even did some serious investigative reporting. As both a television personality and the wife of a prominent investment attorney, Nan became a big fish in a small pond.

Then Tom, Junior went off to Dartmouth to study microbiology and Tom, Senior went off to California with a young beauty fresh out of law school – to hell with his now middle-aged wife. Nan survived, carried on with her head held high, and continued to enjoy her status as a semi-celebrity for another decade. Life was reasonably good until the station was sold and the new owner decided to clean house, replacing old hands like Nan with younger talent.

Again Nan pulled herself together. She invited a good friend to lunch, Gina DeVito, who had recently been laid off by the shrinking local newspaper. The pair decided to set up their own PR firm and managed to sign a number of good clients. But as time passed, it became obvious that the firm wasn't going to pay off well enough to support two people. The partner dropped out when she got an opportunity to run a Pennsylvania weekly.

Nan persevered, but public relations, like journalism, was becoming an online enterprise – not her area of expertise. She still had good contacts, and occasionally ran special events for some businesses and non-profits, but now found herself doing mostly *pro bono* work. Which was why she was wearing a not-so-new dress to the symphony gala. It was eight years old, but she knew she looked good in it, even if no one noticed. She still looked good, period. Her thick, glossy dark hair had only a dusting of gray, but there was a platinum streak on one side of her forehead. The best hair stylist in the area had cut her hair to accentuate the streak, and it had become her trademark. There were not too many wrinkles around her eyes; she had a long, straight nose and high cheekbones that the camera had loved. Her mouth was rather wide, with deep laugh lines, but she still had full lips sans the benefit of collagen injections, which was more than a lot of women her age could say. And she'd be damned if she'd ever "have some work done."

So here she was, well-preserved with nerve endings intact, attending a party with a gay guy while another guy bumped into her and spilled her drink without even looking at her. Nan was approaching high dudgeon when she saw Alex resume his escort duty at the side of Dorothy Vandencamp and engage in some banter with her and her friends.

She approached the group and addressed Alex.

"Excuse me, Mister Rayburn. I'm Nan Holloway, in case you've forgotten."

He looked at her with a neutral expression.

"I know who you are."

"Well you just bolted past me and made me spill a drink on my dress."

Alex looked her up and down as if searching for wet spots.

"I wasn't aware," he said evenly. "Just send me the cleaning bill." And he turned back to the group.

Not even an apology! The arrogance of that man! There was nothing Nan could think to say that wouldn't involve a total loss of dignity so she stalked away. Where was Stephen? She was more than ready to leave.

As she scanned the room, her eyes met those of a man she hadn't encountered before at the party, but who seemed vaguely familiar. There was something about his posture, a bit stooped, but he looked to be only 40 or 50. This happened frequently to Nan. She had interviewed a lot of people over the years and couldn't recall all of them, but this man was disturbing in some half-remembered way.

After his eyes met hers, he quickly lowered his head, and his hang-dog posture again seemed familiar. Perhaps he didn't want to be recognized, perhaps he had secrets to hide, just like - no, it couldn't be *him*. This man was well-dressed, well-groomed, with a nearly-trimmed mustache and beard. And he was here, at this elegant function. The man in her memory was supposed to be in prison for murdering his wife.

In a flash, Nan forgot Alex Rayburn, the party, and her spoiled dress. She smelled a story!

2

DAYBREAK SPLASHED THROUGH French windows, washed across a hobnail carpet, and swirled into the eyes of detective *cum laude* Alex Rayburn. "Oh, God," was all he could muster, eschewing the early hour of day.

Morning had always been disagreeable to this bachelor detective now squirming and turning under his covers. Sleep usually presented a way for him to stop the usual velocity of his life and take some time to decompress. His last well-paying case involved the rapid pursuit of the ugly facts of divorce, and had taken a serious bite out of his quality time. Still, he readily admitted, he enjoyed sometimes doing with warped pleasure what others thought invasive and despicable. When two people are as rotten to each other as they can conjure up, how would divorce proceedings be possible without those special facts no one wants to have brought to light?

Of course the truth is necessary, he told himself time and again, if for no other reason than to maintain his personal integrity. Along with his occasional cynicism, Alex kept an optimistic attitude about life. He had witnessed some dreadful circumstances but refuses to be encumbered by them.

Now, as he lay illuminated in the glorious sunshine of morning, the great detective pulled more of the paisley bedspread around his head. Too early. The memories of last evening's party shuffled through moving clouds of consciousness in his head. Amy Huffton had been on his mind lately, and she had been there last night in full splendor. Blonds weren't usually his choice, but this one was a raving beauty, all stops pulled out. The luster of her skin could almost be felt easing along his eyeballs as he examined one of the finest creatures he'd yet seen on Planet Earth. Her gracious demeanor would have even the worst misogynist eating out of her hand. What a pleasure to include her in his mind's Hall of Fame.

With some effort, he made his way to the shower, reviewing last night's embarrassing episode among those he'd always referred to "polite company." He hoped the remarkable Amy had not noticed his drinking so much. Gad, I made a fool of myself.

He had agreed to escort Dorothy Vandencamp, an old family friend, to this fund-raiser for the symphony. There were laughs constantly. Dorothy was a sassy woman. It was hard to believe her energy at her very senior age. He'd always liked her. Still does. She had been responsible for getting a symphony orchestra formed for an area not really big enough to support one. When he had become a bit unsteady on his feet last night, Dorothy had giggled and played at holding him up. But she had wisely opted to take a taxi home

Many gatherings, soirees, parties and cocktail hours had passed under the bridge since Alex had sloshed in the spirits to such great depths. While P.I.s are known for drinking oceans of the stuff, Alex had his good family name to consider. During his stint on the Buffalo police force, the evils of booze had become apparent. Besides, drinking is prerequisite to disaster when people are pursuing you.

Alex had driven the Lamborghini Miura, one of his favorite cars, to the event last night, but it had proven an unwise choice as the constant jostling of the sporty car caused him to feel queasy on the return trip. But in the chill of the night, with the windows down and slumber a short mile away, all was well. He drove down Market Street in the merchandising area of the city to his top-floor apartment. No matter where he went, a city's downtown, even in a small city, was always his favorite scene.

Life had been good to Alex Rayburn. All the money he needed, respect in the community, a history of working internationally. All were irreplaceable, in his estimation. His favorite writer, Mark Twain, alluded to the benefits of constant travel when he said that "travel is the doom of prejudice and bias." Once one has lived among the native people of any country, one's perspective dwells on a more understanding plateau. Alex spent much time in Europe among family friends, and had worked in the Middle East for two years.

Alex figures he's been near every personal disaster one could imagine, encountering cutthroats, con men and women of dubious intent. Such were his days of "living for experience." Now, he finds his hometown situation in this pleasant berg, located among the bucolic hills of New York State's Southern Tier, nearly ideal. For all places and all societies have a need for a good detective once in a while who can mitigate difficult times ahead for an unsuspecting person or vulnerable company. Opportunities here may be a little harder to find for a P.I., but in the end they're just as invigorating as in any big city.

Before last night's event was over, he had tried to get a bit closer to Amy Huffton, she of the Huffton family famous in the Chemung Valley for starting up several glass factory locations, including a science lab on their own private hill and another near the community college. In the early 1800s, a Brooklyn company had been encouraged to move to this expansive area hugging the lower New York State border mainly to avail itself of the good rail service existing in the vicinity. The founding fathers of the town were influential in the company's progress and vice versa. In the marriage between the company and the city, much prosperity ensued from 1850 to the present day, and the company had recently changed the last part of its name from "Glass Works" to "Incorporated." Alex's parents did well in this town, and the family money had risen accordingly with the recent fortunes of the glass company. Related smaller companies were doing well too, with his own stocks splitting occasionally. The glass company had sprouted new wings in the space exploration part of the Twentieth Century, fashioning windows for U.S. space vehicles and exploiting other proprietary patents. The prosperity continues to this day in the Twenty-First Century, and nobody's complaining.

Amy Huffton was a third-generation aristocrat, yet sweet and cordial, and she was Alex's current person of interest. Whenever he felt romantic, his life would suddenly jump from person to person, a trait he abhorred in himself, yet allowed. He half-heartedly anticipated that he would find himself someday. Meanwhile, let 'em guess. He thought it amusing to let people wonder about his sexuality. Gay, no. Straight, no. Bisexual, no. He tried to make it all fun.

He absentmindedly glanced from the steamed-up window in his marble shower room and scanned the world below. He enjoyed showering and watching events happen in the valley from one of the "eyebrow" windows of the upper floor. He often hummed the short verses of *Plaisir d'Amore*, a favorite French tune, and luxuriated in the cool, calcified water coming from the city pipes.

The Chemung River rolled steadily along in a straight line separating the sleepier north side of the city from the more commercial south side. The glass museum shone brightly as a sculpted glass jewel just on the other side of the river not far from the fire department. The fire company was a modern triangular structure with five angled doors and a helipad outside for emergency helicopter landings. It was used regularly by the State Police and the health care system, located at the medical building across the street from the glass museum. He often spotted the choppers coming in and leaving with some poor soul destined for some major hospital in some distant city.

Construction was always going on in a city growing more modern by the year. He noticed the glass museum project just now being completed on the roof. It was a spacious area and under strict secrecy until completion. It had a "strong" look with beams recently cut into the lower floors. Looks like they're going to put something special up there, he mused as he rinsed off. He wondered what the Hufftons have in mind for that little spot. A number of scenarios for its use went through his mind in the steam of the shower, after which his thoughts turned to Nan Holloway.

Nan seemed to be at every gathering he attended these days. His knowledge of her was spotty and she didn't hold his interest. Wasn't she on TV a while back? Didn't she work for a promotional outfit? Is that white streak in her hair real? Alex thought her husband had passed away recently, or perhaps they were divorced. There was something about her...she was intelligent, witty and desirable, and quite handsome at her age - about his age, he thought. Naturally, she would be at the symphony event. Wouldn't you know I *had* to cause a spill on her dress! At the gala, he had dismissed her quickly with some idle acknowledgment because Amy was summoning him and he had to talk with her. His thoughts ran on: I could swear Nan said something angry under her breath. Maybe I'll apologize if I run into her again. Maybe I won't.

At the party, Amy's conversation with Alex had begun simply, with the usual assertions of confidence she possessed in her family's glass company. She was well aware of the company's propensity for constantly turning out eye-popping products which amazed their clients and likewise, the federal government. The business was known for turning one-half of its yearly profits back into the company for research and development, and it was this business dynamic that kept them front and center among the tech companies. Most of the glass geniuses in the world had found their way to this "glass capital," enjoying the high salaries and the accompanying small-town ambiance among the verdant hills of Upstate New York. More experts seemed to come to the company every day. This made for a business preeminent in the fine, clear product produced here under steaming chimneys and bright black office buildings. It was apparent that if a company officer in an aerospace company had a design problem and he thought glass or ceramics might solve it, that knowing executive would go straight to the southern border of New York State and talk to glass people who were unavailable anywhere else in the world.

Then the talk became more personal.

"So Alex, how's business?" she opened.

"You mean the detective business?"

"Yes," Amy smiled. "This hobby seems to be your current favorite."

"I just try to do people some good."

"You don't exactly need the money," Amy noted.

"Yes, you're right. The family fortune is still intact. But everyone needs something to do."

Alex thought for a moment. Was this going to be a snooping job? What possible need could this wealthy woman and personal friend have for his services? Did she even want them?

Amy seemed a bit uneasy as she walked to the draped window. The multicolored books on the shelves refracted the light from several floor lamps into hues of dusty atmosphere from eye-level to the seventeen feet it took to reach the ceiling. Alex pondered Amy's family and was amazed anew at what a man could do with taste *and* money. The old man had favored the richness of teak and walnut when this room, the library, had been conceived, yea those many years ago. Alanson J. Huffton still observed his domain from a giant portrait on the wall above the mantel, with subsequent generations in abundance framed below him. The subject of the latest portrait was Amy herself, far more beautiful than the family pictures now hoary with age.

"Quite a family history here," Alex remarked.

"Yes, the company has been blessed with success ... with family endeavors meant to keep it viable. We've been fortunate. It's nice that our granddads knew each other."

Alex added, "The early family members made us what we are today." He paused, "Which brings us to tonight. I'm wondering. Is there something on your mind?"

"Yes, there is." He could see some concern in her face. "Have you ever heard of the iridium element?"

He stroked his chin. "No. It's completely new to me. I suppose it's somewhere on the Table of Elements."

"Well, in this case it's more than just the element. The object I'm talking about has several rare earths combined in a small composite that our science guys are just getting a good handle on."

"What will they do with it?"

"Good question." Amy walked to her sideboard and unlocked a small drawer. She drew a crystal from the drawer and showed it to Alex.

"This is the composite element. It was recently fabricated by the Shlessinger Company in Frankfurt, Germany, one of our rather secretive subsidiaries, and brought here to Hans Guildermann's lab under strict security. To most citizens, the German company deals with rare earths for computer chips and other small applications. Dr. Hans Guildermann, who worked with NASA and now Homeland Security, maintains a lab in Watkins Glen. He is the genius who spawned the whole idea of using iridium as the essential element in the device, a 'gun,' if you will, that we are now working on. It has amazed our scientists here."

Alex handled the glassy item thoughtfully. "Why show me this?"

"Well, there's more to the story," Amy confided. "For years, we here in this unsuspecting valley have fooled around with technology which, if applied correctly, can build the one thing the U.S. and everybody else wants."

"Wow! Can you tell me more?"

"Yes, but in my employ, if you choose to be so, you must be extremely careful with whom you discuss this – like no one, except the person you will meet shortly, someone you may have met previously."

"You've known me forever, Amy. You don't have to ask." Alex wondered to whom she referred.

"Good. That's what I wanted to hear."

Alex had no trouble staying interested in anything Amy had to say. She had a way of commanding the room wherever she went.

"As I said, our guys have devised a machine for the government which, by including this element will … well, perhaps we should sit down."

Alex was hardly able to contain his enthusiasm. Sit down? What in the world is Amy talking about? She certainly thinks a lot of this product.

"We believe that we have discovered the technology that will shoot a laser beam to the constellation of Arcturus and well beyond."

Alex was confused. "Well, that's quite a feat, but don't we already do this?"

"Shooting laser beams into space is just a ruse," Amy continued. "This gun has more value than that. This weapon will incinerate any satellites launched into near orbit and, more importantly, incoming missiles from any country."

The great detective's jaw went slack.

"What? Is …"

"Is this a reality?" she interrupted.

"Well, I ..."

"No. Not yet. But it's what we call a 'proven theory' in that it will definitely work once this little item is tested tomorrow. It will be done at our facility on Spider Hill, and we don't need an orbiting satellite on which to try it – just that big orb in the night sky. Our guys will literally shoot the moon tomorrow evening as our viewing crew looks on from the telescope at the community college. Handy, that telescope."

"And so....?"

"So, the beam will be aimed in the middle of the Sea of Tranquility as the moon reveals itself. It's supposed to be a clear night up on the hill."

"Wow!"

"Once the iridium crystal is inserted in the forward generator of the weapon and fired, it will make a distinguishable mark approximately one mile wide on the moon's surface. Not much – but it will be made visible by capturing light from reflectors which were placed on the moon by astronauts during various moon landings.

"This is all the testing we need to do to present it to the government. They will take it from there, adding their tracking mechanisms to make it a true defense system replacing that weak attempt at the 'Star Wars' program the government abandoned in the nineties. This will practically assure world peace, for if any country cares to attack us, well, their missiles will be history. It is absolute power for whomever owns the weapon, and better us than them."

"Wow again! I'm wondering what my part may be in all this."

"There seems to be a problem already. You see, Dr. Guildermann's lab was broken into a few days ago and some key papers may have been compromised. I'm officially hiring you to investigate the importance of this happening. Somebody knows we're working on *something*. We're aware that a thing like this is impossible to hush up completely, especially if there's been an attempted theft like the one at Guildermann's. Once this thing is perfected, everyone will want it; security will be tighter than the skin on a snare drum. After our test, security will be the problem of the NSA. Just now, it's our concern - we're the ones developing it."

Alex slumped in the chair. Amy waited patiently for his reaction.

After her almost surreal scenario sunk in, he declared, "I am definitely on board!"

"One more thing. I found a person who will work with you regarding the necessary documentation for the government. We are still a business and we must observe the rigors of the proper paperwork required by various people who have a 'need to know.'

This person is a very good chronicler and might accompany you wherever your investigations take you."

"I always work alone," Alex stated flatly.

"Not anymore."

3

NAN WASTED NO time when she got home from the symphony fund-raiser. She immediately slipped out of her party clothes, wrapped herself in a terrycloth robe and got busy on the computer.

Somewhere, buried in the files, were notes from her interview with Lester Nichols. Ten minutes later she had them, and the memory of that brief encounter at the county jail came jolting back. The local hoosegow wasn't one of those monstrous cathedrals of cages one saw in the old James Cagney movies, but it still held an ominous air of desolation. Certainly Lester, his straggly reddish hair hanging down over his forehead, had appeared desolate. His skin was pale, his hands slightly quivering, his voice lacking in both inflection and resonance. She had felt an immediate distaste for this individual, but told herself to reserve judgment.

Nan introduced herself and asked if she could record their conversation. Nichols nodded listlessly.

"I didn't do anything to my wife," he began, with a beseeching look - the only time he looked up at her from his crouched position, forearms resting on the table between them. "I wouldn't hurt Norma. I loved her. She simply disappeared one day ..." His voice broke and he stifled a sob.

Nan was unimpressed. "So what is your explanation for her disappearance?"

"I just don't know. I tried to find her, to trace her movements that day, but it was hopeless."

"You waited three days before contacting the police. Why?"

Nichols squirmed in his hard chair. "Well, it was embarrassing, you know? A man's wife apparently walks out on him … and I thought she might come back."

"Had she done that before - just leave without an explanation?"

"No, never."

"Did she have any reason to leave you that day?"

"I don't know. I've asked myself that question again and again," he replied shakily, already showing signs of becoming weary of her questioning.

"Well, the police found something. They found dried blood on the kitchen floor - hers."

"How many times do I have to go through this?" Lester complained. "Maybe she cut herself."

Before Nan could bring up the other bits of evidence the police had uncovered, Lester pushed his chair back abruptly and stood.

"I'm so tired of questions. Why don't the cops find Norma instead of locking me up here? This nightmare needs to end." Then, more assertively than she'd heard him speak before, "Guard! We're finished here!"

So there was not much to go on, except that Nan was now certain that the man she had glimpsed at the symphony gala an hour or so ago was Lester Nichols. She believed he had recognized her, as well.

She tried to remember the disposition of the case. It had come to trial; there was a hung jury. Then an appeal for a change of venue and another trial. Again, no verdict. The public and the media –certainly her station, WLED-TV – had lost interest as the case dragged on. How had it been resolved?

Nan recalled that her former partner, Gina DeVito, had covered the story for the local newspaper and doubtless had more in-depth information about it. She would call Gina. But not at this late hour.

Nan yawned, stretched and bent to pick up the clothing she had carelessly shed earlier. Yes, the saffron silk displayed an interesting array of pink splotches. She would take it to the cleaner tomorrow, and yes, she would send Mr. Alex Rayburn the bill. He could afford it.

Next morning, while said Mr. Rayburn was rolling over for a second snooze, Nan was up and on the phone to Gina. Gina recalled the Mysterious Missing Wife case in much greater detail than Nan did.

"Lester was a pharmacist with a somewhat shady reputation. Norma worked as an assistant manager at a gift shop. Modest house, no kids. Likeable, but no close friends. Norma was very pretty, I recall. Lester appeared to be a sort of a nerd. I can't really imagine him killing her. There was circumstantial evidence but no clear motive."

"Well, I just didn't like him, or believe him. He certainly seemed to be hiding something," Nan speculated. "Was he ever convicted?"

"No," Gina replied. "After that second trial, he was released and just disappeared, like his wife. I can't imagine why he would return to the scene of the crime now – if there even was a crime. Are you sure it was him you saw at the fund-raiser, Nan? It's been almost five years."

"I'm 90 per cent sure. He's smartened up his appearance a lot, added some facial hair, but he still gives me the creeps. I wonder if I'll run into him again."

"Are you really that interested?" Gina asked. "Why?"

"Well, of course I'm interested! It's an unsolved mystery, isn't it?"

"Okay, okay. I have one idea for you to follow up on," Gina offered. "Lester had hired a detective to find Norma when the police were unsuccessful, name of Alex Rayburn. Ever heard of him?"

"Damn! Yes, I know him," Nan replied. "And I don't like him much more than I like Lester Nichols."

Gina snorted. "You always were tough on guys. Look, I'll email you a copy of my last story on the case – it includes Lester's photo, and also one of the missing wife."

Nan thanked her friend for the information and promised to get together soon for lunch. Then she brewed a cup of coffee and considered how she was going to get Alex to talk with her about the case. Presenting him with a dry cleaning bill didn't sound like a very promising approach.

Checking her calendar, Nan saw that she had a two o'clock appointment with Amy Huffton at the glass museum. She liked Amy and had previously worked with her on several special events. Amy was young, beautiful and a member of the town's leading family, but she was by no means a spoiled little rich girl. With a master's degree in art history from Stanford, she was now a vice president of the company itself, in charge of practically everything. She also held the position of director at the family's prestigious glass museum, which was a favorite project of hers and a tax write-off for the Huffton Company. Amy had asked Nan to meet this afternoon and brainstorm a gala opening reception for a new collection to be displayed at the museum. "Pro bono, most likely," mused Nan, but Amy was an important contact, and a good person besides.

Nan had noticed Amy and Alex Rayburn in close conversation last night at the fund-raiser before Alex had downed too many martinis and lost focus. In fact, Amy had spirited him off to another room. What was up there? Amy was not one for a mere dalliance, and she certainly wouldn't be conducting it in the family manse. Curious!

Amy and Alex and their families had always been close. Perhaps Nan could explain to Amy that she needed to confer with Alex about a story, but had gotten off on the wrong foot with him. Maybe Amy could smooth the waters and ask Alex to give Nan a hearing.

Gina had asked Nan why she was so interested in Lester Nichols. It was a good question, and now Nan asked it herself. She had responded to seeing Nichols like a punch-drunk prize fighter to the bell. Why? If Lester Nichols were back in the area, it could make a good story, but Nan was no longer the hot-shot journalist of her early days with the network. What would she do with a story if she got it? Beg the local rag to run it? Crawl back to WLED with it? Still, her instincts, so carefully honed over decades spent delivering the news, had never deserted her. Something was up for sure, and she wanted answers. Maybe she could write a book. Or it might make a good reality crime series on television.

She would bite the bullet, ask Amy for help in getting Alex Rayburn to tell her what he knew, and just eat the dry cleaning bill.

4

AMY'S OFFICE IN the dramatic headquarters building of the Huffton Glass Company was not extravagant but, with strategic lighting and a subdued color palette, it served as an elegant showcase for some of the company's famous art glass pieces – and for Amy herself, Nan noted. The impeccably groomed blond sat at a semi-circular teak table. Her desk, lacking the usual office clutter, held a clear glass vase (vintage Huffton, no doubt) with a profusion of out-of-season tulips, a leather-bound portfolio, a decorative pen stand and a discrete communications console.

Amy rose to greet Nan, and gestured to a plush seating area in one corner of the spacious room.

"Thanks so much for coming, Nan. I believe you know Alex Rayburn?"

A tall figure slowly uncoiled itself from the depths of a soft leather sofa and turned toward her. Indeed it was Alex, with a distinctly uncomfortable look on his handsome face. He merely nodded, while Nan, thoroughly nonplussed, managed to croak, "We've met."

"So I understand," Amy said with the hint of mischief in her smile. "Have a seat, Nan."

Nan seated herself in the chair farthest from Alex and awaited enlightenment. What in the name of heaven was *he* doing here?

"I'll cut to the chase," said Amy, and eased herself onto the arm of the sofa where Alex sat. "I've asked Alex to act for the company on a very confidential assignment, and I want you to work with him, Nan."

Nan took a few seconds to assimilate this startling proposition. "But...I thought you asked me here to help plan a reception..."

"That is what I had in mind when I made our appointment, but now, this project with Alex is of prime importance – and it's not another volunteer thing. You'll be receiving significant remuneration."

Nan brightened at that last comment, but was still mystified. "What sort of project?" she asked.

"I'm going to ask Alex to fill you in on it while I run off to a board meeting," Amy said. "I wanted you to meet here to discuss it because my office is soundproof." She picked up her portfolio and breezed out the door in a cloud of Arpege.

"Pour Nan a drink," she called over her shoulder.

Alex took a few steps to an antique cabinet and opened it to reveal a choice selection of wines and spirits. "What is your preference, Ms. Holloway?" he asked, and then, with a disarmingly boyish grin, added "I promise not to spill it on you."

Self-deprecating humor? From Alex Rayburn? Just a tad too charming to be convincing.

The man is trouble, Nan thought. Surely he was no more pleased with this strange partnership than she was.

"Any Finger Lakes white, if you please," she said.

In a moment she accepted the glass with both hands. "I don't know what your confidential assignment is, or why we have to be ensconced in a soundproof room to talk about it, but understand this: I haven't agreed to anything and I won't until you explain it all to me."

Alex proceeded to fill her in on much of what Amy had told him. "And she wants you to sort of take notes and do the paperwork, fill in forms and such."

Nan sent him an evil look. "She could get a good secretary to do that. Why pick on me?"

"Well, she thinks you have the background to be a keen observer, and good judgment in sorting out important facts from the inconsequential."

"She's right, but what do you think?"

"I certainly agree, but I prefer to work alone. No reflection on you, of course."

"Of course. But you let Amy talk you into including me."

"I suppose I did, but I made it very clear to her, that for your safety, I'm in charge."

"Of course," Nan said again, fuming. "Suppose I don't agree to sign on?"

"You will." Alex relaxed into the sofa and regarded her with a steady gaze. "Unless you would rather fuss around with fancy hors d'oeuves and frilly decorations than get the inside track on a good story."

Damn him! "But it's all top secret, right? Where's the story?"

"You'll find an angle to use. And besides, it pays well."

Nan didn't want another minute of Alex Rayburn, but the job was intriguing, as well as the prospect of enjoying a boost to her bank account. "Well, I don't want to let Amy down …"

"Right!" Alex stood and reached for her glass of untouched wine. "I guess we're done here, then."

Nan was not about to let him dismiss her like that. She handed him the glass, carefully letting it tip just enough to spill a few drops on his trousers. "Oops! Sorry!"

Alex took hold of her wrist. "Look here, Holloway. We're going to have to get past this petty spilled drink feud or we'll both end up saturated with booze."

"Make it champagne – that could be fun."

Alex's jaw dropped. He relaxed his grip.

"Finally got your attention, did I?" said Nan, eyes flashing. "My turn. If we're going to work together you'll have to stop being an arrogant ass and treat me like a colleague."

Alex scowled, then laughed and raised his hands in mock surrender. "Okay, okay. Take it easy! It's me and you, Nancy Lou."

Nancy Lou! "Don't call me that!" she sputtered. How did he know? Of course - he must have googled her. He was a detective, after all. Nan had been happy to abandon her maiden name, Nancy Louise Zerwig, when she married Thomas Eugene Holloway, II. What else did Alex know about her? Well, she hadn't been an investigative reporter for nothing. Two could google.

"Please – just call me Nan."

"All right, Nan. Anything I can do for you?"

Nan suddenly remembered that she had been eager to talk to this Alex character with whom she was soon to be halfheartedly allied.

"Alex, on another topic: I understand you did some investigating for Lester Nichols."

"Yes, I remember. I was trying to find his wife. Why the interest now?"

"Well, I'm sure I saw Nichols, just last night. At the fund-raiser at Hufftons'."

"You're certain it was Nichols? It's been a long time."

"I'm sure," Nan insisted. "And I'm wondering why he would come back here? What's he up to?"

Alex shrugged. "I can't imagine. If you see him again, try to find out how I can contact him. I'd be interested to know if the wife ever turned up."

"Wouldn't she have been declared legally dead by now? Maybe he's working some insurance scam or ...whatever. He was sort of a con man..."

"He was a bad actor.," Alex cut in. "But we have a more important matter to concern us now."

"Oh, right," Nan conceded with a pout. "Fate of the world. So what's the plan of action?"

"I hope you're not going to be flippant about it," Alex chided. "Go home and do some real thinking. That's what I'm going to do. When I devise a plan and require your assistance, I'll be in touch."

"Sir! Yes, sir!" Nan saluted smartly and stalked out.

5

FROM ALEX'S POINT of view, Nan Holloway was not the best choice for her assignment. Unfortunately, she was now joined at the hip with that smooth and suave detective currently living in his very own body. He had no choice but to accept her. Still, somewhere in his mind, he thought she might eventually fill the bill, at least for the duration of this job. "We'll see," he muttered.

Nan had alluded to a possible sighting of Lester Nichols, which caused Alex to dig back into a memory, now much dimmed by time. Nichols was one of those guys who held his cards close to his chest, and was more slippery than a wet cat. Why would he be skulking around a fund-raiser? The man was nefarious to say the least, and his loyalties were to himself only, but any evil enterprise perpetrated here would be small potatoes, wouldn't it? What could be his reason for risking being seen? Did he lie in wait to get even with some fellow criminals who had purposely put him out front to cover their tracks? Would there be a great gain with some foreign country?

Before he knew Nichols well, Alex had taken on the job of finding his wife, Norma. But he had soon decided, why look? Was she, too somehow involved in his shady activities? Did she have something on Lester? It's no wonder that his wife had left him, but what surprised Alex most was that Lester's other half had been clever enough to evade her husband. No one was astonished when Nichols' lawyers got him acquitted from the charge of murdering his wife. The evidence was mostly circumstantial and didn't hold up under scrutiny. Also, with no *corpus delicti,* the charges were doomed.

Alex is aware that Nichols, since he had disappeared from the area after his temporary incarceration, has been suspected of everything from the theft of fine art to shady land-grab deals and phone scams. The guy could do anything underhanded that a person could dream up, and even as a cheap hood, was a master of disguise. His is now a low profile existence, presumably because police everywhere are interested in his activities. He slithers around the U.S. carefully, being too well- known in countries that have extradition policies, nations that would welcome him back to a much-deserved stay in one of their iron-bar motels. Nichols comes out of nowhere and goes back to the same. Nan, even though she felt certain, could have been mistaken when she thought she spotted him at the event last night. At any rate, Nan's unusual interest in Nichols was her own can of worms. The great detective has other things to do. Nichols would be on the back burner.

Alex maintained a small office in a downtown loft just to keep unwanted attention away from his residence. Not everyone knew he was quite wealthy, and why inform them? Just a plain little second-floor space would do for investigations into graceless homicides, petty thievery, and other situations known to affect those irascible people in life who act before they think. His duty overseas with the military police had provided him with a good education in all the bad things one person could do to another.

A desk, two chairs, a worn rug, a file cabinet and a washroom were all that were necessary for his business interests. He kept his files in his computer and on paper at the Rayburn family residence, in case of an unscheduled office visitation.

As regards the laboratory break-in, he needed to get himself over to Guildermann's compound and clear up a few facts. Now that Amy needed him, he would swing into high gear and immediately aim the Lamborghini toward Watkins Glen and the lakeside lab operated by the good doctor. His garage door went up, the car roared to life and away he sped down Rt. 414 to a sweet little town with a state park right in the middle of it.

Everyone in New York State and the surrounding areas knows Watkins Glen well. It is more than just a nice town at the foot of one of New York's fabled Finger Lakes, Seneca. It was the capital of open-wheel racing for automobiles of every description and marque in the world, and had been so, for years. It was, it is, America's premier road racing circuit, second to none.

The quaint village is located at the bottom of a gorge for which the state park is named. Thousands of visitors come from every direction in summer, not only to view the racing at the top of the hill, but also to enjoy the ambiance of a sleepy, lakeside town. The usual tourist trappings are in abundance in Watkins, including boat rides, hiking trails, native memorabilia and long docks on which to stroll in the cool of a summer evening. New hotels have made it a grand destination for those who prefer lakes and greenery to mortar and asphalt.

The Glen itself boasts the magnificent gorge, carved through the raging waters of several millennia, with 200-foot cliffs and spectacular waterfalls.

Nearly a hundred wineries surround Seneca and the other Finger Lakes, beckoning the palate of all manner of wine tasters. Limousine rides to the wineries are scheduled by the hotels and visitors are glad to know they can sample as much as they can hold and not have to drive.

At this moment, a certain Italian car roared through the scenic explosion of late summer in lake country and took the road on the west side of the town. Before long, Alex could see Dr. Guildermann's lab come into view, down the hill on the fringe of the lake. He spun off the main road and descended to a side road beyond the salt drilling company. At the bend in the road a winding driveway appeared.

It was plain to see that Guildermann had a staff of lawn care experts, for no matter where Alex looked, the lawn and vegetation were kept pristine, almost overly groomed. The fences were strong and had possibly been installed by the government to protect the man inside. Evidently the government, and Amy's glass company, kept serious security here, even though some clever criminal had dared corrupt it just days before.

The house was a Mid-Century mansion-style typical of monied people who like to live on lakes. On approach to the house, the roadway expanded into a parking zone where Alex finally entered with dust whorls trailing. He walked to the entrance gate and buzzed the intercom.

In a moment, a chubby, but smaller, replica copy of Sidney Greenstreet came waddling down a set of steps and welcomed him.

"Ah, Mister Rayburn, I presume?"

"Right you are, sir. Dr. Guildermann?

"Yes. Here, I'll let you in."

It was indeed a solid gate, the best Alex had seen since the Saudis had redefined the word "security." "Quite a fence you have here," he remarked.

"Yes, a bit too much, if you ask me. I don't know if I'm worth quite this much trouble, heh, heh."

"Amy Huffton must regard you highly."

"Yes. A sweet girl, Amy. I knew her father well."

As they walked toward the house Alex said, "Do you have any idea how someone could get into your place?"

"I have no idea. I just know that my papers were strewn all over the lab, even trailing out the door. I can't tell what they actually took, other than a few notes of mine which won't do them much good. Most of my processes are still locked in my mind, but I can understand that they might have heard of a certain object I have now given to Amy."

"Was it made of one of the 97 elements?" Alex mused.

"Heh, heh. Well, by now you have been made abreast of some amazing possibilities regarding our national security."

"The iridium crystal?"

"'And the use to which it may be put."

As the walk steepened, Dr. Guildermann began to huff and wheeze.

"Would you like to pause here a moment?"

"No, thank you. Believe it or not, I'm in pretty good health. But we probably should sit down on this bench and talk."

"Sounds good."

"Yes, iridium - though it's not exactly a crystal. I merely added my process to the basic formulation, which originated at Schlessingers in Frankfurt. My additions are what made the whole thing work."

He continued. "Laser beams have two distinct properties coming as a result of the nature of how the laser action is actually produced. It is literally 'Light Amplification by Stimulated Emission of Radiation.' The 'simulated' part is the key. Einstein first proposed this phenomenon many years ago and it was not proven until the late Fifties when other enabling technologies came into being.

"Let me explain: normal light is produced by some sort of excitation or reaction resulting in a short-lived energy state. When it relaxes back into the lower state, it can do so by emitting light. Einstein imagined what would happen if, with very high intensity excitation – the new technology – one could produce a greater excitation in the excited state than the lower state. Now a new relaxation process comes into play where the de-excitation is no longer spontaneous, as mentioned earlier, but is 'stimulated' directly from the higher state. This method produces what's called coherent light, meaning that all the light waves are in phase. This in-phase or coherent, part gives rise to two unique properties."

Dr. Guildermann was on a roll as he explained these difficult postulations so common to his advanced knowledge. Alex listened patiently.

"One – the laser beam spreads, or diverges, very little with travel distance, and two – the laser beam can be focused or concentrated to a tiny spot. Both of these are related to wave-like properties which give rise to terms called diffraction and interference. Diffraction is really a term related to the divergence of light, and that, combined with Maxwell's Equations, defines this property and therefore describes the properties and propagation of light..."

Alex didn't even pretend to understand Guildermann's impromptu explanation, and decided it wasn't really pertinent to his mission. "Now if you can explain the inner workings of the internal combustion engine..."

"Haha! Oh, Mr. Rayburn, you make me laugh!"

"Well, sir. I believe I'll have to be content with a certain amount of ignorance."

"But it's really quite simple," Guildermann assured him. "Fortunately, as a scientist funded by the U.S. government, I have developed a theory and the design of a new, sophisticated electro-optic device that requires a special glass composition and a unique geometric structure. When attached to the output of a laser, one can reduce the divergence 10 times below the predicted theoretical diffraction limit. This would also mean that the focal spot size would be similarly reduced, resulting in a 100 times increase in intensity. This, my friend, is what the government wants."

"It's incredible!" Alex responded.

The two lingered a moment in contemplation. Then Alex reminded Guildermann, "Amy has employed me to ..."

"I know. You need to examine this property for clues."

"You're right, Sir. And as we walked up here, I wanted to ask you about that mattress down near the fence."

"What?" Guildermann squinted. "By God, you're right! You haven't been here ten minutes and you've discovered the only way someone could have gotten over the fence –with a mattress! Haha! All this security and it was a mattress that foiled them! They were so confident in their abilities to be everywhere at once that they never electrified the fence. Chalk one up for arrogance!"

Alex assumed that "them" were the security people milling around everywhere.

"It'll be fun to tell those over-paid agents later at dinner," Guildermann chuckled. "Speaking of dinner, would you like to partake later? I have an excellent chef on duty."

Alex realized that there was little else of importance at Guildermann's. He had seen the lay of the land and discovered the thief's entry point. Though he found no other clues, at least he knew that there would probably be no further break-ins.

"No, sir, I'll just look around and be on my way." He tested the doctor's sense of humor and tossed out a little sarcasm."It's plain to see, someone thinks well of your work."

The rotund scientist laughed in agreement. "This damned place is supposed to be a high security area. Come, I'll deposit you in my lab and you can contemplate to your heart's content."

Alex stayed awhile and snooped around in Guildermann's work area, but could only guess that any stolen papers hadn't much of a bearing on anything. Who'd want papers? Wouldn't the ne'er-do-wells want the iridium element itself? Amy had said that there was only one produced thus far, and it was just for experimentation shortly to take place on a hillside facility near a community college telescope. He expected that he would be privy to that event. This had begun to smell like something Lester Nichols might indeed want to involve himself in.

Nah. That couldn't be. Lester was small potatoes compared to this.

6

AMONG THE FEW things that set Nan Holloway's teeth on edge was waiting. How she hated it.

After steaming out of Amy Huffton's office, she had barely reached the elevator before she realized that Alex Rayburn had, once again, put her at a disadvantage. Now, as she waited for the down button to light, she knew that she would have to wait for Alex's summons in order to fulfill her assignment from Amy. It was quite possible that she would never hear from him at all. Alex had also left her with no new information about Lester Nichols, the slimy pharmacist who had escaped a charge of murder only to reappear. She was stymied there, too. What to do?

Amy had said that Nan should help out with the opening reception for the new exhibit at the glass museum "if she had time." She had plenty of time now.

Nan walked across the Huffton corporate campus to the world-famous Museum of Glass. She never tired of visiting the magnificent free-form glass structure with its definitive collection of glass objects through 3000 years of history. There were also intriguing exhibits on the science of glass and the popular demonstrations of glass blowing. Nan's mood lifted the moment she entered.

She picked up a brochure at the reception desk describing the upcoming exhibition of Turkish traditional stained glass and contemporary glass art. The photos depicted the legendary windows of the Topkapi Palace Museum in Istanbul and other polychrome mosaic windows, an important feature of Ottoman architecture. Also to be displayed were works of Turkish glass artists working today. The event promised a feast for the senses.

Nan strolled past the lively glass market, resisting the urge to browse, and into the office of Todd Everingham, managing director for the museum. Todd looked up from a catalog he was studying and rushed to greet her.

"Hello, Nan. I had a feeling you might turn up. Amy told me you would be working on the reception with us."

Todd was a tall, gangling thirty-something with a mop of unruly dark hair, horn-rimmed glasses and a boyish smile. His pedigree included Boston College, Yale and Cornell (for some Ivy League exposure), and the community college in upstate New York, where he'd begun his academics. His acumen with the arts had been sharpened at the Metropolitan Museum of Art in New York City during the three years he assisted the Assistant Curator, and in similar positions at other institutions. But he never felt appreciated no matter what he did for organizations on his resume. His frustration with "spinning his wheels" weighed heavily on his mind. Even though his present position with the glass museum looked good on his resume, he felt adrift and unsuccessful. "I'll show them some day" was his mantra.

Todd struck Nan as an elder Harry Potter and indeed, some of special events he'd devised were nothing short of magical. He had attended Stanford at the same time Amy Huffton was there and became one of the protégés Amy had later placed in key positions throughout the company.

"Amy wanted me in on this reception," explained Nan, "but now she has me working on another project as well, which will take precedence. I'm hoping you can give me the basic info so I can at least be thinking about it."

Todd summarized plans for the venue, which would be in the new contemporary glass wing of the building.

"We'll be supplementing the pieces they bring over from Turkey with some of our own Turkish glass treasures," he said.

"Do you have any ideas for the reception?" Nan prompted.

"Yes, and we're definitely not into the obvious shish-kabobs and belly dancers. We don't want to play up the ethnic angle with Turkish food or music. The Ministry of Culture's whole purpose in touring this exhibition is to demonstrate Turkey's modernity. You know they're keen to join the European Union."

"Good luck on that," Nan scoffed. "Isn't Turkey hand-in-glove with Iran?"

"Not exactly," said Todd. "They are somewhat dependent on each other economically, but hardly what you would call allies. Anyway, they have a glass manufacturer, Pasabache, which is huge – the Huffton of the Near East. And they have an internationally-known artist. We have Dale Chilhouly, and Turkey has Gulfidan Ozmen. The exhibition will showcase some of her work."

Nan found Todd's enthusiasm contagious. "Show me the layout. Perhaps we can stage the reception so that people are led by food and drink stations and live music on a meandering path along the promenade. That way they won't end up crowding the exhibition all at once."

"Good! And we can have the dignitaries on hand right at the exhibition itself rather than greeting people too near the entrance and holding up the flow."

The two continued in party-planning mode as they strolled through the contemporary wing. As always, it made Nan feel proud, elated, and disoriented all at one time. The floors, walls and ceiling of the spacious corridor were white; diffused natural light illuminated the area by way of a unique system of skylights.

To Nan, it felt like moving through a cloud, punctuated with fantastic visions of large-scale art masterpieces, some whimsical, some awe-inspiring.

Todd halted at a darkened, screened-off area.

"This is it. Let me show you the space. See what you think." He somewhat apprehensively pulled a canvas drape aside to let Nan enter.

None of the glamor of luminescent gallery permeated here. It was more like the dingy backstage of a theater with props, set pieces and lighting paraphernalia strewn about.

"As you can see, we've work to do," said Todd, and then, "Good heavens! What's this?"

He knelt down to a crumpled form on the floor and pulled back a tarp. From behind him, Nan could see immediately it was a woman, or rather, the body of a woman.

"Oh, my God!" Todd exclaimed in horror. Nan knelt as well and took hold of the woman's cold wrist to locate a pulse - an exercise in futility, she realized. There was an inch-thick shard of glass protruding from the woman's throat, and blood coagulating on her skin and clothing. A few fine glass slivers were scattered in her long auburn hair and on the floor.

"She's dead, Todd. You'd better call 911 right away!"

She could read Todd's expression. He was shocked, and already worrying about the bad publicity, Nan surmised. She was equally stunned, but knew what to do.

"You have to call *now*, Todd! Any delays will just make the matter worse, believe me."

Todd stood, turned away from the tragedy and made the call on his cell phone.

Nan studied the woman. There seemed to be no sign of a struggle. She had been attractive and was still so, even after what must have been a violent and painful death. Nan felt a wave of compassion and anger. What a waste of a life! And there was something familiar. Do I know her?

"Todd, take a closer look. Have you seen this woman before?"

Todd, pale and visibly agitated, did as instructed. "I'm afraid I do. She's one of the sales persons from the glass shop. This is horrible!"

"Get a grip, Todd. Do you know her name?"

"It's Nora ... Norma, something like that. Nan, I'm sorry. I've got to run and alert our security ... and meet the police."

"Okay. I'll stay here until they arrive." Nan could barely contain her excitement. She knew from the article Gina had mailed her that this unfortunate woman was Norma Nichols, Lester's long-lost spouse! This was mega-news!

She noted a custodian approaching the area with a strange expression on his face, but after a pause, he turned and moved on. Something told her she should note the way the man just walked away. Shouldn't he be more curious? He exhibited a strong military posture...well, no, she wasn't going to concern herself. There was enough here to worry about.

As soon as he was out of earshot, she made her own phone call - to Alex Rayburn's office. Of course, he didn't answer, and she didn't have his personal cell number, an omission she would soon remedy. Trying not to sound as if she were gloating, Nan left a message.

"Alex, I've found Lester Nichols' wife. She's dead, stabbed with a piece of glass at the museum."

She debated giving him more details, but hung up instead. Let him sweat a little. It would serve him right for not taking her more seriously. He knew where to find her.

7

WHY?

Alex couldn't shake the question in his head. Why Nichols' wife? Lester must be more of a "player" than he'd realized. And Lester's wife had been in the museum gift shop all the time? Right under everyone's nose? Even employed there, for God's sake! Lester must have discovered this fact and finally done away with Norma. He would have known that he couldn't be prosecuted twice – it would be double jeopardy.

"I'll bet the son of a bitch got away with murder this time!" he snarled.

His next unwelcome thought was that he now had to return Nan Holloway's call and get this all straight. Nan had dropped the bomb in her phone message, but didn't give many details. In his next call to her, he would give her instructions to meet him at a downtown restaurant and discuss the implications of this development. The prospect of dining with her left a bad taste in his mouth, but what could he do? "Grrr ... that woman!" He would listen to her at The Three Birds Steak House and try to pay attention.

Nan had one-upped him with the revelation of the death of Lester Nichols' wife. Hell, now it would be necessary to go crawling to her for more of the story, a thing he hated. The apparent murder was also a discovery that would shake his preconceived notions to the core. His entire concept of who Lester's wife actually was might be changing. And could Lester somehow be connected with the event going on at the hill lab later tonight? No, Lester wasn't that "big time." He was just a petty crook who had a little luck once in a while. Alex couldn't deny that the whole thing regarding Norma's death could be merely a suspicious coincidence. Still he pondered what Norma's role might have been in this new equation.

"If I could just get my hands on Lester," he thought. Surely it was Lester who'd killed his wife. Or did he? It doesn't make sense. Or does it? The wheels began turning in his mind. He knew the solution would arrive in a matter of time, and that Nan's insufferable attitudes would not be important once his great mind got into overdrive.

"Humph. I know she'll ruin dinner!"

Despite the turn of events, the afternoon had been pleasant at the lab on the hill. The company was readying its big test to prove the validity of Guildermann's theory. Would the electrical discharge cause a visible change in a predetermined spot on the orbiting orb? Could using the iridium element supercharge a beam of light enough to travel 250,000 miles into space and cause a real ruckus on the moon's surface?

In his mind it still seemed a bit far-fetched, although, like everyone else involved, he hoped it would work. Will the United States soon have a weapon to shoot down man-made satellites and incoming missiles? Will this eventually bring about world peace? In Alex's thinking, this was the biggest event to hit national defenses since the first ancient catapults proved useful in combat. All fingers were crossed on the hill, and things were being readied for some late night entertainment.

Alex thought back to the crux of the matter: Who's causing all this skullduggery regarding the iridium? He wondered if it was the machinations of a foreign nation trying to get the knockout capability for themselves, or was another force involved – some group employed by, say, the Russians, to procure the concept secretly? He had no way of knowing for certain, but he was going to give it a go with his own reckoning. He usually wasn't out of the loop for long. Right now, Nan was bugging him and would surely gloat about her discovery of Norma's body.

"Oh Lordy! Damned reporter," he mouthed, grumbling. "I sure hope this arrangement works out. We'll just have to remember that we're working for Amy Huffton, and be graceful about it."

The afternoon was coming up on six o'clock – suppertime for him. He was hungry enough to endure even a dinner meeting with Nan. Looking west off the Chemung River Bridge, he watched the daylight mellow through the open top of his prized Lamborghini. The breeze blew comfortably around the interior as he came off the bridge apron, and turned left onto Market Street.

This city, nicknamed "The Crystal City," was a town built solely on the good fortunes of Amy Huffton's glass company. Glass ruled here and well it should, ever since the business arrived here in 1851 from downstate, where the early Huffton ideas had taken root. The early Hufftons had arrived from England with money and a dream –to exercise their expertise not only in the industrialization of their glass formulae, but also to exploit their art glass. After a while, the company outgrew its Brooklyn beginnings. Thanks to the urgings of some Southern Tier businessmen, the family decided to go along with a sweet deal involving the now "Crystal City" and the various concessions made to encourage their moving the company literally up the river. The equipment arrived in the summer of 1851, some of it by river barge, and the blessed tale of the remaking of this town began. For many, many years, Amy's company had sunk millions into the wellbeing of not only the business, but the valley in general. They had striven to perfect and protect all of 65,000 glass formulas, with patents in the thousands, as well as their business transactions worldwide.

So far as the city dwellers went, prosperity became expected by not only the high-falootin' go-getters, but also by the more mundane citizens, a circumstance true to this day. It soon became a small city unique when compared to other towns of equal square-mileage. Amy was the current potentate of this special company. The establishment has been run for all its existence by members of her family, that non-greedy lineage of former English gentry, who constantly put large amounts of profit back into research and development. Huffton Glass kept an amiable relationship with New York's Southern Tier, in a city that was, essentially, theirs.

Businesses came and went on its main street, but a few of the restaurants had become legendary. In order to meet up with the new, worst vexation of his life, Alex had chosen The Three Birds, an eatery well-known for its beef.

"If I have to work with good old Nan, I might as well eat with gusto." He would carve up the finest steak "The Birds" could offer.

A distance away, in front of the restaurant, Nan looked at her watch. A line escaped from her pursed lips: "Time means nothing to that guy. Where the blinkin' hell is he?" Her thoughts had just taken flight when Alex pulled up in his fire-breathing, noise-making sports car. He slid into a parking spot practically at her feet and forced a smile.

"Hello there, Nan."

"Hi," came the frosty return.

Alex popped out of the car to a general audience agog with admiration. Nan had to admit he was a showman, impressing any and all bystanders with the flashy confidence of celebrity.

"Been waiting long?" he asking nonchalantly.

"Only a few minutes."

"Right this way, my dear."

Humph! *His dear,* she thought.

Like the gentleman he is, Alex led Nan through the door into the classy restaurant which boasted a long, shiny bar and a large, open dining area. The place was a former feed store for livestock and farm deals, then a car repair shop, and now the elegant Three Birds dining spot. It quickly became famous on the street despite several other places of fine repute. The owner orbited the room, smiling widely with a face of blended Viet Namese and North American features and a giant, toothy smile. The excellent food was presented with a master's touch, and Tony Vu was known for treating his workers well.

Nan admired the soft colors from wall to wall in perfect harmony, with a thick carpet beckoning. Shortly after they sat down, her tired feet seemed to slip out of their sandals of their own volition. "Ohhh, this carpet ..." Her eager toes nestled into the softness.

"It seems a woman always needs to remove her shoes," Alex offered.

Nan blushed. She felt the color rise in her cheeks, and even the white streak in her hair seemed to turn pink. She hadn't even been aware that she'd slipped off her shoes. How did Alex know? With his always-perfect comportment, what must he be thinking? It wasn't really ladylike behavior.

"Well, not *always*," she sputtered in explanation. "Only in moments of great temptation."

Oh, dear. That comment wasn't really going to help, but Alex let her off the hook this time with just an amused grin. "Wish I could join you."

Seeing the owner focus on them, Alex spoke. "Tony. How's business?"

"Wonderful, Mister Rayburn. And who is this lovely lotus blossom?"

Nan had missed this restaurant in her rounds, and was duly impressed with the trappings. Tony, however, had just pushed one wrong button. She was *not* a lotus blossom!

"This is Nan Holloway. You may have seen her on local television."

Tony didn't wish to seem out of touch. "Oh, yes, yes! ...er ... I will take your order personally tonight."

Even though Nan liked being treated right, she thought Tony was overdoing it. Alex probably spent big in this room from time to time and the proprietor was sucking up a bit. Still, the place had perfected the ambiance needed for a special evening, if this was going to be one. "Stop, Nan," she scolded herself. "Just enjoy dinner. You can joust with Alex later at the demonstration on the hill."

She wondered why someone so...attractive had to be such a pain. And why had he insisted that she accompany him to the big event? After thinking a moment, she realized that it would be a good idea after all.

Alex looked across the table at Nan and wondered why she had to be such a pain.

Silence reigned, but after ordering – she, the pork medallions and he, the Porterhouse - they were both struck by the same thought at the same moment: Why are we so contentious with each other? Some amazing portal seemed to open in the universe as they decided in the same millisecond to try to relax the situation between them.

In unison, they said: "I think it's time ..." stopping each other abruptly. Again, almost in unison, they said: "Go ahead ..." which brought about another awkward delay. Alex prevailed. "Sorry. But I was going to say, we could try to get along, enjoy the flap between us, and ..."

"...simply make humor of it instead?" Nan finished.

"Wonderful idea! We could have fun without being hurtful. I confess, Nan, I think you're a charming woman and I respect the knowledge you bring to this odd situation of ours."

Without hesitation Nan chimed in. "It does seem like this thing has run its course. I mean, we're both adults. I've always admired you for your civic-minded projects around the city." She sighed, "I'm ready to give it up – takes too much concentration."

In relief, Alex said, "I agree completely."

The meal arrived with Tony nagging the waiter to do his best. "And get more water!"

He glanced at Alex. "Today you can smoke in here –we have the New York State one-day permit."

"Thank you, Tony," Alex remarked. "But I have no cigar at the moment."

Calling to the bartender, Tony said, "Robert! Get Mister Rayburn an Arturo Fuente!"

"No, no, Tony. Thank you. I'm fine."

It was plain to Nan that Alex held a lot of sway in this establishment. But she was happy not to be in the company of *any* fine cigar.

During after-dinner drinks, Alex began with, "Tell me more about your shocking discovery at the museum."

Nan had been ready to jump on him with a drawn-out tale of finding poor Norma Nichols in a heap on the museum floor, but now felt more conciliatory in view of their new tolerance of each other.

"It really was unnerving. At first I didn't realize who she was, but just this morning Gina, an old newspaper pal, had mailed me a picture of Norma from an old news story. Fortunately her features were the same, and recognition was easy. How remarkable!"

"I concur! When I was looking for her, I talked to relatives, friends, did all the usual checking on credit cards and so forth, and nothing turned up."

Nan raised an eyebrow. "I *am* surprised she was able to elude you."

Alex shrugged, "To tell you the truth, I didn't push too hard. I figured she was better off without Lester, and if she managed to get away, more power to her. Under the circumstances, I didn't collect my fee."

"You do have a heart," Nan grinned. "My first thought when I realized she was the victim was that Lester had finally found her."

"Mine, too - it's possible. But the whole thing asks more questions than it answers," the detective mused. "For example, why was she working at the museum in the first place? It's too much of a coincidence."

"You think she might have been involved in the break-in at Guildermann's?"

"Who knows?" Alex replied. "One thing I've learned in this business is that every persona is composed of layers upon layers. We seldom get to the core."

There are certainly layers and layers to *this* man, thought Nan.

Under Tony's watchful eye, dinner concluded pleasurably and Alex made a note to tip the bedraggled waiter a buck or two more for his patience. The polite and easy chitchat coming from both diners surprised each very much. Perhaps Alex hadn't given Nan a chance. He would have to watch himself and be the kind and thoughtful fellow he knew himself to be. Nan also rescinded some of her bias and hoped that her bitchiness hadn't precluded a promising friendship. Things were changing between them, and they both liked it.

"Who's going to be at the event this evening?" she inquired.

"Well, I don't have the official list, but as far as I know it'll be you and me, the Huffton brass, several officials from the Defense Department, Todd Everingham from the museum, and Dr. Guildermann, of course. Beyond that, I don't know."

"Todd? I wonder how he's connected to this event."

"I don't know. Just somebody with an invitation. We should watch carefully. This might bring a ne'er-do-well out in the open."

Alex was pleased that Nan had recognized Norma earlier at the museum, and didn't mind telling her now. "Good job! You're a detective for sure."

Nan replied, "You know, I was thinking the same thing."

8

NAN HAD TO admit it. She hadn't had this much fun in a long time. Riding beside Alex in his hot "Lambo" Miura, she relaxed back against the soft leather seat.

"This car was built in 1968 and has a top speed of 170 miles per hour. It easily keeps up with today's hot rods ...in case you need to know," Alex informed her.

"I'll take your word for it," Nan said. "Keep it under 150, if you don't mind."

The car's open roof in front of the targa bar allowed a cooling breeze to lift her hair from her face and neck. The sports car circled upward toward the community college campus and the observatory. To the west of the observatory, a branch of the Huffton labs glowed in the oncoming night and was abuzz with scientists. Fireflies blinked in the dense woodlands on either side of the road.

Maybe it was just the effects of a fine dinner, capped off with an equally fine cognac, that made Nan feel distinctly mellow. She had expected to hear from Alex after she'd called him about finding Norma's body at the museum, but hadn't imagined that they would be discussing the case over dinner at The Three Birds. What a thoughtful surprise! She had dressed carefully for the occasion in a midnight blue pants suit and scarlet silk blouse. Men like red, she thought But why had she wanted to please Alex with her appearance? Was it just that she didn't want there to be anything about her for him to criticize? She had no way of knowing that her choice of pants suit over skirt might be fortuitous later that very night, as events seem to have a way of escalating when Alex Rayburn is on hand.

Nan had parked her Nissan Sentra in the nearest lot and, as directed, arrived at the restaurant at six o'clock sharp. Of course, Alex wasn't there waiting for her. When he zoomed up in the Lamborghini a few minutes later looking like a European playboy with his cream-colored jacket and aviator glasses, she mentally rolled her eyes. The little Italian car was as yellow as a neon canary - not exactly discreet.

The dinner had eventually turned out to be pleasant. They had discussed their cases and then moved on to general conversation – happenings in town, mutual acquaintances, books they were reading, travel plans. Alex's somewhat old-fashioned courtly manners appealed to her, though sometimes they annoyed her as over-kill. He had surprised her when he told her that she would be required to accompany him to Spider Hill to observe the results of the test. It was an order, for sure, but she was glad to be going along. When he said they would take his car, she even stifled the urge to wisecrack about the many speeding tickets he had accumulated (as she had discovered on the Snoop site) in the interests of their newly-forged *détente*.

When they were on approach to the observatory complex, security measures became obvious; however, the guards at the entrance gave only a cursory glance at the two of them and waved them through. They were directed to the ridge where a half-dozen small but powerful telescopes had been reserved for VIP spectators who were not privy to the large telescope. Alex had told her that the main telescope inside the building was only for Dr. Guildermann and a few other Huffton scientists, government observers and, of course, Amy Huffton.

Among those spotted by Nan at the outside telescopes on the hill were Jerry Corbeno, the college professor in charge of the complex; George Archer, the Huffton Corporation's VP for Communications; and Todd Everingham (whom Nan still thought didn't really belong there). Her IPad came out of her copious shoulder bag. She was, as decreed by Amy, to be Alex's "scribe" and keep a thorough accounting of things as they developed, so she took names. In addition to the invitees Amy had told Alex about, there were a handful of others Nan couldn't identify in the fading light.

"Do you know who these folks are?" she asked Alex.

He was as baffled as she. "Not a clue."

"Probably various Huffton officials or maybe family members," she speculated. One looked somewhat like the curious museum custodian from when she had discovered the body - but surely he would not have been invited.

Alex greeted General Norman Bellis, who came up from behind them.

"Quite a night, eh, General?"

"Alex. Nice to see you! I understand you're part of the security force tonight."

"In some regards, I *am* the security force."

"Well, we'll all be in good hands with you here. If you need anything from my boys, just say the word."

"That might be necessary, sir. By the way, this is Nan Holloway"

Nan stepped up and extended her hand. "Nice to meet you, Sir."

"Pleasure to meet you, Ms. Holloway. Are you with Alex?"

"Yes, in a way. We're both working for Amy Huffton tonight."

"Ah, yes. What a sweet girl. I knew her father well. Alex, take this card. It's got my cell number on it."

"Okay, Sir. I'll call you if I get into trouble."

The General laughed and walked off to his perch in the lab. He would have a very good seat at the telescope with Dr. Guildermann.

"What a guy," Alex said to Nan. "I might have known the General would be here. And there's nobody as thorough as he is. I've watched him deal with mountains of red tape. He always wins."

The detective, now a "company" detective, checked the luminous dial on his Rolex."It's almost time for the test shot." He took his place at a telescope.

Nan began recording on her iPhone. "There's a breathless air of expectation ..." then she stopped herself. How can there be breathless air? Oh hell, I can edit this later.

Looking up from the bright screen, she noted a vehicle about 200 feet away, rolling down a slope to the nearby lab. The engine was disengaged and no lights were on.

Hmmm ...How odd. She continued to stare at the vehicle which seemed to try to hide itself. "Now it's stopped behind the lab."

"Why are you talking to yourself?" Alex inquired, looking up from the telescope.

Nan told him, "Why would that car drift along with the lights off?"

He craned his neck. "Don't know. "That's a Porsche 911 –a very fast car."

"I think it's Todd's car."

"Old Todd has very good taste." His curiosity piqued. "It's probably nothing, but ...good observation anyway. I'll walk over that way in a few minutes. The countdown has begun and we have just a few seconds to go before firing."

As they glanced at each other, the night sky suddenly lit up, with a single beam of searing light rocketing skyward. All the spectators peered into their telescopes, some yelling, "I see it!" With jarring impact, a puff of dust roiled up the moon's surface. There was no doubt; the beam had found its mark. The Sea of

Tranquility had endured a massive hit from the accelerated beam, a beam of nothing more than excited and well-directed light. The beam struck the moon with enough of a ruckus to prove Guildermann's theory which, as of this moment, was no longer just a theory. The experiment worked!

Shouts of amazement went out and into the night air from within the observatory. The scientists who delivered the blow celebrated in the lab with a rousing cheer. The beam was a success and everyone present speculated about its future. Champagne corks popped here and there. The outside public address speakers crackled:

"The test was a complete success! Everyone on the property is urged to attend the debriefing down the hill in the planetarium. Dr. Guildermann will be there shortly."

Hearing the results officially stated, everyone let out a cheer. Shoulders were slapped and bodies were hugged in a cacophony of glee. VIPs spilled out the lab doors.

"Well done, everybody," she shouted. "Let's head for the planetarium!"

All onlookers outside joined the invitees exiting the telescope building as they poured out excitedly. It was a night to remember. The United States had just trumped all nations who were actively seeking this masterful beam that would probably change the course of modern-day history. This pie-in-the-sky technology had Amy entertaining her vision of selling the discovery to the government; the government people were delighted with the flawless result and speculated mightily with one another; and each individual head jostling through the crowd pursued its private thoughts of how this evening related to them personally. Dr. Guildermann was besieged with well-wishers and, not that he tried, could not erase the smile from his face. Nan and Alex were giddy at what they'd seen and thought of heading down the hill with the others.

But the car seen earlier cloaking itself in stealth quickly came back to mind. Alex told Nan to go with the rest of the people while he checked out the mysterious vehicle she had spotted earlier down behind the lab. The lab door was a short distance beyond his own car, but there also was that Porsche pointed down the hill. Alex suspected something, but so did Nan.

"I'm going with you," she flatly stated.

"All right. You've earned it."

Inside the laboratory, General Bellis was taking one last look at the gun. It resembled an actual military asset sitting on a platform which allowed it to gimbal in any direction - up, down or sideways. It was built as a series of snap-together pods, each providing its share of duty to the functioning of the whole unit. Seriously large cables fed mega electro-power to the unit through the rear. Along the sides were the soon-to-be-patented booster units built by Huffton Glass, which changed a mundane light beam into a super-powered photon wave which, as everyone saw, could literally "shoot the moon." The iridium element is specially prepared to be housed in its own pod and is bombarded with all of the electro-glass science that makes it work.

Suspicious of Todd's maneuvers, Nan and Alex entered the building and climbed the stairs to a platform which overlooked the gun below. They arrived just in time to see General Bellis struck hard over the head by none other than Todd himself.

"What ...?" Nan exclaimed, loudly enough for Todd to hear. Todd swung around, not expecting to see anyone else in the building. Four eyes were locked on Todd, still holding a short rod of steel.

"Back off!" he snarled.

He quickly moved to the gun and tugged at the iridium module. To the surprise of all, it detached from the unit. He turned, nearly tripping over the groggy General, and ran with the iridium to the side door where his Porsche was parked

."Oh hell!" Alex snapped. "The rat's leaving with the cheese!"

"Can we catch him?" Nan asked.

9

IN A FLASH, the two of them were in the Lamborghini and Alex turned the key. Vroom! The car came to life with all cylinders humming. Nan shut her door in the nick of time, snagging her jacket sleeve. Forward they went, *molto presto,* up the driveway in the dashing Italian car and on toward the hill road. Alex pulled off his tie and handed it to Nan, who noticed his sweat on her fingers. She had a dread fear of going too fast in a car, but it was a phobia which would soon be excised from her startled psyche. Alex threw the car back into third gear and the chase was on.

"That bloody little stinker," he snorted. "First he steals the element *and* the technology that makes it work, then he is audacious enough to think that the tin can he's driving can get away from this baby. We'll see. Come on, Sweetheart," he said to the car. "Do your thing!"

The back wheels of the Lambo went high on the pavement and momentarily broke from the ground. Over the hump and down Spider Hill road they sped, with a velocity never seen before on this college route. Twists and turns were effectively straightened out under the racing suspensions of the two fast *omologati*. Neither driver would let up, forcing some frightening sideways skids. The Porsche was no pushover, but the Lamborghini had a superior power-to-weight ratio. All Alex had to do was just watch Todd. He could overtake him at will.

"We should watch carefully, maybe from a slight distance. Then we'll see right where he's going."

"I'm on it," Nan agreed, frozen in her seat with eyes staring ahead.

Todd was quickly around the second bend and accelerating wildly. His Porsche did not disappoint. It was plenty fast. Alex was mildly impressed as the black 911 kept bumping up the excitement, well ahead of them.

Up through the gears, then back again; the drivers put the pedal-to-the-metal in an all-or-nothing contest.

The two lanes of roadway directly under them and very close to their butts weren't as wide as they might hope, but these were desperate moments. Todd had to put distance between their cars to affect his escape, and Alex was simply waiting for a long, straight stretch to wind up his rocket and stay close for observation. The stop sign at the street where they entered the city limits was soon a mere memory. The drivers descended down the residential hill through a sleepy part of town toward the waiting interstate. People in the neighborhood stood agape at the spectacle unfolding in evening night shades. The inevitable brush with a baby carriage happened halfway down the hill at the corner of Fourth and Chemung, but the woman and her child skittered off after no apparent damage. Nan saw the missed carriage and let out a horrified shriek.

"Wow, that was close," Alex said.

"He's a madman!" Nan returned.

"I'd pull back a little, but he might elude us!"

"I hope you've got one foot on the brakes!"

He laughed, "It's the only way I drive!"

In disregard of traffic lights, the two cars screeched into a sharp right turn and onto a four-lane parkway leading them quickly out of town. There were times in this city when one wondered where the cops were - this was one of them. No official car was in sight as they headed through the park on a highway never meant to be there.

Alex was always ashamed of the city for taking this sizable land donation and not honoring the last words of the donor family:"This land shall be used for the construction of a serene park. A highway shall never be built through it." This stipulation was soon ignored when the necessity of an east-west interstate connection became an imperative. Also, the donating family had died out, so old promises were easily swept away in this sweet Southern Tier bastion of democracy.

The highway now running under them was indeed the main connector to Interstate 86, still a mile or two down the road. Just beyond this section was the Gibson Bridge which had a "suicide" curve at the far end, but fear never entered Todd's mind when the curve appeared. He knew his car as well as Alex knew his. Even at breakneck speed, he pressed on with his sports car driving expertise, avoiding the hapless drivers who were simply in the way, Alex had to give Todd a bit of respect.

"He's pretty good with that thing."

"He can't possibly think he's going to get away," Nan offered.

"Anything can happen. All we can do is try."

Nan eyed him with some apprehension, "Try carefully."

"Come on, Nan. You're a woman of the world. Surely you've been in fast cars before."

Alex had taken his eyes off the road for a nanosecond. The car shunted sideways before he corrected.

"Keep your damn eyes on the road!" she wailed.

"Sorry. You're right."

After the bridge, exchanging one highway for another was accomplished with gusto. But the pace was getting more worrisome to Nan. "Oh, my God!" she exclaimed several times, reaching for sufficient words. "I hate this! I love it!"

"Kinda grows on you, doesn't it?"

Alex knew they were safe. But Nan remained on edge and looked askance at him. Yes, she was terrified, but Alex seemed to be one with the car. She told herself that he truly deserved to be master of it – if they survived.

After two more tight turns, Todd finally wound-out his vehicle and made it resemble a streak of tail lights zooming away from other cars on the road. It howled down the entrance ramp and onto Interstate 86, a fairly recent addition to the interstate system. Hot on his tail was Alex and the agnostic Nan, who swore new allegiance to whatever boutique deity she was currently involved with. They were going at a fast clip, but Alex tailored his speed so as not to get too close to Todd.

After about eight miles, Todd turned off on Kahler Road.

"Look," Nan said. "That's the road to the airport. He's turning!"

"So that's his game. Okay. Now we have to be very observant."

Nan agreed. "When it comes to that, I'm one of the best."

"I'll bet you are, Cookie."

Nan liked being called by his cute names (except for Nancy Lou), although she was loathe to admit it. Maybe she'd been hasty...no, he was still irrepressibly egotistical. And yet...

In smaller regional airports one can look through the chain link fencing and see what's going on rather easily. Nan she spotted Todd parking his car and carrying an item she assumed to be the iridium element. On the tarmac, a shiny black business jet idled quietly. Even from a distance, Nan could see Todd handing his purloined package off to someone at the rear entrance of the aircraft. The exchange was made and Todd walked to the front entry stairs of the jet.

"Uh oh. I think he's getting away."

"Nan, take this business card and call General Bellis. Let's hope he's recovered from that crack on the head enough to do us some good."

She quickly got the General on the phone and handed it to Alex. It was as if Bellis had been expecting their call.

"General, here's what we've got so far." Alex briefly outlined what had happened to a very agitated military man. In a moment, it was the General's turn to talk.

"Alex, do whatever you can to keep that plane on the ground! This is a matter of national security. I can negate any agency that tries to stop you, right down to the State Police. You officially have *carte blanche*. Just don't let that plane take off!"

General Bellis ordered his aide to get the airport's control tower on the phone. He was about to pull rank and make sure Alex and Nan would have no interference - or uncoordinated assistance. He also knew that in a situation like this, the tower would not be physically able to stop the take-off. It would be up to Alex to formulate a plan of some kind, any kind, to foil Todd's escape. Once the plane was aloft, it would not be found easily.

It was at that moment that the jet's engines pitched higher, and the plane began to move toward the runway's eastern end. The two in the Lamborghini could actually see Todd in one of the starboard seats.

"Oh brother," slipped from Alex's mouth.

"Do I need to know what you're going to do next?" Nan hoped there would be no danger-laden response.

Alex was studying the situation. He saw their deliverance in an open gate several hundred yards away. He looked behind Nan at a recent purchase he had made, a small fire extinguisher, resting on what the car manufacturer called a "rear seat." He looked back at Nan and said, "Hang on, girlie! We've got orders! This is a foot-off-the-brakes moment!"

With a pitiful look, she again said, "Oh God."

"Brace yourself!"

Alex turned the car around and shot through the open gate. Airport workers backed out of the way and watched in awe. Now things would have to be choreographed. It was nitty-gritty time and action had to be decisive. From his military protocols with

General Bellis, fast decisions came easy to him. He was sure his plan would work.

"What are you going to do?" Nan repeated, nearly beside herself. What could they do from the car? What plan had he concocted? This ride was nothing like her earlier experience today in this super-fast car, but she was in it, bristling with anticipation, and powerless to control anything. There was no getting away from the ordeal.

Alex slammed the car into third gear and accelerated *fortississimo* down the taxiway running in front of the airport lounge. Inside, a drowsy patron saw the car whiz past the windows and looked down at his drink. He slurred, "Think is time t' go home."

The usual takeoff direction from this airfield is east to west, due to the prevailing winds. Alex pointed the car east in order to come up to the plane on the starboard side just before takeoff. He wanted Todd to watch the happenings from his comfortable seat, preferably while he had a drink in his hand. There was only one way this aircraft as going to stop. It had to be timed just right. He wondered how Nan would do with the challenge.

"Here. Take this," he ordered.

Puzzled, Nan took hold of the small fire extinguisher and wondered aloud, "What now?"

As they reached the plane, it had just released its brakes and wound-up its engines for take-off. The pilot had not detected the presence of the two pursuers; the copilot was not yet hooked into his seat belt. Chatter went on inside the plane, which contained pilot, copilot and two Albanian "businessmen." If Alex could have guessed, he would have said the Albanians were to blame for the theft. After all, the Albanian mob was in cahoots with the Russian mob on many nefarious endeavors. He and General Bellis were of one mind in those matters, having seen the extraordinary cooperation the two criminal organizations displayed for one another. Human trafficking, prostitution, drugs, slavery, if it was illegal, they did it. Alex had no way of knowing the extent of the involvement of Near-Easterners in this venture, except that in his mind, it seemed like something they would do. Steal a secret element? Why not?

Alex brought the car up under the starboard jet engine and kept pace with the plane as it built up power for takeoff. For once, the Lamborghini's speed was about to be eclipsed. Things had to happen fast.

"Nan. stand up with the extinguisher and turn around."

"What!!"

"Do it!"

Nan did as instructed. In a few seconds she popped up above the car's roof line, standing on the seat with the extinguisher in her hands. The wind scrambled her hair from the back. She blessed her hairdresser, who had recently talked her into a shorter cut. Although it whipped her mightily, she was able to see what she was doing.

Alex pushed the car toward its red line indicators, while the roaring jet effortlessly began to move past them.

"Now, throw the extinguisher into the engine well!"

"Oh, no, no …!"

"Just do it!"

Todd was looking out the window in front of the starboard engine, horrified as he began to see exactly what was happening. "Increase your speed!" he screamed at the pilot, to no avail.

"Okay! I'm doing it now!" Nan yelled. She was just under the front of the engine.

Alex could feel her exertion, and when he guessed the extinguisher had been launched, he veered sharply away from the aircraft onto a taxiing lane.

Almost instantly, the noise from the disintegrating engine was deafening. The car managed to get away from all flying debris, Nan was still bent over at the waist, enduring the whole episode unfolding in front of her. Alex tugged on her; she got herself back into the seat of the speeding car. They both watched as the engine had its final explosive event and the aircraft went careening along erratically amidst smoke and fire. The pilot braked and coasted the aircraft into the area where it had been idling a short time ago.

"Hurray for you, Cookie!" Alex shouted. "That's one canceled flight!"

"I need to change my underwear," she puffed.

They watched as the plane came to a complete stop. Fire truck sirens were heard in the distance. The front hatch opened. The automatic staircase was deployed. Alex and Nan waited for Todd to come down the steps.

The plane was still intact, except for the starboard engine, but now a cacophony of steam, smoke and noise enveloped it from front to back. Three fire trucks and a state trooper were quickly on the scene. It was apparent that the trooper had been briefed by the tower, compliments of General Bellis.

Confusion reigned, but still no Todd. In the maw of steam and smoke, the trucks had deployed their foam-squirting hoses which only added more drama to the unexpected scene.

Alex and Nan had exited the car and hurried toward the forward stairs. He ran up the front steps to engage Todd. But the elusive Todd Everingham was not to be found. For some reason Alex had forgotten about the plane's rear hatch. As Alex made his way back through the rows of seats, Nan let out a shout from the tarmac. "Here! He's out here!"

Alex heard her and peered from one of the windows. He could hardly believe his eyes, seeing Todd run from the rear hatch of the plane to his very own canary yellow Lamborghini.

"Oh, God, no! Not the car!" Alex deduced Todd's escape route. He, too, dashed down the rear foot well in time to see Todd start his priceless Lambo and screech off toward the open gate.

"Oh crap!" he shouted, practically in Nan's face.

"My God! He's got your car! What are you going to do?".

Alex spotted Todd's Porsche parked a short distance away. It gave him an idea. "You stay here and explain it all to the authorities. I just might catch him yet! And make sure to find the iridium!"

10

DUMPED AGAIN!
As she saw Alex speed off in Todd's car, Nan could almost cry with frustration – she would not be there for the triumphant finale of their adventure. She had survived the suicidal ride down the hill without regurgitating the delicious Three Birds dinner. And she had obeyed Alex's unreasonable command to defy death and gravity by slinging the fire extinguisher into the getaway plane's engine. Supple as she was for her seventy-something years, it was a daunting maneuver, and she had aced it. Didn't that count for something? Still shaking from the effort and the adrenaline overdose induced by the events of the last ten minutes, Nan had to concede that she was the tiniest bit relieved not to be presently occupying the passenger's seat of the Porsche, dashing away with Alex.

So here she was, stranded at the airfield. Might as well spend a few minutes following Alex's latest orders, much as she resented being given the grunt work. She hoisted herself up and into the disabled plane while police cruisers pulled in from every direction. She snagged a pant leg on the entryway. Damn. "This affair is going to ruin my entire wardrobe!" she grumbled under her breath..

The interior lights of the aircraft were on full. She began looking for the critical element. Surely Todd hadn't gotten away with it. The item was a bit cumbersome, and he was on high-flight when he exited the rear hatch. She had merely glimpsed it at the observatory and Alex hadn't given her and further clue. He had just said, "Find it!"

Nan didn't know a cockpit from a crockpot. She rummaged around the seats and the floor and some cubby holes containing charts and other mundane items. She groaned with frustration. Then, as she was crawling toward the murky rear foot well, her knee hit something sharp.

Damn! Another reason to wear somebody else's clothes when out with Alex Rayburn.

She aimed the glow of her cell phone at the offending object. There was a hazardous materials icon taped to it, and the iridium element peeked out at her from a glass panel.

"This is it!" she cried excitedly. It was the box that Todd had ripped out of the oscillating unit, right under the noses of the celebrating scientists and General Bellis. That two-faced traitor Todd must have been more concerned with escaping than keeping his hold on the element. He won't get it now, thank the gods.

Nan quickly punched Alex's cell number to let him know that the element was safe (he had given his number to her at dinner, as evidence of their truce). Of course, he didn't answer – yet there was a humming sound on the other end of the line. What was it? Nan left a message anyway, explaining that she had recovered the element, and it would soon be returned to the authorities for safekeeping.

Unfortunately, Todd, now riding hell bent for leather in the Lamborghini, had discovered Alex's cell phone on the seat. With a touch of a button, her words had gone into the wrong ears. Now an agenda change was in order. He might not try all that hard to leave the Southern Tier as previously planned. But there was one particular rendezvous he'd keep, one that would pair him, once again, with Lester Nichols.

Nan didn't know whether to be upset or amused that Alex was now on a wild goose chase for the element. But he would want to apprehend Todd anyway and retrieve his beloved sports car. So all she could do was silently wish him luck.

She dialed her boss next, to bring her up to date on the situation. Amy Huffton picked up the phone immediately and was ecstatic to learn that the element had been found.

"Amazing!" she exclaimed. "And what a wild ride you've had! Are you all right?"

"Yes, although a little worse for wear," Nan sighed.

"You two are worth your wages!"

"Thanks. But I'm stuck here, I have to find a way back to my car, It's parked at The Three Birds."

"Our security people will bring you in. I'll send a car for you and the element as soon as I can find one. It shouldn't be long. And don't worry about the police," Amy reassured Nan. "General Bellis has been in touch with everyone. Hang in there. I'll see that the element is put under lock and key."

"Thanks. But I'm a bit worried about Alex," Nan said. "Is there any way to track him? He's pretty resourceful, but if he tangles with Todd ..."

Amy gave a short laugh. "If Alex tangles with Todd, Todd will be sorry. Alex can take care of himself. But Nan, call me in the morning, first thing. One way or another, Todd is no longer in my employ. I'm going to need your help with the exhibition – yours and Alex's." Amy ended the call with "Thank you for everything."

The police took stragglers who had been on the plane into custody to begin figuring out the whole scenario. Nan, however, was to wait for the company car. The General's agents would handle the iridium element.

Nan tried to make herself presentable, but decided it was hopeless. And she didn't much care. She couldn't shake the exhilaration of adventure. She felt fully alive and was entertaining one emotion after another. She had to admit, it was a breath of fresh air to know Alex Rayburn and experience how fast things can sometimes happen. What an amazing day this had been!

In the evening darkness, Amy's personal limousine finally found her. Two men jumped out, one taking the iridium from her and the other hustling her into a rear seat. A third security man hopped in and proceeded to debrief her. She had quite a story to tell, but it was a difficult story for him to believe - his skepticism showed occasionally. Finally Nan insisted, "Just drop me off at The Three Birds restaurant. I have to get my car. If you have any more questions, ask Alex Rayburn - if you can find him."

Once safely back in her apartment, Nan headed for a warm shower, soft pajamas and a cup of tea. Soon curled up on the sofa, she replayed the events of the evening. She longed to share the story with someone more empathetic than the rather stoic security man in the back seat. It surprised her to see it was just 10:15 pm - not too late to call her good friend Gina. This wasn't a story she should share with a newspaper editor, but it would be comforting to just chat with a friend. She would set up a lunch date. Gina answered on the second ring.

"Nan, what the hell is going on up there?"

"What are you talking about?" Nan replied. How could Gina have found out so soon?

"The murder! Word gets around, you know. Even in a small Pennsylvania burg."

"But it was just this afternoon!" Nan had moved the murder of Lester's wife to the back of her mind in the excitement of the past few hours. Poor Norma, she lamented again. "But how did you find out so quickly?"

"Al, of course," said Gina. "Al told me."

Al MacPherson, Gina's significant other, or friend with benefits, or whatever they were calling themselves these days, was a retired county sheriff who was still very much in touch with events via the police radio band.

"And the victim was Norma Nichols. Wow!" Gina said. "There's a story here, all right."

"Look, Gina. I owe you one regarding the whole Norma Nichols development. How about lunch tomorrow? I'll fill you in on what I know. But whatever you hear from me must be off the record, for the moment."

"Well … all right, I'd love to meet you. How about noon? Our usual spot?"

"That will be great," Nan replied. She felt easier just hearing her friend's voice, and thinking about seeing her tomorrow. Now if only Alex would call. In a moment, she would try to reach him again.

Despite Amy's nonchalance about the outcome of the car chase, Nan was worried about her erstwhile partner. Might there have been a crash? If he did safely overtake Todd, what would Alex do next? Did he carry a weapon? Did Todd? Damn that man! Although she suspected she'd never get to sleep tonight, after a Netflix movie, she might.

Unfortunately, the events at the airport kept interrupting the on-screen action.

11

ALEX HAD BEEN elated to find the keys in Todd's Porsche.

"Great! I'm outta here, Chickie!" he had yelled at Nan.

The detective, unhappy to be stuck in someone else's car, soon fired up Todd's wheels. "What a turn of events! I'm in the wrong car, but I've gotta try."

In a flash, Alex was off and running in the direction of the regional shopping mall. Todd was far ahead of him, but not out of sight. The Porsche should be able to keep up if the driver could adjust his driving techniques a bit. He let the car lead as he familiarized himself with the German interior. This was indeed a driver's car and it was pleasing to compare the Lambo to this stoic beauty. The Porsche is not a slow car. If he could just keep Todd in sight ..."Should be easy. The Lambo's bright yellow."

His optimistic thought, however, did not take into account that it was now nine o'clock at night. The sun had set and things had darkened quickly. He sprinted ahead with his usual arrogant confidence, calling on that particular character trait which had saved his life more than a few times in the Middle East wars. He reflected for a moment on his time with General Bellis, acknowledging him for the great leader he was then, and is now.

"I'm sure glad Bellis cleared the way tonight," he thought. "This would have been ludicrous without him."

As Alex roared along at a speed unwise to road conditions, he began to suspect that his current vehicle was outmatched. "Damn! What a position to be in – chasing my own car!"

On he drove, trying to keep Todd in view. Often Todd would disappear, and then pop up again. It was quite dark now and the shadows had deepened. Oncoming lights so interfered with his view that he finally lost the bright yellow beast in the fogs of night. In the end, Todd disappeared somewhere around Newfield, just before sighting Ithaca. Alex resorted to language that offended his gentile nature. "Most unbecoming of a gentleman," he scolded himself.

Before long, he was orbiting the hills around Ithaca and getting nowhere. He cursed himself for even imagining that he could keep up with his own car.

Todd, in the meantime, had found his way to a prearranged meeting place beyond an old covered bridge in Newfield. He had sped around a curve, across the wooden structure, and on about a mile into an open garage, dousing the lights. In the black of night, he watched Alex drive by, just below the driveway.

"Heh, heh. Can't find your own car, Alex Rayburn?" He turned and went into the house.

Earlier, using Alex's cell phone, he had contacted the one who was vital to the success of his operation. Lester Nichols was the individual who could now help retrieve the iridium element currently housed and protected at Amy Huffton's Museum of Glass. Todd had been delighted to hear Nan spill the beans when she was trying to message Alex.

"So now I know. You didn't think *I* was listening, did you, you dopey woman?" he crowed. Such slips amused Todd. No matter the situation, he loved one-upmanship. But someone didn't take to his humor kindly.

"Talking to yourself again, Todd?"

Lester Nichols stepped in from the other room. He had used this abandoned house to hide in during other capers.

"Can I help it? Some things are damn funny."

Lester fancied himself as one of a more professional group of thieves and con men than the academic Todd: "You're the apprentice here, don't you forget it!

"Well, you need to show your stuff now. I overheard on Rayburn's phone that the element is being held at the Museum of Glass. Maybe we can snatch it during the Turkish Exhibition when there's lots of distractions…" Todd was thinking aloud. " It's going to be a very formal event, invitation only. But nearly everyone who'll be there knows me…."

"Don't worry so much. I told you - I'm a master of disguise." Lester preened.

Todd snorted. "You'd better be. Or our Russian friends will lose patience with us."

"Us? Or you? You almost blew it all tonight"

Todd was nonplussed. "How the hell could I know those two were going to disable the plane? Nobody does what that … that … bloody skunk-woman did! That engine blew up every which way it could!"

"All right, all right, calm down. You did the right thing; you got away. Now it's up to us to get into the museum and finish the job."

"What about Alex Rayburn's slightly obvious car?"

"Let him find it if he can. We'll dump it at Guildermann's, just to confuse him."

12

A FTER A FITFUL night, Nan actually overslept. She was stiff and bruised from her rocky ride in the Alex-mobile. She had just enough time for a cup of coffee and a couple of Aleve before phoning Amy. Nan wasn't sure what Amy considered "first thing in the morning," but she guessed 8:30 would do. The secretary put her right through.

"Nan. I'm glad you called. You'll be happy to hear that Alex is fine. He wasn't able to catch Todd, but he got home safely. He called me about eleven last night."

"That's good news," Nan replied.

She had worried about the man. She had tossed and turned for hours, but he hadn't called *her*; he'd called Amy. Well, Amy was their employer, but *she* was his partner. Didn't she rate a call? "I swear I'll never waste another minute worrying about Alex Rayburn," she vowed silently.

"Nan, I'm going to need you full-time and more between now and the opening Friday," Amy said.

"I'll do all I can, of course," Nan replied. "But I'm surprised the police are releasing the crime scene so soon"

"General Bellis took care of that. We really can't postpone the opening because of the Turkish government's expectations. This exhibition was designed to earn some points for the current administration. There's an election coming up, and the president wants to show the voters and the EU and the world how progressive he is." Amy sighed. "I was counting on Todd to pull everything together. I still can't believe that he turned on me. I trusted him, the creep."

Nan had never known her current boss to lose her composure like this. She sympathized.

"He fooled us all, Amy. I really liked him and was looking forward to working with him on the reception."

"But what a mess he left us in. We've only got three days."

"Well, at least you've got the element back," Nan reminded her.

"Yes, you're right. That's the important thing. And we're going to display the element at the exhibition, too. We'll show the world how progressive *we* are."

Stunned, Nan spoke up. "In view of what's happened, are you sure that's a good idea? What does General Bellis think?"

"Norm Bellis is all for it," Amy replied. "In fact, he suggested it. Alex likes the idea, too. He thinks it might bring Todd back for another try, and we'll be ready for him this time."

"I see," Nan responded noncommittally. So I'm to plan the party and Alex is to guard the element. Humph! Typical gender role assignments. And from Amy, a female VP, no less!

Amy continued. "Alex will join me in hosting the visiting dignitaries. He'll be very useful - he speaks a little Turkish."

Of course, he does, Nan fumed. He probably plays the zither and grills perfect kabobs, as well. She wondered if Amy could hear her eyes roll.

Nan told Amy, "I have a lunch engagement today, but I'll be able to spend the afternoon and evening catching up on things. I'll be at the museum by three."

"Sounds good," Amy agreed.

Nan granted herself a leisurely morning to enjoy her home. The condo was a re-purposed school building halfway up the hill to the college; her apartment was a spacious former school room with tall windows lining three sides. As she eased through a reassuringly domestic morning, Nan wondered if Alex would call to fill her in. She hadn't heard from him by 11:00, when she took the condo elevator down to the garage and settled into her sensible Sentra.

Nan's destination was The Hand of Man in Owego, New York, a small antique and gift shop with a cafe overlooking the Chemung River. The charming little town is stretched out along the river. Lovely old Victorian homes and civic buildings are interspersed with more contemporary structures, all shaded by tall elm trees which somehow survived the elm blight of the early 1900's.

Gina had arrived first, eager to hear about the murder of Norma Nichols, and had two Negroni cocktails waiting. The women exchanged greetings, placed their order, and then Gina declared, "Enough of the pleasantries, Old Buddy. Spill!"

When she heard that it was Nan who had discovered the body, her eyes widened and she interrupted, "Can I publish any of this?"

"It would be risky at this point, Gina. I told the police I *thought* it was Norma, but there's been no official identification yet. What if I'm wrong?"

"Not you, Nan. I'd bet on your instincts every time."

"Thanks, but some other things have been happening that are bigger news than the murder – all off the record." Nan went on to tell Gina about her dinner with Alex.

"You really had a date with Alex Rayburn? Gina interrupted. "May I touch you?"

Nan felt herself flush. "Oh, it wasn't a date. We were just talking over this business that Amy asked Alex to look into –a break-in at one the company's scientist's home on Seneca Lake. After dinner, we motored up to a company lab on Spider Hill to watch a test". Belatedly, Nan remembered that Amy had sworn

Alex and her to secrecy. "I really can't tell you any more. But I could use your help on something: See if your friendly policeman Al has heard anything about a theft and a car chase. If he has, then maybe I can comment – for your ears only."

Nan was still smarting from Alex's habit of overlooking her phone calls. She knew she was giving in to a natural desire to share exciting news and had to stop herself. Had she already said too much?

Gina leaned back in her chair, crossed her arms, and cast narrowed eyes at her friend.

"You can't just leave me hanging like this. I promise not to print anything. Just answer one question. Did the car chase involve the notorious Lamborghini of a certain Mr. Rayburn?"

"It did. And I was in the passenger's seat!" Nan confided gleefully.

"No way! You are living the dream of half the women in the Southern Tier!" Gina exclaimed. "I'm dying for the details!"

"You know, I'm not completely sure myself what happened. And I've absolutely no idea how it's going to end," Nan said. "But Amy Huffton wants me to take charge of the reception for a new exhibition of glass from Turkey that opens Friday at the museum, so I'll be too busy to concern myself with the murder, or with Alex Rayburn's activities."

Grinning widely, Gina said, "You're lying of course."

Nan screeched a happy guffaw. "You know me too well, sister! But seriously, I'm really curious to know if Al has heard anything on his police scanners. Ask him and let me know, will you?"

"Sure. From one snoopy journalist to another, I'm on it. She added, "And as soon as you can, please tell me everything!

Nan promised, although she was a bit ashamed of herself for sharing too much about her adventure with Alex. Thankfully, she felt her energy and general good humor return while driving to the glass museum to meet Amy. The lunch, the drink and the camaraderie combined to boost her spirits and she was ready to dig into the job at hand.

She met Amy in Todd's former office at the museum. It had been given a thorough going-over by the authorities, including General Bellis. Amy had retrieved all the documentation of plans for the mounting of the exhibition, as well as the opening reception. The files pertaining to the reception she quickly handed over to Nan.

She explaineded, "Actually, all the contacts have been made and orders placed with the caterer, the florist, the musicians and so forth. Just look them over and see if you can recommend any changes or improvements."

"Is the location the same? Nan asked. "I mean, it was the site of the murder."

"It's been thoroughly cleaned up and it's ready to go. It's the most appropriate spot logistically and artistically. Just try to forget the murder, Nan."

Nan bit her lip. It seemed that poor Norma was being swept under the rug as a mere inconvenience.

"Have you heard any more about the investigation? Do the police have any idea who did it?"

Amy was tired of talking about it. "The local police are off the case. General Bellis has the Feds working on it. I'm sorry about the woman, but it's not our problem, now."

Nan found both the information and Amy's attitude disturbing. It wasn't like Amy to be so unfeeling, but of course, she had a lot on her plate with Todd, the rotter, out of the picture.

Still, Nan felt like poking her friend. "And the element? Where will it be displayed? It's not glass, you know."

That remark got Amy's attention. She was nonplussed, but replied smoothly, "Alex and General Bellis are coming in to talk about that at four-thirty. I'd like you to take notes and get a summary to my desk tomorrow. The meeting will be here in Todd's old office."

"I'll be here," Nan assured her as Amy hurried off toward the executive building.

Humph! Back to being a secretary, she lamented. And how did Amy manage to bet in touch with Alex, when he couldn't care less about contacting me?

Nan turned her attention to the paperwork regarding the reception. Amy was correct, the project was well organized. She looked over the menu items – just a few Middle Eastern specialties along with elegant continental fare. Champagne, of course, but an interesting array of top-of-the-line non-alcoholic beverages as well.. Table linens would be white layered over scarlet – the colors of the Turkish flag. Music would be provided by members of the string and woodwind sections of the area Finger Lakes orchestra.

Flowers? Tulips, the Turkish national flower, would be the natural choice, but Todd avoided the obvious and opted for red and white variegated lilies, including the fragrant Stargazer variety … but wait! Nan noticed something unexpected. The florist's order was authorized by Norma Nichols, the murder victim, not by Todd Everingham. She quickly checked the rest of the correspondence in the file. All the correspondence for the arrangements, indeed, had Norma Nichols' signature at the bottom.

She had evidently been more than just a sales person, as Todd had identified her, and much better known to him than he had let on.

Nan thought back to Todd's reaction when they had discovered the body. He had seemed genuinely shocked, but had given no indication that he and Norma had worked so closely together. For how long? And how closely? Nan pondered this in her wily way. Was Norma aware of Todd's plan to snatch the element? If so, it might be a strong motive to put her out of the picture. Nan's head was whirling with postulations of plots real or imagined concerning the death of Norma Nichols, a murder yet to be solved by the authorities.

A chilling possibility occurred to her. Was Amy aware of the Todd/Norma collaboration? Was that why Amy was so willing to gloss over the murder that had taken place in the museum that bore her family name? Nan didn't want her opinion of Amy to

change, so she vacated the idea. But her restless mind continue
the his five o'clock meeting with Amy. Forewarned is fore-armed.

"Damn it. Alex, pick up!" she pleaded aloud.

Where Alex Rayburn was concerned, Nan was mightily
frustrated, as usual. She left a terse message outlining what she
had discovered, called him a few names, and hung up.

But it was a frowning Todd Everingham who got the message.
He was still in possession of Alex's cell phone.

"Very enlightening. That blasted woman knows too much,"
he said to Lester Nichols, his partner in hiding. "We'll have to do
something about her."

13

UNABLE TO GET through to Alex by phone, Nan had hoped to deliver her information in person before the meeting. But Alex, Amy and General Bellis, with a somewhat fake-looking bandage visible under his cap, arrived together.

"I hope you're feeling all right, General." Nan said after the mutual greeting.

"I hope you are, too, after your exploit of last evening," he smiled at her.

"Never better," Nan replied. She set up her laptop and began taking notes as Amy began the meeting...

"For the reception, we'll create a sort of alcove to one side near the entrance," Amy outlined, "and place the element on a specially-designed Huffton Glass pedestal. Leading to the pedestal will be a series of platforms stacked at different angles. Each platform will have a podium with a short video telling part of the story of the element, the gun's development, and its significance for national security and world peace. There will be a panoramic screen backdrop showing outer space videos from NASA."

"Wow!" Nan exclaimed, looking up from the laptop. "That sounds spectacular, but won't it detract from the Turkish ..."

"Not at all," General Bellis interrupted. "The display will be angled so that it will not attract the attention of people who are entering for the reception."

"Yes," Amy elaborated. "The display is designed to be seen on the way out, and the General will invite people to see it after his welcoming speech to the Turkish delegation."

Nan wasn't sure of this strategy, but she bit her tongue. Obviously, the matter had been previously decided. And why was the General speaking at this event, anyway? If they wanted a national dignitary, how about a New York senator – her favorite, Kirsten Gillibrand – or someone from the State Department?

"We have the Turkish glass display just about completed," Amy announced. "Nan. How's the reception coming along?"

"Ready to roll," Nan replied. "I see that 132 invitations went out, and we have 92 acceptances so far – unusual! I should let the caterers know how many folks will be in the Turkish group, and how many from Huffton."

"I'll have that for you tomorrow," said Amy.

"I can tell you there will be seven from Turkey," said Bellis. "Todd Everingham was going to be their wrangler before he turned traitor. Alex, I want you to take over that role, if you would, please. You can keep them out of trouble without their noticing, and play the genial host, answer their questions about the museum. Also this gives you a presence near the iridium display."

"Good thinking, Sir. I'll be pleased to do it." Nan noticed that Alex seemed to defer to the General in everything, nodding in agreement to his pronouncements, whereas Nan wanted to ask a few pointed questions.

Here Amy asserted herself. "I would like our head designer to accompany Gulfidan Ozmen. They've met before at international conferences and are good friends."

"Noted," said Bellis. He turned toward Nan. "I will have a number of plainclothes security people here. Don't be concerned about the caterer's count for them - they won't be indulging," he said with a grim look.

"Do we really need them?" Amy asked, a bit peevishly. "We have our own security people stationed throughout the gallery."

"Your people are here to guard the collection – not the element," Bellis reminded her. "And we may well have to foil another attempt to steal it."

It seemed to Nan that a fancy reception would be an unlikely place to pull a heist like that. Why was Alex still nodding in agreement? Maybe being in Amy's presence rendered him speechless. When he wasn't hanging on the General's every word, his eyes were fixed on Amy. Was it infatuation or could he possibly have the same suspicion she had?

Nan more of less tuned out the balance of the meeting, which produced nothing worth recording. Finally Amy said, "That about wraps it up." She turned to Bellis.

"Can you join me for dinner, Norm? We'll try The Three Birds over on the south side of town. The steaks are something special."

Nan grabbed Alex by the arm before he had a chance to follow them out. "I was worried about you! And I wanted to know what happened. Don't you ever answer your damned phone?"

"Well, it's not exactly me who's been ignoring you, sweetness. Surely you realize by now that Todd has my cell phone from the Lamborghini – y'know, that beautiful yellow vehicle of mine which he copped? I thought you knew. I couldn't find him last night."

Nan was immediately contrite. How stupid she'd been! "Oh, that … that's right. Sorry. Well, if you retrieve your phone some day, you'd better not listen to your voice mail. You'll get an unpleasant earful..."

Alex continued her sentence, "... which probably amused Todd. And no doubt your messages tipped him off to some of our confidential information."

Oh my God! Worse and worse! After a pause, Nan said contritely, "I feel I haven't been much of an asset to you in this affair."

"Nonsense," Alex stated. "Who stood up on the seat of a speeding car and tossed a fire extinguisher into a jet engine intake? Wasn't me, I was driving."

"Scared the crap out of me!" Nan recalled.

"But you did it. And having you along has helped keep me stay focused. You're more important than you think."

"Thanks, Alex," she said gratefully. "But now I think I can add some real detecting skills to the mix."

Alex was amused. She had done more than she realized. What was this new aptitude she was about to reveal? The thought gave him a chuckle. She went on to tell him what she had discovered about Norma Nichols' role in performing Todd Everingham's job.

"Hmmm ..." Alex said. "That information certainly throws some light on the picture. And also raises a lot of questions about how Norma's murder relates to Todd's master plan."

"Sure does," Nan agreed. "And I'd like to run an idea by you that I'm pretty sure you won't like."

Alex was happy to see Nan's enthusiasm.

"Okay, shoot!"

"Well, I was wondering if Todd was acting alone and how he got all his information. And why Lester Nichols suddenly reappeared out of nowhere. And, of course, where does Lester's mysterious wife, Norma, fit in?"

"So? Any theories?"

"Well, you remember, Lester turned up at Amy's fund-raiser. She must have invited him. How? Why? Do they know each other?"

"Hmm ..." Alex listened.

"Amy hired Todd, and possibly Norma, as well. She's very hands-on in personnel matters. And Amy knew all about the element from day one. She invited her pal General Bellis - Norm, as she likes to call him - here for the test, and knew that she could count on him to impose a police and media blackout if anything went wrong."

"Are you implying that Amy could be masterminding the theft of the element?" Alex asked coldly.

"Well look at the facts. Who's in a better position?"

"I can't believe it!" Alex was astonished.

Nan persisted, "I thought that you, a *real* detective, might weigh those facts and become suspicious."

"Nan. How can you imagine such a thing? You *know* Amy."

"I realize you're fond of Amy. So am I, but ..."

Alex's eyes narrowed. "Are you perhaps a bit jealous? Is that possible?"

Suddenly it was Nan who was not amused. "That's a low blow, Buddy." She was shaking. "If I were jealous of every woman who was younger, richer and prettier than me, it would include half the female population of New York State. No. this isn't about jealousy. It's about logic!"

"Really? So what *logical* reason would Amy have to formulate some devious plot to steal her own company's creation?" Alex fumed. "Give me a motive or give me an apology."

"If I'm wrong, I owe Amy an apology, not you!" Nan retorted angrily. Then, totally deflated, she dropped into a desk chair. "Okay, she doesn't have a motive. I should have thought of that. But do you have the ability to think outside the box, here, O Great Detective?"

"Yes, I do," Alex said, composing himself. "But I'm not telling you anything. You might accidentally call my cell phone and spill the beans to Todd!" He stalked out of the office and shut the door, firmly.

14

"GENERAL?"

"Yes, what is it? Hurry, soldier! I need this phone to be clear."

"What do you want us to do with this car we found parked here at Guildermann's compound? It's a yellow... er, Lamborghini something or other."

"Good work! Yes, we'll retrieve it. Meanwhile, sit on it and guard it carefully. I'll send somebody to get it."

General Bellis was instantly happy for Alex, for no matter what might occur over the next few days, Alex was a bit special to him. But he wondered why Everingham would leave the Lamborghini there? Was this some odd surprise he hadn't counted on? And where was Lester Nichols? Was he with Todd?

The General had some decisions to make. He'd begun to wonder if he would be able to trust these two sneaks he'd employed to run their plan all the way to the end. After all, it was his own future he was immediately concerned with, not theirs. He didn't care about further dealings with two hired thieves who expected a whole lot more than they were going to get. This was *his* party, and all the planning to get the iridium out of the country had to rest on his connections. He reckoned he must not be construed as a turncoat. No, not after his splendid record with the U.S. Army and the years of yearning to break free from it all. He could not continue to share this escapade with two rogues who were comparative amateurs. He was "The General" who had organized the Army corps on the Eastern Quadrant of the country and was known for his good decisions during skirmishes in the Middle East. And he was "The General," recognized far and wide as a possible candidate for the presidency of the United States. This, only if he chooses to do so. For this, he would have to be extremely careful. No spot could be on his record. He must now remain unblemished as he carefully deals with the Russians in this matter. The Russians could be a great help in future elections but ...

Norman Bellis pondered, as he often did, running for the highest office in the land. The election might be a triumph or a disaster. Perhaps he would opt instead for buying a major part of the Seychelles archipelago and have Manhattans delivered to his hammock on the beach. One way or another, he was going to have a great life, with or without his wife, whom he considered expendable. He would not hurt her in any way, of course, but perhaps leave her behind to visit the graves of their three stillborn children. He would set her up with plenty of money so she would be able to do as she liked. He couldn't include her in his rather heady plans - too many variables. She was a simple woman, and would be content to carry on without him. He was the important one here, and this iridium element, along with all he knew about it, was poised to make him richer than rich, and indeed, untouchable.

The idea of the presidency began to lose its luster. Again, too many variables. "Do I want to put myself through all that malarkey?" he asked himself for the one-hundredth time. "I don't think so."

He knew that once he was in that Indian Ocean nation, it would be a new day for a man who'd never been a bad sort, just a man wanting unparalleled freedom. His health was good and really that's all one needs to get on with having a good life. It doesn't hurt to be filthy rich, either. The iridium element wasn't all that important in the scheme of things – his scheme, anyway. After all, it wouldn't be long before every advanced country on the planet had the technology. Now one question weighed heavily on his mind:

"Can I trust Todd and Lester?"

The "somebody" that the General had referred to earlier on the phone was a grateful Alex Rayburn, still relegated to driving Everingham's Porsche (though learning to like it). The General had relayed the word quickly to Alex after that phone call from one of the men guarding Guildermann's lab. Nobody in the country was more relieved to recover his unmatchable car than Detective Rayburn. He would leave Todd's car at Guildermann's, and good riddance.

"Thanks, General. I'll pick it up, myself. I'll head up there in the morning."

The General was sincere. "I'm glad for you."

"Thank you, Sir. Are you staying in the area long?"

"I'll be gone when the time is right. I'll certainly stay long enough to take in the Turkish exhibition. I want to see how Amy displays the iridium element to the public. I'm letting her do so as a courtesy; after all, it's her company that turned Guildermann's theory from fiction to fact." Norman Bellis made the effort to continue projecting his present persona, even though the seeming sentimentalist was going rogue. "We have to have strict security, you know. After it's on display for a day or two, I will personally move it to Washington, D.C."

"See you tomorrow, General."

At sunrise Alex awoke happy, knowing his toy was safe. He rushed around with enthusiasm and decided that it might be a good idea to pick up a very unhappy Nan Holloway for the hour's ride to Seneca Lake - if she were still speaking to him. Then he realized it might be a bit too early in the day for the formerly globe-trotting Nan.

"I wonder if she's got her face on yet," he snickered into his house phone. After this call, maybe he could smooth things over with his female consort when they were on their way to the lab on the lake. It would be good to have his prickly partner as well as his priceless automobile back. Unfortunately, he wouldn't be getting his cell phone back, too, he lamented, but he would grab a spare.

"Hello?" Nan answered her phone.

"Rise and shine, Cookie."

"It's about time, you self-absorbed show-off." Nan was still upset, and amazed herself with the remark.

"Wha ...? Alex tempered Nan's ugly mood with a laugh as she dabbed her face with a freshening towel.

"Let's just live in the present and forgive it all," he said. "We have other things to concern us. I'm picking you up shortly for breakfast at McDonald's. Just look outside, you'll see me. I'll explain the rest when we talk."

"Okay." Nan was happy to hear his gracious tone. I suppose he's not so bad, she thought, then howled, "Oh my God! Look at my hair! And what does he mean by *shortly?*"

Ten minutes later, Alex came rumbling up to her condo in Todd's Porsche. Another ten interminable (to Alex) minutes passed. Then Nan appeared, reasonably garbed and groomed, and got in.

"I'm really embarrassed about the Amy thing ..." she began.

Alex cut her off. "Forget it, Nan. It's all a part of being human. Goofy things are what we humans do."

He reckoned that now, at long last, she was solidly with him. No more jousting for advantage; no more hurt feelings over nothing, and no more rude comments. It was over. She liked him, and he liked her. "Ready for some fast food?"

"More than!" she clipped, with a cheery smile. Alex's penchant for fast food was legendary. He judged that it was not only quick, but actually had more quality than people gave it credit for. Still, for fun, he had often told friends that he was a monument to questionable foods. "I work hard at having my arteries seize up," he would say, using a favorite quote. On this day he was very happy to have Nan in the car, since they'd begun to unfreeze again.

After a breakfast sandwich or two, they were on their way to Watkins Glen and the Guildermann compound. The car hummed along Route 414 north through the verdant hills of upstate New York with the shadows playing across the hood on Todd's shiny vehicle. Nan remarked about the clarity of the day. It seemed that each leaf on each tree on the surrounding hills was perfectly delineated.

"Not much humidity today," Alex posted.

"These are the nicest days of the year," she returned.

"After we get the car, let's have a drink at the marina."

"Sounds good," Nan agreed. "What will you do with this car?"

"Just leave it. I suppose the government will impound it."

"Too bad. Nice car."

His tone was conciliatory. "You're a truly great lady, Nan. You're able to put up with me."

She replied, "Well, you're not so bad yourself. I don't give you enough credit. Your life, especially when you were a cop, must have made you the confident person you are. The military, too. And you have a good friend in General Bellis."

"Yes. Good old Norm, steady as Gibraltar," Alex mused wryly. Then, "You're a good partner, Nan."

"Thanks."

Nan rather liked the Alex she hadn't known before today. Words were softer between them as small talk began to dominate the morning. Conversation came from everywhere, on every topic. They were truly comfortable with each other for the first time since the incident at Amy's party.

They passed the small houses in Beaver Valley and continued on to Seneca Lake.

"Answer one question for me, will you? Nan said.

"Okay, shoot."

"Why no marriage?"

"Never thought I had time. Managing the family fortune is a full-time job. There are holdings here and yon, some in Switzerland, some in Asia. Seems like I'm constantly on a plane bound for somewhere. Really, I like the freedom to determine what's next, day by day. It's probably a lame excuse, but there it is. Real freedom."

"So, you're not gay," Nan teased.

"Heavens no," he laughed. "But hey, who knows," he continued to chortle.

Oh, great," she thought. Is he just playing with me?

Alex liked the easy interaction. Things had improved immensely between them.

"I have a spare cell phone," he disclosed. "You might want to record the number."

Nan blushed, remembering her *faux pas* with the misdirected messages.

"I think I'll just wait for you to call me from now on."

He gave her hand a squeeze. "I will, y'know. You can count on it. But really, always feel free to call. Right now, I'm a bit worried about you. Because of the intercepted phone message, Todd knows what you know about poor, murdered Norma, and your other suspicions. You could be in danger."

"Me? I'm not important enough."

"But he must know you're working with me, and with Amy. He could want to silence you the way somebody silenced Norma."

Nan tossed her hair with an air of bravado. "Too late now, isn't it? He'll certainly realize that you and I have spoken. Maybe we're both in danger."

"Perhaps," Alex conceded. "But I'm used to it. Are you?"

15

"DIDN'T WE JUST pass my Porsche heading for Watkins?" Todd Everingham craned his neck to observe two people in the quickly vanishing vehicle. He was in the passenger's seat of a rented Toyota; Lester Nichols was at the wheel.

"By God, it is! That must be Rayburn and Nan Holloway. I only got a glance. I'll bet he's heading for Guildermann's place where we left his Italian canary."

"Yeah, that Lamborghini is really yellow. He's lucky we didn't trash it," Lester added.

"No, you can't trash a car like that no matter what your motives are. You'd be destroying a work of art. Hell, I might want to buy it someday, ha ha."

"I could destroy it."

"That's your trouble, Lester. You're not a very classy guy."

"Oh, and you are, smart ass?"

"Yes, I am, actually. I just wish I could get my Porsche back."

"My heart bleeds for you," Lester said sarcastically. "If we can get that damned element, we'll both be able to buy what we want, when we want."

"You're right about that, anyway, assuming Rayburn doesn't screw it up for us."

` "Doesn't matter what Rayburn does," Lester said. "He has no idea where we are or what we're doing"

"We hope! I don't think he fell for that fake break-in ploy of yours. The mattress-over-the-fence maneuver went out decades ago."

"Maybe. But it worked. And it sure got Amy Huffton in an uproar, didn't it?"

"Yeah, and that's why she put Rayburn on the case. Thanks a lot!"

The feuding felons were heading for Corning to complete the plan roughly outlined by their boss. How they managed to pull it off was up to them. They needed to make careful preparations.

"I picked up Nan Holloway's messages on Rayburn's cell phone. Did I mention she was at the museum when we found Norma's body? She thinks I might be the murderer."

"Is she right about that?" Lester queried. "Did you get tired of forcing yourself on my wife? Or did she get tired of you? You're a cold-hearted bastard, Everingham."

Todd gave a mean laugh. "Very funny. I know who killed Norma."

"Well, don't think you can pin it on me, if that's what you're implying," Lester objected. "I wasn't anywhere near the museum when it happened."

"And when exactly did it happen, Nichols? I've been wondering how long she lay there with a piece of glass sticking out of her neck."

"Poor Norma," Lester moaned. "She didn't deserve it. But I agree, it's just as well she's out of the picture. She knew too much and kept wanting more. Maybe she was blackmailing you, Todd."

He gave his contentious cohort a sideways glance. "Good for Norma!

Todd ignored his comments. "And now, Nan Holloway knows too much. Rayburn, too. Something needs to be done about them or they're sure to mess things up."

"I have good reason to hate them both. I could arrange some accidents."

"Don't go by what your stupid emotions tell you!" Todd warned. "We need to stick to business. Stay on point! The boss wouldn't like you murdering people for the fun of it. It complicates things, you moron. The General won't pay for a botched job. Act like it's a business. No emotions!"

"All right, all right. Take it easy. Let's turn the car around and wait for them. We know they'll use this road; it's the most direct. There's a store in Beaver Valley. We can hang out in the parking lot. Then, let's see where they go, and when opportunity presents itself, we can grab Nan Holloway.

"Not a bad idea," Todd conceded "Rayburn's going to want Nan back in one piece. I've still got his cell phone, so we'll wait for his call. I guarantee, he'll call his old phone knowing I'm on the other end. But remember, Nichols, this is just something we're going to do off the record. Keep in mind we've been hired to get that element. That's our number-one priority, got it?"

"Yeah, I got it," Lester moped, already imagining how he might terrify Nan. Everingham was no fun.

"All this with Rayburn and Holloway might have to wait to till *after* we get the element for the boss," Todd cautioned him, further dashing Lester's dreams of vengeance.

Meanwhile in Corning, the General reflected on the past few days. They had been rough on his nerves and he was particularly concerned about the law: local, state and national.

"Somebody's going to put it all together," he worried. "Perhaps they'll investigate Norma Nichols' death and come up with the right answers."

But no, he felt reasonably safe from scrutiny. After all, he was "The General," a favorite of Amy Huffton since her childhood. Now she was heading an industrial titan and was probably the most influential person in the region. Her good will was a safety net.

Still, he kept thinking about Norma Nichols.

Todd Everingham, sitting in a convenience store parking lot, was thinking about Norma, too, and how things had gotten out of hand. Was it just three days ago?

At that time, after an energetic early morning encounter at his apartment, Norma had tousled his dark hair and said, "So tell me about it –The Big Plan."

"You know everything already, Babe," Todd had answered, still breathless and sweaty.

"No. I mean the *real* plan. I thought we were going to make off with a priceless Turkish whatchamacallit."

"For the tenth time, it's a *ewer*," Todd interjected wearily.

"Well, that was the plan as far as I knew it. I've been helping you all along the way, Mister Big Shot Ivy League guy. You may be able to tell a Matisse from a Modigliani, but you couldn't even organize a tea party without me." Norma rolled out of bed.

Todd sat up. "What's this all about?"

"Just for you, lover, I even recruited my slime-bag husband to help out, after I had carefully eluded him for years. And now you're going to cut me out, aren't you."

Todd scowled. "You're talking B.S., Norma."

"Oh, am I?" She started getting dressed. "Well, I found that 'secret' cell phone you use to talk to General Bellis, and I played back some messages."

Todd was fully awake now. "I can explain all that."

"So can I." Norma zipped up her skirt.

"Oh, come on, baby," Todd smiled boyishly and opened his arms in invitation. "We're not done here, are we?"

"Oh we're done here, all right." Norma slipped a sweater over her head. "We're done, period, unless you want to cut me in on whatever you and the General are planning."

Seeing that the games were over, Todd sat up and faced her, his expression suddenly serious.

"Norma. What you don't know can't hurt you. So believe me, you don't want to know."

"Okay, then. She slipped into her three-inch heels and retrieved her hand bag from the night stand.

"We'll talk about it again at the office. Or I'll talk about it to Amy Huffton."

"Stop!" Todd called uselessly after Norma's angry exit. He sighed deeply and picked up a cell phone from a drawer in the stand. His communication was succinct.

"General, we have a problem."

General Bellis had listened to Todd's story without interruption. Finally he spoke.

"Tell Norma I would like to meet with her at the museum, somewhere out of the way."

"There's no one working at the exhibition site now."

"Fine. Bring her there."

Norma had been pleased when Todd told her that the General wanted to speak with her. She trotted along happily beside him, fluffing her long auburn hair.

"Do I look all right?"

"Oh, for heaven's sake, Norma!"

When they reached the site, General Bellis was waiting, an impressive presence in full uniform.

"Mrs. Nichols!" He held out his hand.

"Just Norma, if you please."

"Of course. Norma."

She took his hand. "I appreciate your taking the time to see me."

The General continued holding her hand. "My pleasure. Todd tells me you're unhappy. What is the problem?"

"Well, I think I've been an important part of this project. Now I've heard some conversations between you and Todd which lead me to believe there's a lot more going on than I'd thought. Things which I've never been informed about. I think I deserve to be included."

The General looked down at her in a fatherly fashion.

"It's true, you've been invaluable. And we're grateful. But now your role is over. You'll be paid well for your services. Ten thousand dollars – how does that sound?"

Norma pulled her hand away. "It sounds like stalling."

"If you continue with this, you'll be in over your head. Better to make a graceful exit now."

Todd saw the ice in the General's eyes. Bellis had not made a suggestion; he had given an order.

But Norma, distressed with the tone the meeting had taken, was not in an obedient mood.

"You just wait a darned minute! I know there's going to be a huge payoff at the end of this little enterprise, and you intend to cut me out of it. If I were to tell Amy Huffton what I know, I'm sure it would be worth a great deal more than ten thousand to her."

"Careful, Norma," Todd cautioned her. He had seen the General transform from teddy bear to grizzly before, and he sensed it was about to happen again. Norma, unfazed, plummeted on.

"I have a feeling you could be much more generous with me if I agreed, as you say, to make a graceful exit now. Otherwise..."

"No, Norma!" Todd sensed disaster.

The General had turned red in the face. He was breathing heavily. He moved close to the petite woman and took hold of her shoulders, nearly engulfing her.

"Yes, you're going to make an exit *now*!" His face a mask of rage, he seized the nearest deadly object at hand, a Persian 14th Century glass bottle, and dashed it against the corner of a display case. He circled Norma's neck with his hands, implanting the jagged neck of the bottle in her throat, and squeezed.

Norma's frantic eyes sought Todd's as she thrashed about.

"Stop!" Todd squeaked out. Not usually an empathetic individual, he was horrified now, yet unable to move to Norma's defense.

Bellis squeezed tighter, half-lifting the woman from her feet, and shook her violently. Todd, limp with horror, knew Norma was beyond help.

The body fell in a heap, and the General shoved it into a corner with his foot. Her blood had spattered slightly on his dark uniform.

"Problem solved! Make sure no one finds this for at least fifteen minutes," he commanded. "And let someone else discover it." He strode down the long corridor and out an emergency services entrance, leaving Todd to ponder his next shaky move.

Todd couldn't forget "discovering" Norma's body with Nan, a truly shocked Nan, just a scant half-hour later. He remembered bending over Norma. She was still warm and smelling of the flowery scent she had worn earlier that morning. He'd almost gagged.

Back in the present, he knew he would never be involved in a murder again if he could avoid it. He and Lester would foil Nan and Alex without another horrible scene like Norma's demise.

16

HANS GUILDERMANN, RELAXING on his dock with a fishing rod, heard the Porsche arrive in the circular drive. He had been alerted that Alex would be picking up the Lamborghini. He beckoned to Alex and Nan to join him.

"What are you catching?" Alex inquired, as he ambled across the lawn to take a seat on one of the sturdy Adirondack chairs on the dock.

"Nothing!" chuckled the professor. "It's the wrong time of day for the fish to be biting, but I love just sitting here with a line in the water."

Nan joined them. "It's a sort of like meditation, I imagine."

"Exactly." Guildermann concurred. "That's why I chose to build my home on the lake. After a long session in the lab, it's like a vacation just to look at the water. And the view is never the same twice."

"I've noticed that too, through the years," Alex agreed. "I wouldn't live anywhere else but the Finger Lakes region."

Nan, whose heart still throbbed to the beat of The Big Apple, said simply, "It's very beautiful here."

They sat together in companionable silence for a few moments, just surveying the glassy surface of lake, its surface a mirror reflecting the deep green of the surrounding hills.

The scientist retracted his fishing gear. "Can I offer you some coffee? With some of my favorite sticky buns?"

"Thanks, but we've just had breakfast," Alex replied.

Guildermann chuckled again, his eyes twinkling. "Breakfast together... that's nice."

Nan blushed.

"Well, Alex, I've been wanting to ask you about the break-in here," Guildermann changed the subject. "I know you discovered how it was done, but do you know why? Whoever it was made a mess of my papers, but it appears nothing of importance was taken."

Alex nodded. "It all seemed rather pointless to me, too. Amateurish, in a way. The only explanation is that it was a red herring.'"

"Red herring? Oh, yes, a diversionary tactic. So! No real harm done, and the test of the device was a huge success. I could say my role in this endeavor is over. But how about yours?"

"We were successful in recovering the iridium element," said Alex and described the car chase and Nan's exploit at the airport. "We hope to apprehend the thief in a matter of days."

"What a feat, Ms. Holloway! I congratulate you, both of you!" The professor escorted them to the parking area where the Lamborghini awaited its owner. With Nan at his side, Alex departed a happy man.

Todd and Lester, who had thought to intercept the couple in the yellow sports car at Beavers Corners and possibly snatch Nan, gave up after twenty minutes and returned to their Finger Lakes lair. They had a task to complete and a plan to perfect.

After they created and discarded several scenarios, Lester lost patience. "It's just too risky, no matter how you look at it. Why don't we just snitch that Turkish ewer thing, like you told Norma we were gonna do. Isn't it worth a bundle? I know a lot of fences. I've got contacts all around the world."

"You idiot! The ewer is a work of art, immediately recognizable. You can't break it apart like jewelry to sell piecemeal."

"Don't I know that? I was thinking of collectors, who would want it intact ...."

"For what? To show off to their friends? Or to store in the attic until the price for glass ewers goes up?" Todd was indignant. "You can't deal with a masterpiece like it's... a hunk of expensive metal. And it's breakable, dummy."

"Just cool it with the insults, Everingham. I've got the kind of expertise and experience that's needed here, whether you like it or not."

"Yeah, you've told me often enough. And you're a master of disguise. So how is that going to help us? I'm tall, and practically everyone who will be at the exhibition knows my face," Todd objected. "And Rayburn and Holloway have seen you."

"Exactly!" Lester smirked. "That's the point'"

Lester explained his scheme to Todd, who grudgingly admitted he didn't have a better idea. They spent the balance of the day on the phone, setting up meetings, interviewing. The next day - the day before the exhibition - was spent working on timing and rehearsing for the big event.

"This had better work, Nichols," Todd growled, "or if General Bellis doesn't kill you, I will!"

"Stop grumbling and concentrate on making it work," Lester replied. "If it doesn't, we're both dead meat."

Nan, too, was busy preparing for the exhibition, although with more optimism. The reception would do Amy and the museum proud. When her cell rang with a call from Gina, Nan immediately began sharing all the delicious details until Gina interrupted.

"Look, I've been checking with Al, like you asked me to."

"You sound serious. What did he say?"

"He's puzzled," Gina replied. "He's discovered nothing about the car chase or the theft you mentioned - or the murder! It's very unusual for the local police to be shut out like this when there's a murder on their turf. The FBI might step in if there's a known felon on the Most Wanted list involved, but they generally work *with* the locals."

"Well, Amy mentioned that General Bellis was taking over the investigation of 'a situation at the test site' that sent Alex off on that car chase. I suspect the military hushed it up. Perhaps the murder was related in some way so that they preempted that investigation, too," Nan offered, her mind racing. What was the connection? It had to be more than a coincidence.

"The General may be a powerful man, Nan, but he can't unilaterally declare martial law," Gina shot down her suggestion. "No, Al says there is every sign of NSA involvement. National security! What have you gotten yourself into, Nan?"

"I ...I'm just planning a party here And helping Alex. He's close with the General, but he hasn't told me everything, I suspect. He likes to keep the upper hand."

"Of course he does, but please be careful, Buddy. I thought this Alex thing was just a lark, but whatever games you're playing could be really dangerous." Gina paused, and Nan could hear some low grumbling in the background. "Al's here with me now. He says whatever you do, don't get on the wrong side of the Feds'"

"Tell Al thanks, but honestly, all I'm doing is checking on flowers and food."

"Sure you are. Just be sure to give me the story first when it's all over." Gina concluded the somewhat ominous call.

Nan hadn't really thought about being in danger, although Alex had mentioned it, too. What could be more dangerous than what she'd already done? But then the vision of Norma Nichols, crumpled on the museum floor with that deadly glass shard protruding from her throat, made Nan think again. Someone involved in this affair had committed a murder, Todd or possibly Lester. If they were desperate enough to do that, what might they do to her, or to Alex, if they got too close to the truth?

And the NSA? The element had been recovered, so what could be their concern now?

Nan shivered.

17

COLONEL WINSLOW WAS incognito.

He'd been watching the iridium device proceedings in the Southern Tier for weeks, performing a special task requested by the President of the United States. Any good plan that involves secrecy is never delegated to the oversight of a single man, not even the esteemed General Bellis. The General wasn't aware of the watchdog known as Winslow who was all over town, watching and reporting on a special phone line every night to the President - a watchdog who was involved enough to play the part of "mole" at the museum exhibition as he had done several times before. The Turkish glass would be interesting, but Winslow was to be on hand to observe the showing of the iridium gun. The events were planned to be presented simultaneously to divert excessive interest in the device. The idea was to play down the importance of the gun while still informing the general population of the existence of said item. No general announcement had yet been made to news people because the president wanted the populace to get used to the device gradually.

Still, here it was, birthed in relative obscurity. Washington insiders had realized from past miscues that it takes the public time to absorb something like this. This was hot stuff and had to be "handled."

Winslow knew that the recent construction on the roof of the museum was the first implementation of the iridium knockout weapon which would eventually be placed at other locations across the U.S. For the security of the country, a plan had been devised for the distribution of the weapon to various sites, thus creating a chain of exposure to the glide path of not only satellites, but also incoming missiles. Each gun would cover a certain section of the United States mainland. It would accomplish blanket coverage of the type desired when the ill-fated "Star Wars" proposa; was voted too expensive decades ago.

This new edition was better and cheaper, thanks to the Guildermann discovery and the scientists at Huffton Glass who perfected the device. Each gun would have an east-west, north-south segment of the United States land mass as a designated protectorate. One quadrant would terminate, another would begin its effective range, and so on.

Out of deference to the Huffton scientists who devised the method of channeling light into a super knockout ray, the first public deployment of this ultimate light-concentration weapon would be located in the just-constructed area of the glass museum roof. A second gun (the first was now in the museum destined for exhibition) was recently installed in the roof enclave. It was now fully operational and known only to Colonel Winslow, Amy Huffton, and soon, Alex Rayburn. The scientists who installed it were sworn to secrecy.

Later, as people began gathering in the museum vestibule, Amy saw Alex approaching one of the custodians, presumably to clear him for his duties this evening. She had an amused look on her face as she walked toward them.

Alex was just able to nod to Nan, who was flitting from person to person in the reception area. "I'll be right with you," he stage-whispered.

Amy touched Alex's sleeve. "I'd like you to meet someone." The custodian turned and gave Alex a penetrating look. Amy spoke to him.

"Colonel, this is Alex Rayburn. He a trusted friend and has been hired to oversee the security tonight."

The two shook hands.

"It's good to meet you, Alex. Amy has a lot to say about you."

"Nice to meet you, Sir." Alex looked at the way the man was dressed. "But ... but what is your connection with all this? Are you really a Colonel?"

"Yes. Full Bird Colonel – Air Force. And you might say, I'm security, too."

"Oh?"

"You know, there's nothing as paranoid as the Defense Department. As you may realize, we have people watching people, and then people who watch those people."

"I can imagine, sir. Wow! What a get-up!" citing Winslow's attire.

"The President asked me to remain covert; to just come up here and watch everything."

"Well, you fooled me. I had no idea you were around."

"As you know, *that* is the point."

Alex filled in a few details that might have eluded Colonel Winslow. Generally they were on the same page with their conclusions.

"Bellis was not made privy to the rooftop area just constructed, which, in the natural order of security policies, was exactly the proper procedure. No need for him to know. It was textbook artistry, resulting in the best use of security divisions available to the person known as POTUS,"

"Good thinking, Colonel. But I would expect it from a Full Bird."

The Colonel ignored the compliment and went on to explain to Alex the deployment of the weapons across the United States which would create network of impenetrable defenses to cope with to any incoming missiles and aircraft. Also, any satellite which appears threatening, from any nation in the world, would be imminently subject to be neutralized at will for questionable activity. The network of weapon sites will be coordinated by the Defense Department in one of the newly constructed out-buildings at the Pentagon.

"So," Alex interjected, "the strange little construction cupola on the roof of the glass museum, which I first saw from my shower room, is in fact the housing for the second weapon, already now in place and fully operational."

"That's right. This will be the best defense system ever devised to keep us all safe. It'll probably end war - that is, in all places except the usual Middle Eastern countries."

"I see what you mean, Colonel," Alex agreed, more or less.

"The first version, the one that shot the moon, is the one on display for the general public tonight at the exhibition, along with the Turkish things."

"So I understand."

"Be sure to tell no one what you know, especially Bellis," Colonel Winslow concluded.

After they parted, Alex sought out his current employer.

"Looks like a nice turnout, Amy." It was a formal affair, as fancy as one would bother in the laid-back atmosphere of the Southern Tier. Amy was in full bloom as hostess, wearing an ivory chiffon cocktail dress, undoubtedly the creation of a top designer.

"You are matchless tonight," Alex complimented her, meaning every word.

Then he sought out his partner. Nan had taken her position at the reception and was abuzz with bouncy repartee. Things were going swimmingly as she watched the invitees devour the delicious foods, both sweet and savory.

"I don't know how you do it, Nan" Alex said, admiring the saffron silk ensemble upon which he had once caused wine to spatter.

She modeled it. "Like it? Does it look familiar?"

"Lovely! Breathtaking! And yes, I remember it well. Did you save the cleaning bill for me?"

"I believe I have it right here," she replied, patting the deep V-neckline of the dress.

They had a good laugh realizing that the original spill at Amy's party had, in its way, brought them together.

Despite the supercharged atmosphere of waiting to see if this night would prove dangerous, all seemed well at this exhibition of the most remarkable glass pieces, ancient and contemporary, formulated and accomplished by the talented Turkish people. A hubbub of stimulating conversation penetrated the reception and display areas. The iridium device and its precious element was off to one side near the exit, as specified in the meeting with Amy and General Bellis, not to be revealed until the General made his announcement.

18

GENERAL BELLIS WAS strangely absent as the evening wore on, Alex Rayburn noted with some concern. Even Colonel Winslow, the super-secret agent assigned to the case just before Norma Nichols' death, had lost Bellis somehow in the party atmosphere. Both men wondered if something could have delayed the General.

Nan was elated. At Monday's gala, Alex Rayburn had all but insulted her. Tonight, he made a point of admiring her. Not so bad for a seventy-something has-been. All she had had to do was endure a death-defying ride in a sports car and risk her life performing a daredevil stunt with a jet engine to bring about this miraculous change in his attitude. What next?

While she had bridled at being assigned to serve as a party-planner, she was enjoying the success of the event immensely. Still, she wondered what was happening behind the scenes with Alex and General Bellis, and the anticipated reappearance of Todd and Lester to swipe the precious element. That's where the real action was, her journalistic instincts told her. With her sense of adventure much revived by her experiences with Alex, she was impatient to be with him for more of the same. It was like a deep breath of fresh morning air, a welcome awakening of new capabilities, a brightening of the colors in the painting of her life.

Amy Huffton, ever gracious, strolled over to commend her. Nan thanked her in return, seeing Amy as a vision of peaches and cream and golden hair. Oh, to be forty again! No, I am not jealous, she reminded herself.

She spotted Steve Smithfield admiring the exhibit and went to chat with him. His sizable annual donation to the museum fund had earned him an invitation for this event.

"Hi, Steve. Are you having a good time?"

He turned and grasped her hands. "Much better now that you're here, darling. I can't wait to see Gulfidan Ozmen. Her work is amazing. That emerald ewer is divine!"

"Yes, it's truly a treasure," Nan agreed. She debated letting Steve know that Alex was not gay, but why not let him dream on? And there was still a chance that Alex was playing her.

"Gulfidan will be officially introduced with the Turkish delegation by General Bellis." She checked her watch. "About ten minutes from now."

"Great! I'll watch for her," Steve said. "By the way, you look smashing tonight. That dress is always so flattering."

Nan grinned. "Thanks. That's why I wear it so often."

"Oh! I guess that sounded like a backhanded compliment...I didn't mean..."

"Don't worry. We're pals." She left him in the hands of Alex's last "date," Dorothy Vandencamp, and went on to greet more patrons.

Alex, meantime, had his eyes peeled for Todd and Lester. As he had rather expected, they showed up as part of the Turkish delegation. Considering Lester's skill in disguise, Alex was surprised at how obvious they were in their traditional Turkish garb while the rest of the delegation was in modern Western dress. "What the hell ..." he wondered. At least they would be easy to keep track of during the evening. Maybe too easy. Something isn't right, the detective deduced. And where was Bellis?

Amy Huffton signaled for the musicians to conclude and made her way to the podium.

"Ladies and gentlemen, good friends of the museum, I'm Amy Huffton. I'm so happy you have come to share this very special evening with us. To officially introduce Gulfidan Ozmen and the delegation who accompanied her to the Crystal City, here is General Norman Bellis of the United States Army. The General is a not only a personal friend of long-standing, but also a world traveler who has visited Turkey, and a great patron of the arts. General Bellis."

The General appeared on cue to make his remarks.

"Where were you, Sir? Is everything all right?" Alex whispered as he escorted him to the podium.

"Just tending to some final arrangements," the General replied cryptically, with a strange smile on his face.

There was warm applause as the guests crowded toward the podium for a better view of Ozmen and her entourage. It was then that Nan spotted two men in caftans, part of the Turkish group, hurrying in the opposite direction. One was tall and dark; the other moved with a slightly bent posture. "My God! It's them!" she thought, and then "Where's Alex?" The two were headed toward the exhibition area, not the iridium display site. What were they up to?

Nan was torn between following them and finding Alex. Where was he, anyway? Probably fawning around General Bellis or Amy near the microphone. By now, there was a whole crowd of people blocking easy access to the podium. Nan decided to follow the two felons and stop them, whatever their game might be. Had they given up on the iridium element and decided to snatch the priceless ewer instead?

The General was in full pre-presidential mode, beaming as he made his introductory remarks. He mentioned the members of the Turkish delegation one by one, shaking the hand of each as they came to join him around the podium. Two were missing: "I suppose they are busy sampling the baklava," he quipped good-naturedly.

"And now, the woman whose immense talent we are here to admire and honor," he began, continuing with a biography of the artist and citing her many awards and accomplishments. "I give you…"

He was interrupted by a shriek from the other end of the corridor.

"Stop them! Somebody! Help!"

Nan had found her voice and it was loud and clear. She had followed the two men in caftans as they gingerly approached the emerald glass ewer in the display area, which was now bereft of people. It was apparent that they were intending to pilfer the priceless *objet d'arte*, so deliciously unguarded and practically inviting abduction.

Nan grabbed a lighted candle in a heavy glass holder from one of the food displays and hurled at the back of the tall man. It brought him down. Her confidence rose dramatically and she bashed the other bandit on the head with an empty crepes pan. He, too, went down to his knees with a groan. Was this the "danger" she had been dreading after Gina's dire warning? She was loving it! "Damn, I'm good!" she congratulated herself.

"Holy cow!" Alex exclaimed as he circumvented the melee and arrived with two security men. They roughly dragged the would-be thieves to their feet. Alex saw immediately that the two were not actually Todd and Lester, although they had managed to fool people for a time. The culprits were eager to talk.

"Hey, we thought it would be a good joke," the tall man moaned.

"We're just actors," wailed the other. "From Elmira Little Theatre .- you can check."

"That's right. Two guys with a lot of costumes and make-up hired us to impersonate them""

The shorter one added, "Some dude in an Army uniform was there and said it would be okay."

By now a thundering herd of excited and giddy guests had stormed the exhibition area, privy to the added attraction of an attempted theft.

Alex Rayburn, the great detective, slapped his forehead. "Oh God! The gun!"

19

ALEX, TWO SECURITY men, and Colonel Winslow, still dressed as a custodian, ran hard toward the position of the iridium device. It was near the exits which led to the ground floor garage and the roof.

"Crap!" he yelled as they closed in on the gun's location and he saw that the the iridium element was gone from its special pedestal.

One of the exit doors was ajar.

"They've headed out the exits!" Winslow spouted.

"Get down to the stairs, now!" Alex shouted.

He and the men ran down the stairs in time to see a car roar out of the lower level garage with three men inside, one looking suspiciously like General Bellis.

"Why you dirty dog!" Alex shouted after him. Then, to Winslow, he shook his head and said, "How far do they think they can get in a car?"

The getaway vehicle glided fast up the ramp and toward the street. At the same moment, a helicopter buzzed over their heads, close to the ground as if watching the speeding car.

Alex again: "I wonder who's in the chopper?"

Colonel Winslow said, "My car is right over there. I'll get after them."

The detective searched his mind for any clue as to where they might go. A helicopter might be a convenient variable in any escape equation, and seeing the craft fly over caused him to remember his time in the Middle East. He knew that standard military practice was for choppers to arrive exactly when necessary to foil escape attempts by Taliban fighters and various other thugs. His experience brought back the sharp thinking and deductive prowess he was known for.

"I think it's heading for the fire station parking lot, three blocks away. It's the only place around here big enough to land a chopper," he shouted to Winslow, who was halfway to his car.

It finally dawned on Alex. "Hell! That's how they're going to get away!"

He noticed one of the scientists who had fired the gun a few nights ago at the hill had sprinted through the museum and down the stairs with them. Alex seized the man's arm.

"You! Come with me"

He practically tripped the man as he pushed him back up the stairs to the roof of the museum,

The upper door flew open onto a walkway leading to the cupola where the second gun was housed. They hurried across the tarred roof toward the small enclosure.

"Does this thing work?" Alex puffed.

"Yes, it's fully operational," the scientist said.

"Well, get that baby warmed up 'cause you're about to use it!"

"I don't have the key to get in," the man objected.

The cupola door had a hasp lock which, truth be known, wouldn't have slowed anybody down, especially not Alex Rayburn.

"Stand back," he ordered

He slid his Walther PPk out of its holster and fired two shots at the hasp. The second bullet spun the hasp off and allowed entry.

Once inside, the technician brought the gun to life with a loud hum as he got the devise ready for use.

"How the hell are we going to fire it?" Alex said with desperation, knowing they were inside a building.

"Watch this!" the scientist said, happy as a kid to show off his new toy. He pulled a lever, which hummed, whirred, and caused the building's entire canopy to fold back like a convertible car top.

"This was installed in anticipation of its eventual use for chasing a missile or satellite."

"Glory be!" Alex shouted exuberantly to a blue sky, not yet darkened by evening shades.

The gun was now open to the sky and not a moment too soon. Alex could see clearly, 360 degrees around.

"Wow!"

The glass museum was just high enough to afford a perfect view of the fire station, two blocks away. Alex could see, on the city streets below, the car approach the fire station parking lot with the helicopter also in view and coming down. He surmised that General Bellis had thrown his weight around enough to get his own chopper to land and take off quickly, thus effecting a perfect escape.

"Swing it around," Alex told the operator. "Can you see the fire station?"

"Yes, it's in the viewfinder. I can see the car stopping on the tarmac."

"Can you set this thing on a lower power, like maybe *stun*, or something like that?"

"I think so."

"I hope so," Alex said. "I want those guys back alive."

"A lower setting will probably render the helicopter engine useless."

"Good." But he worried. "Hurry! Time's a'wasting!"

From his excellent vantage point he could see that Colonel Winslow had taken a wrong turn somewhere on the north side of town and had become confused. He would never arrive in time to stop the chopper from lifting off. It was going to be the iridium gun or nothing as the escapees were now at the helicopter entry portal.

"Wait! I have to charge the forward coils," the scientist remembered.

"There's no time!"

"It'll just take a second."

Alex didn't want the chopper shot down from a height. It would kill all aboard and that precluded their prosecution. He wanted to know the reason a respected Army General would even try such a stunt.

"For God's sake, man! Fire that thing!"

The chopper had loaded its humans of dubious character and had just closed the door. Bellis, Todd and Lester were dreaming of foreign shores where they could live out a great life with all the money the Russians might pay them. Belted in their seats, they were confident that the transportation problem was licked. Which, they thought, was their final step.

The General said, "Well boys, we did it. Look out the window and kiss Corning, New York good bye." They all laughed at the ease with which their ruse was accomplished. The biggest thing on Bellis' mind was that he'd escaped discovery as the killer of Norma Nichols. He was relieved that she was no longer a factor. Everyone got away, and that was good!

On the museum roof, Alex was frustrated.

"Oh, crap! They're lifting off! They're beginning to fly over the river and outta here!"

Alex had just got the latest expletive out of his mouth when the gun flashed its payload through the Crystal City sky and into the chopper. There was little more than a puff of smoke at the tail, but something had happened. The craft spun slowly around and tilted backward The main rotor slowed considerably letting the 'chopper sink slowly toward the shallow waters of the Chemung River. People on the bridge watched in amazement as it settled down on the only island in view, never to fly again. It sizzled and popped and blew steam into the air. The brief escape flight was finished. The rotor stopped.

On board, the impact was great enough to make Todd painfully bite his tongue. Lester, severely shaken, stared at the bulkhead and reviewed his life's mistakes.

General Bellis sat in pure shock Here was the ending of a brilliant plan and an equally brilliant career. Shame and despair hit him at the same moment. His family would have to live with the stigma of an Army man turning on his country with no better excuse than the money he would be paid by some dictator. It was a heinous act of treason perpetrated on a trusting country, the finest democracy on earth. Now dazed, he could hardly move. The ride was over, literally, for the three of them, and their dreams were dashed upon the rocks of a tiny island in a placid river in a place known as the Crystal City.

The General was aware of the curious onlookers on the bridge and river banks gawking at his humiliating downfall. Fire trucks arrived on the bridge, manned by men no longer surprised by his visit to their station a mere six minutes ago. In the company of thieves, Bellis was dead in the water ...

... as he would someday write from his cell.

20

THE PRESS CONFERENCE was scheduled for nine the next morning at the Huffton Glass executive building's auditorium. Amy, in an appropriately somber dark suit, welcomed members of the media who had converged on the Crystal City everywhere from Boston to Washington, D.C. and points west. General Bellis's quickly appointed replacement presented a briefing on the now-named Project Clear Skies. He cited the contributions of Dr. Hans Guildermann and the other Huffton scientists in its development, and followed with an outline of the plan for its deployment across the nation.

The task of informing the public about the twice-attempted theft of the crucial element fell to the hero of the hour, Alex Rayburn. Alex had been present at the all-night debriefing of General Bellis and his infamous associates. Todd Everingham had proven truculent, repeating vehemently and frequently that he was "not a crook." Lester Nichols, who knew *he* could make no such claim, had merely sulked and cursed his luck at getting involved with "non-professionals." Only the General had exhibited sincere remorse for his actions; in fact, his distress was so great that he was put on suicide watch.

Even Alex, who had suspected the General's role in the plot to steal the element, had been shocked to hear Bellis confess to the murder of Norma Nichols. Colonel Winslow had had his suspicions, but was dismayed as well with the extent of Bellis's loss of humanity in his pursuit of wealth. The Colonel, obviously, did not wish to elaborate on his part in the proceedings, and so had delegated Alex to cover the ground with the media.

Although attempting to outline the activities of the past few days dispassionately, Alex was unable to repress a certain degree of exuberance in telling the tale, noting particularly the exploits of his partner, Nan Holloway. And Amy Huffton made a point of publicly thanking the team of Rayburn and Holloway for their invaluable assistance.

Alex was particularly happy to know that one of the iridium units, critical to the functioning of the national missile protection system, would be permanently attached to the roof of the glass museum in his hometown. Because it had already performed so efficiently, the whole world would soon know about it, and that it was fashioned right here in Upstate New York. Soon Project Clear Skies would be operational and everyone would sleep a little better.

Nan, seated with some of her old media pals, was only slightly mollified by the mentions of her role. She was still mightily annoyed for - again! - not being in on the conclusion of the adventure, and for being excluded from the debriefing. But when the press conference drew to a close, she was approached by a representative from her old New York City network for an exclusive on-air interview. The local television station, suddenly proud to claim her as an anchor *emeritus,* invited her to come in and discuss a weekly talk show. Nan remembered that she had promised Gina first crack at the story - it was too late for that, but she would write a firsthand account for Gina, which could then be syndicated. Her dark mood lifted dramatically. She was a journalist again!

After accepting copious thanks, congratulations and accolades in his usual casually gracious manner, Alex found Nan and steered her away from the crowd. "We should talk. Let's have lunch."

"Okay. I have a lot of questions for you, Mister."

They walked to the executive parking lot where the canary yellow Lamborghini awaited.

"You sound just a little touchy," Alex said. "Am I in trouble again? Should I have let *you* shoot down the helicopter?"

Nan couldn't help laughing. "No, of course not. By the way, I think you were brilliant with that maneuver."

Alex opened his eyes wide with feigned amazement. "Approval; from you? I am indeed honored."

"Come off it," Nan chided. "You know you're a hero now."

"And you are a heroine," Alex returned. "What do you plan to do now that you're famous again?"

"Enjoy the heck out of it," she enthused, with a toss of her head. "I may even write a book about our little caper."

"Oh, no! That's what I was planning to do," Alex objected.

"Well, we can't both write it," Nan declared. "We'd kill each other. And *I'm* the journalist."

Alex wisely bit his tongue.

They arrived at the car.

"So where are we going for lunch?" Nan asked. "The hotel?" referring the popular Radisson close by.

"I thought we'd go somewhere special to celebrate. How about the Aurora Inn?"

The Inn is a handsomely restored mansion dating back the days when the Wells Fargo stagecoach stopped at Cayuga Lake. "It's a fine day for a long ride."

"Wonderful! I agree!"

As Nan climbed into the passenger seat, Alex gave her a friendly smack on the bottom. "It's me and you, Nancy Lou!" he sang.

"Damn that man!" Nan thought for the umpteenth time, and grinned happily.

The Unlikely Adventures of Alex and Nan

Adventure Two: Unrelated Incidents

Horton-De Wolfe

1

NAN HOLLOWAY CHECKED her makeup, adjusted the collar of her shirt, and ran her hands through her glossy dark hair – one didn't want to appear too carefully coiffed. As host of the "Nan About Town" show on WLED-TV in upstate New York, she wanted to make a good appearance, although it was scarcely as crucial as it had been when she was a rising star in network news down east in the City. That was what – forty, fifty years ago? she reminded herself. She was performing well below her capabilities now, but at her age, she felt lucky to be working at all.

She and her husband had first moved to this surprisingly sweet part of New York's rust belt to raise their son, away from the frantic pace of big city life. She had easily landed an anchor job at WLED and held on to the spot through two decades and a divorce before being put out to pasture in favor of younger talent. She was only back on the air now, she well knew, because of the notoriety she'd received thwarting the theft of a top secret scientific device alongside the dashing detective, Alex Rayburn.

Nan had invited Alex to be her first guest on "Nan About Town," but he had declined with an uncharacteristic display of modesty, declaring that she didn't need him. Nan suspected that modesty had nothing to do with it – he simply didn't want to be part of some else's show. He was accustomed to being the one to run the show and liked it that way. The man annoyed her to distraction and attracted her mightily, and she already missed the excitement of their recent collaboration.

Still, she loved being on air again, even if it wasn't in an investigative reporting capacity – her forte. Being charming to people was second nature to Nan, and she knew that asking the right questions and really listening to the answers made for a good talk show, as well as a good story.

She looked over her notes on today's guest, Billy Blackhorn, who was the writer in residence at the Rockwell, a museum of western art located in Corning, New York and affiliated with the Smithsonian of Washington, DC. A Sioux from North Dakota, Blackhorn wrote heartbreaking poetry about his peoples' lost lands, lost way of life, lost dignity and purpose. He also wrote gritty essays and news editorials bemoaning the pending desecration of his reservation through the construction of a pipeline and the leasing of lands to oil companies for the purpose of the highly controversial fracking process of natural gas extraction.

Nan had heard Blackhorn read his poems a few years earlier at the Rockwell and knew he was attractive, articulate and charismatic. She looked forward to the interview. She began by outlining his itinerary while in the area, and then asked him to read from his latest poetry volume, rather unattractively titled "Carrion." With his compelling looks and deep voice, it hardly mattered what he read – he would make an indelible impression on her mostly-female viewers.

They chatted about the Native American heritage of the surrounding area, dubbed by the tourism bureau as "The Gateway to the Southern Finger Lakes," noting the towns named Horseheads and Painted Post. They spoke about prominent Native Americans of the area such as Queen Catherine Montour, Ely Parker and Red Jacket. Billy professed a special admiration for Red Jacket, a Seneca, who had negotiated with the new United States after the American Revolutionary War. Noted as a powerful orator, Red Jacket addressed the U.S. Congress advocating freedom of religious belief and civility.

"His words have resonance today," Blackhorn stated, quoting some of them.

Blackhorn also declared himself a great admirer of the Finger Lakes region, with its fruitful hillside vineyards, deep forests, sparkling streams and waterfalls.

"You live in an exceptionally beautiful part of the world," he said to Nan, his eyes earnestly shining into hers. "I hope you won't let it be spoiled." Nan was ready for it.

"You mean fracking?" She then explained for the viewers, "Fracking is a process used to extract oil and natural gas from the earth by injecting water and chemicals into the ground under pressure."

Blackhorn continued, "I know it's tempting to land owners in an area with a depressed economy, but leasing land to the oil companies for fracking is not the solution. The process can poison the water you drink, the water that nourishes your vineyards, the water of the lakes themselves and thus, your tourism industry. It will disrupt the landscape, perhaps drastically. Did you know that the Pawnee Nation in Oklahoma sued the oil companies because earthquakes, induced by fracking, increased from 20 in 2009 to 623 in 2016?"

He went on to read passages from a manifesto adopted by some of the Northwestern tribes: "Whereas we are responsible for protecting Mother Earth from any pollutants that may cause harm to citizens, land, water and air, and whereas the National Historic Preservation Act requires Federal agencies to consider the effects of their action on historic properties, and whereas the fracking process could endanger tribal water resources; therefore be it resolved, the Nation prohibits in perpetuity hydraulic fracturing or any process that is toxic to the lands ...”

Blackhorn read with great passion and intensity and Nan, although enthralled, checked the time remaining for the show and had to interrupt him.

“But what about the argument that fracking will not only enrich land owners, but also create jobs in the community?”

Blackhorn was direct. “But not jobs for local people. You’ll see an inundation of pickup trucks with license plates from Oklahoma, Texas, and Alabama – the experienced oil hands looking to make lots of money. And they’ll overrun your motels, so you’ll need to construct ‘man camps’ to house them. You’ve probably read about the difficulties they cause, not always being the world’s most civil gentlemen.”

Nan was indeed aware. “Yes, and you’ve touched on some of those problems in your latest book. Could you please read, ‘She hoped he would take her away’ for us?” Blackhorn proceeded to read one of his most poignant poems. Nan thought it was a good way to conclude the show. She thanked Billy; the interview was over.

Off the air, Nan asked him if he really thought fracking would eventually come to the Finger Lakes. She added, “Our governor is against it.”

“Politicians can be bought,” he scoffed. “You’ll find these people will stop at nothing. Bribes, dirty tricks, threats. Do you believe this?”

He drew an envelope out of his jacket pocket and showed her a note. In heavy block letters it read:

SHUT YOUR MOUTH WHEN YOU’RE IN NEW YORK

OR WE’LL SHUT IT FOR YOU PERMANENTLY

Nan, dumbfounded, looked up at him. “Who would send this?”

"The usual suspects, I suppose. I can't believe they followed me here. I came to read poetry, not make trouble. But now I want to shout it to the world."

"This letter came for you at the Rockwell?" Nan queried. "Hand delivered?"

"Must have been," he shrugged.

"Are you going to the police with it?"

"No, no. I've received threats before, but only out in North Dakota, where I have a bit of influence." Then he repeated, "I can't believe they followed me here."

"But how can you continue with this hanging over your head?" Nan wondered. Of course he was here to promote his work and build his reputation, but espousing the anti-fracking cause couldn't help with that. Was he really so dedicated to the environment?

Billy shrugged, "I really don't want to make it a police matter, Nan. It might upset the Rockwell people, and they have been good to me." He folded the note into his pocket.

"I shouldn't have shown it to you, but I thought someone should know. You seem to genuinely care about the issue." He sent her a piercing look, tempered with a shadow of a smile.

Nan melted. "I think I know someone who can help," she blurted out. "He's a detective in Corning. I'll call him tomorrow... early."

If there's one thing that sits pleasantly on Alex Rayburn's mind, it's the smoke of a good cigar, especially if it's well-aged. And it's even more enjoyable when puffed at the third oldest cigar store in the United States, in the presence of chums who seem to come and go regularly. Not only are the cigars aged to perfection, but so are the store and all who enter in. It's the stuff of retirement, and oh, how Alex loves it. His wealth and notoriety never bother anyone. They were all high school pals and none of them were exactly poor.

When dawn broke over "his" city, Corning, New York, on a day promising to be like most others, his first waking thought was to haul himself out of bed, complete the necessary bathroom itinerary, squirt a little cologne under his collar and vacate the premises in favor of Smith's Cigar Store. He'd done it since "retiring" a few months ago. He loved it, and in case he showed up at the establishment with no cash in his pockets, his credit was good.

Today Eric, one of the customers inhabiting Saturday mornings at the store, would be there with his baked-up concoctions for all the "old boys" to try. Alex certainly wouldn't want to miss that. Also to be considered was the act of unwrapping and "pulling" on a premium cigar sold to him by one of the three sibling owners. Once at the store, all would be well in the mind of this 76-year-old bachelor, now retired, rich, in good shape and good to look at.

"Ah, life in the Crystal City," Alex ruminated.

Yes, he considered himself retired, but after spending a time with the Buffalo police department learning how to investigate people who didn't talk much, turning the tables on crooks was in his blood. There was also that time in the Middle East when the Army had considered him one of the best investigators they'd had. After that, snooping seemed like a natural proposition for him. Would the supposedly retired Alex Rayburn investigate *any* case? Only if it mixed curiosity with adventure.

His current interest brought back memories difficult to expunge. Before he knew it he'd chosen a noble pursuit predisposed to creating palpitating hearts and unending adventure. He'd often said that to really know if you like what you're doing, ask yourself, "would I do it if I weren't being paid?" Nothing seemed more fun than being a private detective, especially if he didn't actually *have* to. Since the family fortune took up most of the room in the vault at the Community Bank, payment for his services was always given to several charities near to his heart.

This small city in upstate New York, "The Crystal City" as Corning is known, wasn't quite rural enough to hear the cock crow, but an early morning whistle at the local employer would quickly tell a person walking toward his factory job if he might be in danger of being late for work. At the whistle's shrill, the current time would stand accurately on the hour, or fifteen minutes before the hour, depending on one or two blasts.

Alex let his mind wander as he showered. The whistling unit has been preserved from the early days of operations at the glass factory, when few people had wristwatches and most walked to their employment at the plant. Heading for the factory in the morning, a person would hear either two blasts or one. The employee could tell from the timing of the sounds if he were running late, or if he still had fifteen minutes to arrive. Two blasts would tip him off that he still had the additional time buffer. In a short time, one blast had better find him at his work station or the boss would want to know why.

The city fathers recently made known to the company that no matter how much the hierarchy improved or updated the plant, the presence of the whistle was sacrosanct and could never be considered for termination. Alex agreed. He knew the company president personally and mentioned his enthusiastic agreement. Visitors in the local hotels were startled by its unique morning sound heard weekdays all over the valley, but somehow, they liked it too. Its timing was now made perfectly correct, according to the "atomic" clock located halfway round the world in Bern, Switzerland.

Life in this town still fashioned itself around the omnipresent whistle, but weekends, everyone slept. Alex knew that Saturday morning sessions at the cigar store weren't considered a party until he got there. Unfortunately, this morning his mood was tempered by a phone presently buzzing in his pocket.

"Hello?" he said flatly.

"Alex, thank God you're home!"

He immediately recognized the voice of one cool customer, a woman not given to emotional outbursts or worry; a local talk show host, a former international feature writer, network new correspondent, and generally exclusive confidant by the name of Nan Holloway.

"Well, hello, Cookie!" He was genuinely happy to hear her voice, though it seemed tinged with foreboding.

"I've got to see you right away. I have something to talk over." She began to speak excitedly, launching into the story of Billy Blackhorn and the threatening note he'd received.

"Wait a minute. Slow down. What are you talking about?"

"Something I hope you'll want to investigate!"

"Who's Billy Blackhorn? Sounds theatrical."

Nan bit her lip. "It's his real name. Stop making light of this!"

"All right, all right," he chuckled. "Sounds deadly."

"Damn it, Alex! Sometimes you're such a pain!"

"Okay, calm down. I've learned from our last caper that you can be quite serious. I respect that in you. But Nan, keep your sense of humor," he added with another chuckle. "We're not trying to stop a jet plane from taking off."

He was reminding her of an episode from their first adventure together. Everything had worked out well (although badly for the aircraft). Their successful recovery of a strategic scientific development was what had helped Nan get a job in journalism again with her old TV station. She was happy as a clam these days, as she recaptured public attention with a nice new show of her own.

"Okay," she conceded. "I see what you're saying. I'm cool."

"Shouldn't Mister Blackhorn go to the police?"

"Alex. I've just finished working with you. You are a known commodity to me and better than any police detective I know," she announced. "Though you shouldn't let that go to your head."

"It's going to my head!" he mocked her good-naturedly.

"Sorry," said Nan, although she wasn't.

"Okay," Alex returned. "Why don't I come down to your place in Elmira? I can be there in a half hour. We can go to McDonald's again, like old times."

"Sounds good. Fast food for fast people."

"Whatever made you move to Elmira, anyway?" Alex inquired.

"To be closer to a McDonald's, of course."

"...Hmm. I see you've retained your sense of humor."

Alex had asked her more than once why she'd left her unique Corning apartment in a remodeled hillside school building. She had explained that the Elmira residence was much closer to the WLED-TV studio, and she needed to broaden her circle of activities and acquaintances as resources for her talk show. And there was a different sort of vibe in Elmira. In Corning, Huffton Glass Incorporated held sway and operated as a sort of benevolent dictator, an enthusiastic and reliable supporter of the community. Elmira had no such advantage, and the "old money" which had built the city and helped it thrive through past decades had died out, or moved south. The current generation, for the most part, sought greener pastures elsewhere. As a result, there was an influx of new movers and shakers who were taking advantage of the opportunities in the area (including amazingly low rents). A new city was emerging, one where progress was being made by a combination of creativity, persistence and a lot of hands-on hard work. Nan found this scenario stimulating and quickly became a part of it. In Corning, the fine old families still held sway, and Nan had never felt she really fit in.

Alex, on the other hand, was a part of the Corning establishment. How could she tell him that he was one of the reasons she'd left town? She saw him everywhere in Corning, interacting easily with a wide variety of citizens and obviously in his element.

And often, there would be a lady on his arm. Nan was shocked by her own reactions when she would pass by a cafe and spot Alex at a table enjoying coffee or drinks with an attractive woman. Or she might attend a concert and notice Alex seated with one of their mutual friends, like the stunning Amy Huffton, a vice president in her family's corporation. Then Nan would get an odd feeling in the pit of her stomach, and would repeat again the mantra, "I am not jealous, I am not jealous." After all, her relationship with Alex was not a romance. She had no special claim on his time and attention. But she couldn't help how she felt.

Now, living in Elmira, when she saw Alex it was intentional. Their attention was focused on each other. Nan much preferred it that way.

As a bonus, her apartment was a dream. It was located in the center of a few acres of greenery in Elmira's Near Westside Historic District. The house, almost a mansion, was 180 years old and meticulous renovated to preserve its charm and character. Nan's particular delight was the 40-foot long balcony just outside her door, where she could sit and savor the first cup of coffee in the morning, or sip a glass of wine and watch the sunset. She could also, on occasion, watch Alex Rayburn drive into the parking area in one of his snazzy automobiles, a dashing figure with his silver hair and year-'round tan. Life was very good for Nan Holloway these days.

2

ALEX CHECKED HIS Rolex. The rendezvous with Nan in Elmira had concluded with his luke-warm promise to meet with Billy Blackhorn and see how the land lay. Unlike Nan, he was not convinced of Billy's sincerity or the authenticity of the threatening note. But he would give the guy the benefit of doubt.

Alex maintained excellent relations with the Native Americans he encountered. He had been honored with the friendship of Duce Bowen, an elder with the Seneca nation 200 miles west of Corning in the mostly-Indian town of Salamanca. For several years he had listened to many beloved tales served up by Duce, hearing them in personal conversations with the man he respected so much. He didn't have to wait for Duce's historic speeches to hear the stories.

And too, his friend was intimately familiar with the Rockwell Museum in Corning. He provided the museum with stories from his marvelous life, mixed with the deep experiences of Native American lore. Duce had passed away last year after a career of addressing colleges and universities around the country. To Alex, no one could tell a story like his special friend Duce. He also respected the strong attachment of the Indians to the land which was originally theirs. Duce was sorely missed by the Corning detective, and by all, especially for his forgiveness of the old white settler hijinks perpetrated by the ignorant, early Europeans. "That was then, this is now," Duce would say. "That's all there is to it." Alex wondered if Duce had known Billy Blackhorn.

After dropping Nan at her apartment, he aimed himself at the on-ramp of Interstate 86 for the 18- mile trip to Corning. Ordinarily he chose Route 352 which trailed along the Chemung River; however, if he hustled, he could salvage an hour or so of convivial banter with the gang at Smith's, where he would light up one of his favorite Arturo Fuente cigars.

Today, Alex was driving another car from his collection, a 1982 Lancia Zagato. Though not as powerful or exclusive as his favorite Lamborghini, it was a sweet ride which beckoned the driver to take off into the country and use the roads for cornering. Even the devil couldn't roll this sporty car over upon itself, he'd reckoned. After negotiating road curves that he shouldn't have lived through, Alex often yelled to no one, "What a car!" He always thanked the founder of the Italian company, Vincenzo Lancia, with a shout.

Arriving in Corning, the Lancia growled its way down Market Street toward the cigar store. A large group of onlookers was clustered near the store entrance. He stashed the car quickly and beat a path to the front of the establishment where he could hear the owner, Barry Brown, shouting to a police lieutenant.

"I've got to get her back! We love her. She's been part of the family since 1903! Do you have any idea what she's worth?"

Alex advanced through the crowd. When no one stopped him, he entered discreetly and went to the side of his friend. He had quickly ascertained that "she" was not Barry's feisty sister Sue Brown, co-owner of the store, but another precious lady, Queen Catherine, the store's iconic cigar store Indian.!

Alex was very familiar with Queen Catherine Montour. Barry had often related how the sculpture had been discovered by his grandfather in an old tobacco barn in Big Flats, a community contiguous with Corning which was a major tobacco farming center in former days. Like the historical character herself, the carved wood representation of the Indian female dated back to the late 1700s. She had been valued at $150,000, despite a shaky provenance. The valuable carving stood about five feet tall and was painted with pale coppery skin (Catherine had been one-quarter French). She had large dark eyes and glossy black hair, parted in the middle. The patina of her hair was particularly shiny, generated by hundreds of hand touches from the store's patrons.

Catherine Montour had married a Seneca chief and, after his death, she became a chief herself. Her community, before it was destroyed by American Revolutionary War soldiers, had been located near the present-day town of Montour Falls, which boasts the magnificent She-qua-ga Falls. The tumbling water is still an overpowering sight from the town's main street.

Her wooden statue wore a plain yellow headband and a long fawn-colored jacket over a brightly striped skirt. Alex, like Barry, thought she was a lovely piece of art from a bygone era. It wasn't a thing most Native Americans regarded highly, but as Duce had said, "That was then, this is now."

At present, Barry was repeating to the police for probably the fifth time that somebody had kidnapped Queen Catherine during the night when the security system was inexplicably offline. In fact, after opening for the day, Barry hadn't noticed the theft, until Lou, a local CPA, came in and exclaimed, "Where's Catherine this morning?" It was then that Barry noticed things slightly out of placement, and the statue, gone.

"When I saw that she was missing I almost passed out!" Barry confided to Alex. "Please Alex. Find her for me!"

Alex, of course, promised. His first thought was, why did this very good security system fail?

In Elmira, Nan hadn't expected a call from Alex so soon. They'd begun their association a few months ago with a nerve-wracking adventure involving a government project, almost science fiction in nature. Her nerves had finally calmed down after that romp in his Lamborghini and the nefarious plot they'd finally foiled. Now her big concern was protecting Billy Blackhorn from the nebulous threats which were the result of his fracking activism. What did Alex mean with these new words on the phone?

"Another case. Believe it or not."

Nan had mixed emotions. She had hoped Alex would concentrate his efforts on Billy Blackhorn.

"Not another secret ray gun, I hope," she said dryly, referring to their first, and what she thought would be their only, case. She had happily helped him once. But again?

"No more ray guns," Alex laughed. "But this one is important to me."

"And what I need is not important?" she was ruffled again, as only Alex could accomplish.

"Of course your Indian friend is important, but something else has come up."

Peeved she stated, "Then we'll just have to take care of both."

"Good. I knew I could count on you."

"Ooh, that man!" she ground through her teeth.

He went on to describe his friend Barry Smith's dismay at the disappearance of his prized wooden queen.

"You could really help, Nan. I remember that you interviewed an antiques expert on 'Nan About Town'. I always listen to your program. You could get some ideas from her about how to trace missing sculptures."

Ignoring the patronizing, Nan bristled. Here we go again!

"You mean, you're going to investigate a death threat to a real live Indian, and I'm to go on a wild goose chase for a wooden Indian?"

There was a pregnant pause as Alex registered Nan's dissatisfaction. Here we go again!

"Come on, Nan. Be a sport. I agreed to help you. Now you can help me. Tit for tat, you know."

Nan sighed. He was right. She was a bit too prickly where Alex was concerned.

"Sorry. I'll be happy to help, of course. But no more speeding cars, if you please!"

Alex was delighted, for despite their needling of each other, he knew Nan had a good mind for abstract thought. He could accomplish this job, or both jobs, with a confidant whose pragmatism was her biggest asset. We'll get something done, now. He could feel it.

"Does Barry have a photo of the statue?" Nan inquired.

"Only a few hundred. I'll ask him to email some to you."

"Good. Are the police going to be working on this?"

"Yes. The cops get their cigars in the store, too. And everyone loves Queen Catherine. But the cops don't appreciate the emotional element. Barry is really suffering and his sister is distraught. He doesn't want to wait for the usual wheels to turn. We'll go places the cops don't go. We will get quicker results for him and Sue, I'm sure of it."

Nan rolled her eyes. She was a pushover for cats and dogs, but couldn't understand this masculine attachment for inanimate objects, like Alex and his cars. However, she understands the kindness one harbors for a friend.

"As soon as I get the photos from Barry, I'll contact Lydia Esterbrook at Antiques Unlimited."

"Thanks, Cookie."

"Don't you dare say 'It's me and you, Nancy Lou!'" Nan interrupted. Alex loves to tease her with the couplet, an unhappy reminder of her grade school moniker.

"I wouldn't dream of it, Nancy Lou."

Billy Blackhorn was worried. The note in his pocket said, "Shut your mouth in New York State or we'll shut it for you!" He had shared the cryptic note with Nan Holloway and a few other empathetic individuals, thinking that should trouble follow him here from North Dakota, others would be on the alert and ready to support him. If they believed the source of the note to be some despicabl, hired minion of Big Oil, so much the better. Billy had not lied to them. He merely allowed them to draw their own conclusions.

But Holloway had proven disturbingly proactive. She had sicced her detective friend on him. Billy doubted that a rich guy from Corning, New York, even if he was a pretty decent detective, would be the sharpest arrow in the quiver. However, it wouldn't do to underestimate him. Billy would now have to fabricate a feasible story that fit the facts. He ran some fingers through his thick black hair to gain strength from his long locks. Could he do it? He was tired, so tired of the game. All he really wanted to do was write and give lectures.

Could he actually trust this detective with the truth? It would be a relief to have someone really understand his situation. Billy fancied himself a good judge of character. He would see what this Alex Rayburn was made of, and then decide.

He had arranged to meet the detective at the Radisson Hotel for coffee in the lobby. Billy arrived five minutes early, bringing with him a copy of the local paper, *The Leader.* He first read the feature written about his speech the evening before. The newspaper gave it a bold headline: "Native American Poet Claims Fracking Destroys the Land." Coincidentally, a front page headline cried out, "Queen Catherine Stolen from Smith's Cigar Store." A shiver ran up Billy's spine. But no, how could there be a connection between this incident and his trouble back home? Was it just a coincidence?

"Mister Blackhorn?"

The man who addressed him was older than Billy had expected. He was finely, if casually, attired and physically fit. He didn't look like a gumshoe; he looked like a college professor or a merchant. Billy rose and extended his hand.

"Yes, I'm Billy Blackhorn. Are you Alex?"

"Alex Rayburn, at your service."

"Thank you for coming, Mr. Rayburn."

Alex responded with a pleasant nod. The two men sat down, each in a high-backed chair in the sunken lobby area. Alex liked the place because a snap of the fingers brought a waiter from the dining area with a pot of coffee. Alex was known here, mostly for his sizable tips and kind handling of the wait staff. The staff would watch for him and decide whose turn it was to serve a man of such inherent grace. Billy was impressed, which added to his mistrust. A server brought them a pot of coffee and some Danish cuts. They took measure of each other, sipping the dark brew while Billy indicated the front page story.

"I see there has been a theft. I wish I'd had a chance to see the statue of Queen Catherine. She was a remarkable woman."

"Indeed she was. And the statue was remarkable, too," Alex replied. "She belonged to friends of mine. The owners are frantic."

"I'm sure they are. Are you going to help them find it?"

"I'll do everything in my power. One thing you'll learn about me, Mister Backhorn, is that trust in these matters is essential… from me *and* from you."

3

A LEX HAD SAT with Billy and "jawboned" for about an hour. He'd never considered that fracking the country might be as bad as the liberal element of U.S. citizenry made it out to be. Billy certainly had lots of reasons to feel the way he did, being a Sioux Indian of the first calling. Alex knew his feelings were genuine, and ended up respecting the guy. In the moderate, intelligent, receptive mind of Alex Rayburn, the disgraceful Indian reservations located in the middle-western area of the United States were shamefully inadequate to human life, and fraught with all of the unnecessary crimes of a people continually frustrated by Uncle Sam, even to this day. Regarding the friction evident between the two factions, it seemed that nothing ever got resolved. He wished his friend Duce had not left the earth as soon as he had. A little good Seneca advice might be in order right now from a guy who really knew the score and yes, Billy was acquainted with his late friend, Duce Bowen.

But this fracking thing was a burr under Billy's saddle and might get him into more difficulty than he could foresee. Surely if someone were out to get Billy, the ne'er-do-well would have to trip over the great detective from Corning, for it was easy for Billy to convince him to help. In the heart of Alex Rayburn, a fondness for the Indian prevailed above all. He reckoned the Native Americans are smarter about the land than any big company executive could be. Experience is the best educator.

When Billy was talking at their downtown meeting place, Alex had drifted into thought regarding Barry Smith's cigar store Indian. Are these two incidents related in any way? No. Why would they be? On the other hand, why not?

It so happened that Alex knew a character who called Market Street his home. Tommy Barber was a drifter who had come into Corning and decided he liked it. In the five years he'd endured life on the street, he'd come to know just about everybody in town and was considered pleasant and harmless. The YMCA allowed him to shower, even providing the soap and towel. Though he had to be rousted out from under the Bridge Street bridge occasionally, the cops generally left him alone to check out the trash containers along the street for the cans and bottles which allowed him a meager subsistence. Tommy hung out in Centerway Square soft-soaping anyone he met into buying him a hot dog or two from Jim's Hot Dog emporium, and because he was such a low-key operator, again the cops looked the other way. Heather, Jim's worker, would sometimes serve him a dog with all the trimmings and pay for it herself.

If an unwary citizen irritated him, Tommy a little on the outspoken side. He once told a cop that he was so stupid he "couldn't pour the piss out of a boot if there was a hole in the toe and the instructions were on the heel." When he related that story to Alex, the great detective nearly lost it, laughing uproariously well into their good conversation. Humor served Tommy well. It was the major personal attribute that made his low position in life easier to bear.

Alex, wealthy as he was, could see the grinding situation of Tommy's existence and throw him some cash to help him along.

He figured that the types of characters who inhabit the streets had more to say than people gave them credit for. Why shouldn't Tommy's wisdoms be rewarded? The two of them would often be found sitting on a bench together at the nearby city fountain, while Alex drained Tommy of his street knowledge, complete with more than a few harrowing experiences. Alex had tried to help Tommy get an apartment, but his unhoused associate preferred the cold, hard life of a "road scholar," as he called himself, versus the amenities of living comfortably. No, they could be friends, Tommy might say, but he wants to remain independent according to his own sensibilities.

For Alex, it was fortuitous that Tommy also knew the modest underbelly of this small city in upstate New York. He seemed to be everywhere at once. Initially, squad cars had been called out to various locations because some desk cop saw a blip on one of the many surveillance screens located at the police station. But after a while, the cops would see that "It's only Tommy", and would ignore his rustling around in some downtown alley. He was generally considered honorable despite his mean existence and odd habits.

Tommy might now facilitate the answer to a small problem that puzzled Alex: How was the security system at Smith's Cigar Store compromised? Did he see anything? It was fun for Alex to think that he actually had his own confidential informant (CI) in a city as small as Corning. He'd used Tommy before. The results were surprising.

"Tommy."

"Hello, Alex. How's everything in the social stratosphere?"

"Very nice generally, but sometimes disgusting."

"I don't doubt it," Tommy answered.

"Talk with me, my man," Alex said, kicking out a chair from his table in Centerway Square. Tommy wiped the recent rain from the wrought iron seat.

"You've been in Smith's Cigar Store. Tell me, have you seen any recent problems out behind the place?"

"Like what?"

"Well, the store was broken into and the only things taken were a few cigars and the Indian statue, Queen Catherine."

"Oh, so that's what they were doing. That's a pretty statue."

"Go on."

"I think it was Thursday night. It seemed strange to me that anybody would be working on the roof late at night. I thought someone was fixing a leak or something."

"Well, that was the night of the theft. Did you get a look at anyone?"

"Nah ... wait a minute. Those two guys both had red shirts on – one of 'em had a mustache you wouldn't believe. The other one took orders from him."

"Do you think you'd recognize them if you saw them again?"

"Maybe. I was sittin' on a beat-up old chair behind the Pathways office. Some employees sit there and smoke from time to time. It's kinda hidden between two trash hoppers. They didn't see me."

"Good. I'm glad of that."

"And they were drivin' a van with 'Phillips Lighting' on the side."

Alex remembered that the Phillips plant in Bath had closed about ten years ago. Someone must have acquired one of the old vans.

"I saw them bring a large object out the rear door. Wow! I was watchin' a robbery and didn't know it!"

"Okay, thanks a lot. Keep this under your hat for a while, will you?"

"Sure 'nuff, boss."

"And Tommy, here's a little cash. You're pretty important to me."

"Nice to know I'm workin' again, heh, heh."

Alex was delighted. He now had more information than anyone else. These nuggets from Tommy were invaluable. He wondered, should I share the information with the cops? Not yet. In the meantime, he would go on high alert and keep his eyes open. The city is not big enough for two crooks in red shirts to evade him. That late at night, the criminals, probably out-of-towners, must have stayed at a local hotel or motel. Let's see. Where might that be?

A gumshoe, as he called himself in fun, has to be ready for a lot of grunt work in order to have a good result in the end of his investigations. Alex spent the next few hours exhaustively checking from hotel to hotel for two men of Tommy's description. The Radisson? No, they were probably too cheap to do that. The new Hilton Garden Inn? Nothing there. The Ramada in Painted Post? No.

He finally pulled into the parking lot at the Red Carpet Inn outside of town. Success! Alex knew the young man at the desk who easily remembered two men with red shirts who'd showed up rather sweaty and unkempt. The two of them had "overlooked" putting their license plate number on the register slip, but Bobby Cravits, a family friend, born under the sign of the Virgin, noticed the van they came in. Being a Virgo, and thus very organized, he'd seen them park their van earlier, and slipped out later to view the license tag for the sake of keeping his records complete.

"But I got their tag number anyway."

Alex chuckled. He was a Virgo too, and knew how Virgos think. Anything to stay organized, neat and complete, he mused. "I had a feeling you'd have it."

Unfortunately, by then the men had checked out. Alex pulled out his trump card. The local police were aware of his prior stint with the Buffalo force after a time on foreign shores with the Army. They trusted him whenever he needed a license number search, never asking any questions. He poked some numbers in his cell phone.

"Corning Police Department, Sergeant Wilson."

"Hey, Jack."

"Oh, no. Not you again."

"Hey, wait a minute – we're on the same side. How're you doing?"

"Okay."

"How's business?"

"Oh, you know – a robbery here, a murder there. Same old stuff."

"In The Crystal City? Never! You guys buy more donuts than anyone else."

"Did you want something, or are you just bugging me?"

"Yeah, I do. I've got a problem."

"Not another international incident, I trust."

Jack was one of the cops assigned to the "iridium" case a few months before. It was a rather sensational event for a town this size. The helicopter crash that ended the escape plan of the bad guys had made headlines around the world, after the local cops had finally made sense of what happened. Jack had gotten very little sleep for a week.

"All I need this time is a license plate owner."

"Okay. What is it?"

Jack took the plate number and put Alex on hold. In a few minutes, the sergeant came back.

"That van is registered to a Ronald Pegler, up on Sunset Drive."

"Thanks, man. I owe you guys a box of donuts."

"Well, don't bring 'em here!"

Alex realized, too, that Nan was depending on him to find out more about the threatening note to Billy Blackhorn. Two things going at the same time always bothered him. Could they be connected? He didn't see how.

He wondered how Nan had made out.

4

"… I offer you the wild rose sweetness of my desire,
the smiles of my people before Columbus came,
our hearts that break yet keep round dancing
back into song …"

BILLY BLACKHORN WAS reading a poem by Susan Deer Cloud, a contemporary Native American poet from New York, as part of his lecture on Native American spirituality at The Park Church in Elmira.

Nan Holloway, part of the audience in the spacious sanctuary of the huge historic building, listened with a rapt expression on her face, but she was not experiencing the words only. She was drifting to the cadence of Billy's voice, admiring his soulful eyes and sculpted cheekbones. She imagined him bare-chested on a white stallion, black hair streaming behind him, as he galloped by and swooped up her much younger self to ride with him into the sunset.

Get a grip, Nan, she scolded herself. But why did the Creator give us imagination if not to utilize it in playful daydreaming?

The lecture was well attended. The Park Church has a strong history of liberal thought and social justice dating back to its founding in 1846. Among the founders was Jervis Langdon, the father of Olivia who became the bride of one Samuel Clemens aka Mark Twain. It's been said that Langdon, active in the Underground Railroad, as well as Livy herself, had much to do with the Southern-born author's evolving attitude toward slavery and black people.

The Park Church congregation has dwindled in both size and financial resources over recent decades, but members remain dedicated to their heritage of social activism. Environmental protection is high on their list of concerns, and several members have carried non-fracking signs only to wind up in jail for their trouble.

Perhaps the most concerned with fracking in the Finger Lakes area were those with businesses, summer homes, or boats on any of the lakes, Nan conceded, but self-interest was certainly not the driving force. She was acquainted with the earnest young Peter Fenton and his wife Alice, members of the Park Church choir, who had organized and participated in numerous protests and rallies.

Billy followed the poetry portion of his talk with a description of traditional and current Native American beliefs and practices. In conclusion, he delivered an impassioned plea to continue the good fight to keep the Finger Lakes region free from fracking. Nan was somewhat surprised by the noisy approval of the rather staid-looking crowd.

A reception in the church hall followed, and Nan approached Peter and Alice.

"What do you think of Billy?" she inquired.

"He's wonderful!" Alice enthused, Peter agreed.

"A great speaker! And I appreciate his support for anti-fracking But he's coming rather late to the game. The drillers have pretty much cleared out."

Nan said, "Really? When we spoke about it after my show, he seemed to think there was still a lot of danger."

"Well, we have to stay vigilant," Peter agreed. "But we've moved our focus to the refugee problem now."

He went on at length to speak about the activities he had planned. Alice slipped away to join the throng around Billy, Nan's smile began to glaze. She interrupted him.

"Maybe you can come on the show some week and talk about it." This nebulous invitation to claim some air time usually satisfied people with a cause to promote.

"I'd love to!" Peter replied.

"I'll call you," said Nan, feeling a bit ashamed of herself. Well, she would call him – sometime. Peter was personable, enthusiastic, articulate, tall, dark and not hard to look at. He resembled Billy Blackhorn without the charisma. He would do a decent interview.

But something Peter had said nagged at Nan: "He's come late to the game, the drillers have cleared out." If that were indeed the case, and the oil companies had tossed in the towel, what was the threatening note to Billy about? Were they culpable? If not, who?

She wondered what Alex had discovered when he'd met with Billy. She would have to call him and find out. The man was not a prince when it came to sharing information.

As the crowd began to thin, nourished well by the fine lecture and famous Park Church punch, Billy beckoned to Nan.

"I met your friend Alex," he said. "He's quite a guy."

"I'm glad you got along," Nan replied. "Is he going to help you?"

"He's going to try, but it's complicated."

Before Billy could continue, the pastor of the church burst into the room.

"Is Doctor Prentiss still here? There's been an accident! It's Peter. On the street, in front of the church."

Billy was forgotten as everyone rushed to assist one of their own. Nan joined them.

"Has someone called 911?" she asked, running alongside the pastor.

"Yes. Help is on the way."

They found Peter seated on the front steps of the church, with Alice holding a blood-soaked cloth to his head. Dr. Prentiss knelt beside him, asking the necessary questions to determine the extent of his trauma. A head wound was never good news; the doctor was being very careful. Nan was relieved to hear the siren of an approaching medical team.

She soon learned that Peter and Alice had been standing with several people on the curb waiting to cross Church Street when a motorcycle pulled up. The rider had swerved close to Peter, struck him on the head with a pipe or bat, and roared off. Alice had stepped back just in time. Attentions were on Peter, and no one could adequately describe the man on the bike, except for his cowboy hat and a kerchief over his lower face.

"Why would anyone do this to Peter?" Alice was crying. "Why?"

Why indeed, Nan thought. Perhaps it was because Peter might easily be mistaken for Billy Blackhorn, who had been warned to keep his mouth shot and who instead had trumpeted his message plainly at the gathering. Was this incident a deadly replay of cowboys vs. Indians in the Old West? Nan didn't see Billy anywhere near the accident scene, nor could she find him back in the church hall. He had made a quick exit, for whatever reason.

She was about to call Alex when she realized she had not yet kept her part of the bargain – to help find the Smith's Cigar Store Indian. Damn! She had better have something to tell him before she berated him for not sharing information with her. It was just 4:30. She still had time to catch Lydia at the shop.

Antiques Unlimited is an enchanted place, one which always delights Nan. To follow the stone path through the pergola into the scented interior was to leave the everyday world behind. Here were all the fondly remembered treasures of the past, illuminated by Tiffany lamps and chandeliers. Lydia Esterbrook also dealt with vintage clothing, and her wardrobe consisted of items from many different decades which she combined with creative abandon. This afternoon, as she floated to the entrance to greet Nan, her small frame was adorned with a loose, long-waisted mauve shift, a purple paisley shawl and an gem-studded Twenties-style headband. Somehow, it worked.

"You look lovely, Lydia," Nan complimented her.

Lydia gave a tinkling laugh and took Nan's hand.

"Come in, come in! I have something wonderful to show you!"

"Really?"

Since moving to the grand old house in Elmira, Nan had started adding some choice antiques from Lydia's shop to her own mostly contemporary furnishings. This time Lydia led her to a bevel-edged oval mirror with a pattern of leaves and vines etched into the glass.

"It's a very heavy, silver-backed, early Twentieth Century beauty!"

Nan checked the price and gulped. "I'll think about it, Lydia. I'm not sure I have a spot for it."

"Oh, a mirror looks wonderful anywhere, darling." Lydia assured her. "You'll be back for it, I know."

Nan opened her handbag. "Now, I'd like to show you something." She brought out the photos of the Queen Catherine statue that Barry Brown had emailed to her.

"How does one go about tracing a stolen antique, Lydia? Is there a central registry or something?"

"Oh, my!" exclaimed Lydia. "I know this piece. It's the Smith's Queen Catherine, isn't it?"

"Yes," Nan replied. "It was just stolen the night before last."

"I saw something about it on TV," said Lydia. "What a shame. It's such a beautiful thing."

"I understand Browns are quite undone," said Nan.

"Come with me," Lydia instructed. She led Nan behind a counter of heirloom jewelry through a small door (Nan ducked) labeled in fancy script, "Ye Olde Office."

Once inside, the old-fashioned charm of the shop dissipated, replaced by sleek, modern technology. Lydia slipped into an ergonomic swivel chair, put on a pair of orange cat's eye glasses and punched up a website on the computer.

"There are a number of registries with databases on antiques and collectibles where owners can register their items. Then, if one disappears and the registry is notified, the information goes out to all dealers and auction houses worldwide. No one wants to get stuck selling stolen goods." Lydia had transformed from a sort of wispy nymph playing dress-up to a knowledgeable business owner.

She continued. "Of course, the police have access to all these sites and will have checked them by now. Is Queen Catherine insured?"

"I really don't know – I imagine so."

"Well, if she's insured, there will be a good provenance to prove ownership," said Lydia. "Are you familiar with the provenance?"

"No. I only know the statue has been in the cigar store for decades."

"Do you know the sculptor?"

Nan was beginning to feel woefully uninformed. "Maybe there's a mark on one of the photos."

Lydia picked up the photos, one by one, and examined them closely with a magnifying glass.

"Aha! See this mark? It's a Joseph Bleyden."

"Oh, a Bleyden!" Nan exclaimed, trying to match Lydia's enthusiasm. Who was Joseph Bleyden, she wondered.

As though reading her thought, Lydia explained, "Bleyden worked from the late 1880s through the 1920s. He was from Ohio, but had a considerable following in New York, Pennsylvania and beyond. Bleyden might well have received a commission in this area to do a Queen Catherine, or maybe he heard about her and was inspired to depict her," Lydia mused.

"Well, there was a lot of tobacco farming in those years in Big Flats, and some old tobacco barns can be seen to this day." Nan said. She knew much of the land between Corning and Elmira was used for that purpose. The growing season was never really long enough around here, plus the occasional hailstorm would poke holes in that precious commodity – the leaf itself. Everything went south, literally, away from the unreliable weather.

"Tobacco was king here for a while," she mused. "The Smiths owned land in the Chemung Valley. Their cigar store dates back to those days."

"I wonder ..." Lydia leaned back in her chair and looked at the ceiling for inspiration. "Native Americans in general never approved of having their images used for merchandising purposes. And the statues were often stereotypes. It's possible some descendants of Catherine want her to be placed in her home territory rather than being exploited to sell a few cigars."

"This *is* her home territory," Nan reminded her. "I don't know what other location could be more appropriate."

"Of course, some rich dude might be interested in showing it off in his billiard room to his beer buddies," Lydia offered.

The shop owner was certainly letting her genteel little lady mask slip with that comment, Nan thought.

"I'll bet not," Nan said. "You know the human race as well as I do Which group of buddies could keep a secret like that?"

Lydia continued speculating. "Most likely it's some sort of prank, Nan. Or maybe someone has a gripe with Barry Brown and wants to annoy him."

A little affronted, Nan said, "Commit a felony just to annoy someone?"

"True. No sane person would do such a thing. Does Barry have any enemies?"

"I sincerely doubt it. The store's been there for decades. Barry is a jovial guy and keeps his business beyond reproach, in spite of all the rules conjured up by our benevolent State government. It would be easy to go crazy with the constantly changing tobacco regulations. Still, it's a friendly store, respected in the community."

Nan thought for a moment.

"Lydia, might Queen Catherine have been kidnapped for ransom?"

"That has happened with jewelry and fine art occasionally," said the shop owner. "But not successfully. Of course, we wouldn't know about it if it *were* successful."

"How about blackmail?"

"The same. But the Queen Catherine statue would be worth no more than $150,000, by my reckoning. She might mean more than that to Barry, but would the risk be worth the reward?"

"You're right on all counts," Nan sighed.

"I think you need to go to the police on this one. I have a contact in Connecticut who had a unique mermaid weather vane ripped off the roof of his barn by some guys in a helicopter! The police found it two years later in Atlanta, selling for a quarter of its value."

The women shared a chuckle and Nan departed, promising to think about Lydia's overpriced mirror.

Lydia's professional smile faded to a frown. She checked her special client list and punched in a number on her phone.

5

NAN TRIED TO get Alex on his cell phone, but eschewing those modern digital marvels, Alex had left it behind in his downtown loft, a nook he referred to as his office.

"Damn that man," Nan growled. "What's he got against progress?" She had no way of knowing his whereabouts, and she was desperate to talk with him. It was important to fill him in on the latest happening at the church, where her friend and sign-carrying cohort, Peter Fenton, had been soundly hit over the head by a speeding motorcyclist. It was a bold act and possibly very injurious to Peter.

Evening had darkened in Corning, and Alex, sans cell phone, had business on Sunset Drive. He parked his Lancia in a city lot at the bottom of Sunset. With stealth, he walked forward and up to an alley behind the house where he hoped to find Ronald Pegler's van. The inadequate street lamps bore witness to his shadowed walk past thick vegetation crowding both sides of the narrow alley. He stumbled in and out of the usual Corning potholes.

In a moment, an opening appeared in the trees showing the van resting behind Pegler's house. Moonlight splashed its silvery glow around the vehicle as Alex crept down the driveway to get a closer look. No one around, he thought, and no sounds to be heard.

A back door opening suddenly illuminated the porch with a shaft of incandescent light from a single bulb in the kitchen. The intrepid detective jumped sideways into a dense cloak of trees and vines. Two men came off the porch and sidled up to the back hatch of the van.

In light just bright enough to see by, Alex spotted a large object carefully wrapped in a rug – about the size and length of a cigar store Indian! The men added a few small boxes to the remaining floor space, paused and lit cigarettes, talking unintelligibly. The interloper Alex waited in the thicket, slapping an occasional mosquito and becoming impatient. The men returned to the house leaving the back hatch open. It was a perfect time for his curiosity to sneak in for a closer look.

He quickly traveled a few paces to the open van, and, with a tiny flashlight, peeled the rug back from the statue of Queen Catherine. The viewing was good enough for him. He instantly felt disgust for people who rob others, and backed away just in time to avoid the eyes of the two men returning to the vehicle. "We'll see who gets away and who doesn't," he chewed through his teeth. His intention was to be a major stumbling block in the lives of these two malefactors and chase them to the ends of the earth.

His next action was to clear out and head back to the parking lot. It was obvious that the men were hurrying to go somewhere, and he knew they would have to pass by his car at the bottom of the hill. The alley is a one-way lane, descending behind houses to the traffic light. It was a distance to his car, causing him to huff and puff before reaching the door handle. He was convinced they would come. He waited in the dark, a street light here and there providing some reference points.

He had only been in his car for a moment when a motorcyclist rumbled past him and went the wrong way up the alley. The rider had given Alex a glance, which seemed to mean nothing.

"Humph! You could only do that in Corning," he muttered. But from his vantage point he could swear the bike went into the driveway where he'd just used a quart of his best adrenalin. He couldn't be certain it was the right driveway. He would see what developed.

On an evening sweet with the air of lavender and pine, he gazed out over the city and wondered if anyone else was involved in the senseless heist of this cigar store Indian. He was bent on tailing these guys. The car was gassed-up, and the not-really-retired detective was ready for anything. He'd always said that health was his best asset. He breathed heavily, but happily.

One thing nagged at him, however. Why had these two ruffians been at the hotel? Good thing Tommy Cravits got their license number. Did they meet someone there? Did they pick someone up? And why would anyone use their personal van in a robbery?

Just as those thoughts occurred to him his erstwhile informant walked in front of the car.

"Oh my God! There's Tommy!"

The window in his Italian car rolled down too slowly. Tommy was just ambling by in his usual slouching gait.

"Past! Tommy! Over here!" Alex said quietly. "I'm glad to see you."

Tommy slipped into the car with a quizzical expression.

"What're you doing here, sittin' by yourself?" Alex knew how much Tommy liked the cloak and dagger angle.

"I'm watching crooks. That van you saw the other night behind Smith's Cigar Store is two driveways up this alley. I'm hoping they'll come down here shortly so I can follow them."

"Wow! Can I come along?"

"Er, no. Too dangerous. I have to do it alone. But I want you to do something for me."

"I'm your man!"

"Keep an eye on that house. You've got my cell number. Message me if you learn anything."

"Okay, boss!" Tommy was giddy. "I'll let you know."

Alex perked up. "Hey, the van's coming! Quick Tommy! Get out and get in those bushes!"

"Okay, boss. See ya."

The light on the van nearly illuminated Tommy as he flung himself into the brush. Alex ducked down and the headlamps swept over them. The van went down the hill further to the four-lane parkway – the last traffic light on the roadway that cuts Corning in half. A right turn heads east into town, and a left turn heads west and beyond the city limits. Alex let the van pass. Two men could be seen plainly in the glow of their cigarette lighters as they turned left at the parkway. Was the cyclist with them? Where was he?

When they were a safe distance ahead of him, Alex fired up the Lancia and tore off after them. He was happy not to have to race to keep up with them. Crooks usually don't break speed limits – being questioned by the police would not be pleasant.

In a few minutes they reached the highway crossover at Painted Post. After an approach curve in Riverside, the intersection of I-86 and I-91 yawned before them. The van swung onto I-86 and again headed west. Alex reasoned that this episode might take quite a while. He hoped they weren't going too far.

"Damn! I forgot my phone. I've gotta be more careful." It struck him that Nan would be livid, for sure. But what could he do? He was resigned to finding out more about these guys and accomplishing the first thing on his list. Surely, when Nan knew about this impromptu journey, she'd understand.

The two in the van were brothers. Ace Billings and Johnnie had been bending the law for many years and had never been caught. Ace had the brains, as well as the mustache; the younger Johnnie was the mule, a big- bodied blond individual who could easily heft extraordinary pounds of dead weight. He had once lifted the back of their Simca car while Ace changed a tire. They were a good pair, they thought - not good, but a pair anyway, and that first car they'd had together was well known and eventually, feared. Their neighborhood in Buffalo had put many demands on them while growing up, and it had made them hard and angry. Ace would shoot his mouth off and Johnnie would clean up the resultant mess, breaking the bones of several no-goodnicks of other underworld persuasions.

Once, when Ace had owed money to "Hats," a notorious bookie, Johnnie broke bones, noses and kneecaps straightening out the debt. It was promptly forgiven and Hats, a beast of a man, decided to leave them alone – too much for his nerves, bothering with their kind of bad. All bookies have nicknames including Hats, who, surprise, had lots of hats.

"Looks like we did it!" a voice in the van exclaimed. Johnnie was always optimistic.

"Yeah, we've still gotta get up to Buffalo and drop this piece of wood we got in the back."

"Yeah, Mrs. Sandbag will be waitin' with our money."

Ace said, "It's Sandberg, you idiot. How many years did you stay in the Buffalo school system? Twenty?"

"Stop makin' fun of me Ace! I ain't as smart as you. Anyhow, you only went to a stoopid tech school anyways."

"Okay, okay, sorry. You're a good guy. You're my brother."

Johnnie grinned big. "Aw, that was nice of you ... Brother." Johnnie looked up to his big brother despite the ugly, despicable, life of lawlessness he continued to heap upon him. Ace knew that a few kind words always got Johnnie to settle down. The road to Buffalo would be peaceful now. Things were calm and normal. At least his biker friend Phil (aka Junior) got a good swipe at one of those anti-frackers in front of that peace-loving church in Elmira. I hope it didn't kill him, Ace pondered. That's *all* we need!

"Where's Junior?" he quizzed. "He should be catching up with us by now."

"You know he doesn't like 'Junior'!"

"Yeah, I know. He can just get over it."

Alex was coming along behind the brothers at 60 mph keeping them in sight, but not too closely. They were dictating the speed. Alex hung back carefully and wondered what he'd do when the van reached its destination. He decreased his speed temporarily to 35 mph to keep the distance between them consistent. Would there be others? Were they headed for Buffalo? What about the motorcycle guy? All good questions for a contemplative mind.

The fearless detective from Corning was in his element. Though he had been born with a silver spoon in his mouth, it was the rough, seamy side of life that fascinated him. Why don't criminals just get a job? he wondered. They work so hard at deception and usually go to jail anyway. Why not put that energy into being a good citizen?

Alex increased his speed to make the distance right again.

Not too close, he reminded himself.

He was awash in thought when from out of nowhere a cyclist sped up beside him and fired a shot through his open windows. The bullet buzzed past the back of his head and pinged off a road sign on the other side of the car.

"What the hell …!"

When the cyclist righted himself for another shot, Alex by instinct went immediately sideways and struck him at his side, smartly and decisively. It caused the biker to run off his lane and shoot out into heavy brush beyond the east-bound lanes of the Interstate. A Western-style hat flipped off his head into the wind and frisbeed into the trees. Responding to this latest shot of adrenaline, Alex declared, "Damn! It must be that biker I saw earlier!"

Alex was shaken, but unrepentant. He watched the debris fly in his mirror. These guys are playing hardball! Damn!

Ahead, the two crooks thought they'd heard a tire blowout.

"What was that?" Johnnie said.

Ace said, "I don't know. Something happened behind us. I can't see anything."

Johnnie felt bad. "We should turn around and go back."

"No, little brother! If anybody has trouble back there, we can't get involved." He searched his mirror but couldn't make anything out. "We've got a job to do. They're on their own."

Alex wasn't going back either. In the flash of the moment, he had recognized the rider as being the same one he saw earlier turning into the alley in Corning.

"That certainly ups the ante! Who are these guys?" He noticed the van motoring along as before and surmised, "They must not have seen my little nudge." It was reasonable to assume these three were connected somehow.

Unaware that Alex was having his own dangerous encounter with a biker, Nan was trying for the fifth time to reach him on his cell to tell him about the cowboy cyclist's attack on Peter Fenton – which she was sure was intended for Billy Blackhorn since they resembled each other somewhat. She wanted desperately to know what Billy had confided to Alex and how he planned to protect the poet/activist from harm. And she wanted to fill him in on information gleaned from Lydia Esterbrook. But as so often happened, she was stonewalled by Alex's inability to remember his cell phone.

What's the point of working together, she grumbled, if we can't communicate? Sooner or later (probably later) he would call her, full of cheer and charm, completely ignoring the fact that he had driven her crazy in the meantime.

She sighed. With no further threads to follow she would stop at the Elmira hospital and see how Peter was doing. She would firm up a date for him to appear on the show, too – that would cheer him up.

But she would not see Peter. Alice, still distraught, greeted her on her way through the lobby.

"Nan. Nice of you to come. They're keeping Peter overnight because there are some signs of concussion."

"I'm sorry, Alice. I certainly hope there's no other serious damage."

"Well, enough for 15 stitches and a fractured cheekbone. And lots of swelling and bruising. He's a sight, and in Technicolor!" Alice attempted a small laugh. "But he'll be fine, the doctor says."

"That's what matters," Nan said comfortingly. Then, because she couldn't help herself, she asked, "Have the police talked to you? Do they have any idea what this attack was all about?"

Alice looked troubled. "They know about his anti-fracking crusade, of course, and asked if he had any enemies. I couldn't name any. There are individuals who wish he'd go away, but they aren't this violent or stupid. What would they gain by making a martyr out of Peter?"

Nan nodded in agreement. It seemed unlikely. Although Peter might be hated by some of his opponents, he also had strong ties to the area environmentalists, many of them with important positions in the community. Sometimes in this and other local matters, they take up the standard and lead the way. They were a good buffer between Peter's passionate group and the average extremist.

"Alice," she ventured, "You know the attack happened right after Billy Blackhorn's lecture. Have you noticed that Peter and Billy resemble each other physically? Could it be a case of mistaken identity?"

"It's possible, I suppose. But if someone were after Billy, why strike him here?"

"Why not?" Nan countered.

"We've already won the fracking battle – essentially."

Nan realized that Alice didn't know about the threatening note to Billy.

"I wonder. It seems to me Billy is correct – politicians can be bought most any time." She didn't pursue her theory and let it drop.

But she continued to probe. "What does Peter think?"

Alice provided little additional information. "The police are still waiting to talk with him. As soon as we got to the emergency room, the doctors put him under sedation. They probably won't question him until tomorrow morning, but they're trying to trace the motorcycle."

"Peter didn't say anything on the way to the hospital?" Nan persisted. Oh, dear. I'm being obnoxious, she realized.

Alice gave her a sad look. "How much can a man say when his head is swimming?"

Nan decided not to push it any further.

6

PENELOPE PARKER SANDBERG
drummed her heavily ringed fingers
on the gleaming surface of her mahogany *escritoire*. She had just ended
a disturbing phone call from Lydia Esterbrook, the antiques dealer
in Elmira who had assisted her in amassing a stunning collection
of Native American artifacts, specifically items referencing the Six
Nations of the New York State Iroquois Federation. Lydia had been
very understanding of Penny Sandberg's passion over the years, even
to the extent of fudging a few provenances. But this time Lydia had
delivered a warning.

"Penny, I don't want you to make any disclosures to me, but
if you had anything to do with the disappearance of a Queen
Catherine statue from a Corning cigar store, you have crossed
the line."

"Whatever are you talking about?" Penny had responded with
convincing nonchalance.

"Don't say anything. Just listen. I just had a visit from Nan
Holloway, from Elmira. She has a show on local TV here in the
Southern Tier and she's quite a journalist. She's also a pit bull when

it comes to digging out a story. She asked a slew of questions about the statue and how stolen antiques can be traced on the internet. There's already been news coverage, and the police are involved."

Penny feigned shock. "I should say so, Lydia! It must be very valuable!"

"Just listen please, Penny. Nan Holloway is associated with a sharp Corning detective named Alex Rayburn who is good friends with the Smith family, owners of the Indian effigy. Nan and Alex are a formidable team, and they are hot on the trail of Queen Catherine. Rayburn Alex has plenty of money and lots of time. I wouldn't want the two of them after me."

From her sumptuous sitting room, Penny Sandberg said, "Oh I remember those two! They were responsible for ending that intrigue down in Corning a while back – something about a secret weapon, wasn't it?"

"That's right. So if you or any of your cohorts are thinking of adding the Queen to your collections, I'm advising you to back-peddle very quickly."

Penny laughed. "Don't in an uproar, Lydia. You know I wouldn't *steal* a statue, or any other piece of art."

"Of course not, Penny. But some of your friends might."

"Now, we're not that obsessed," Penny forced a little laugh.

"I'm just saying *if.*" In spite of warning her, Lydia didn't want to antagonize a woman who had been important to her sales success.

"Take care, Penny."

"Thanks for the heads up, Lydia, even though it's unnecessary."

Lydia bade her goodnight and hoped Penny was truly clear of any involvement. She had been a valuable client over the years. Surely she would now remain above reproach in this debacle.

In her Buffalo mansion, Penny put her phone down with a scowl.

Damnation! What now! She began to pace the length of a masterful forty-foot Persian carpet tied especially for her in the back country of Iran. How she loved the knotted beauties, appreciating the Isfahanis for their peerless workmanship and their signature blue hues. It blended well with the wealthy Ms. Sandberg's home among the astonishing mansions and castle-like edifices in the downtown area of Buffalo's Delaware Avenue. Most of her neighbors had similar residences, but hers was the crowning jewel. How the money had flowed in the Buffalo, New York of earlier days! Many fortunes came to town as a result of the clearing of old timber, now absent since those days of shysters and robber barons. The houses were built while the heyday of lumbering was in its glory. In the present, it would be impossible to duplicate any one of them. This section of Delaware Avenue became history, itself.

Penny stashed many of her treasures throughout her home not only for decorative effect but also to discourage visitors from harboring suspicions about her "real" collections, located in the climate-controlled vaults of the lower level. Soon there would be a stunning addition to the hoard, beautifully Native American, of course.

Penny was a trustee of the Albright-Knox Gallery and the Buffalo History Museum. She wanted to bequeath her collection of Iroquois artifacts to the museum. It would then be heralded as The Penelope Parker Sandberg Collection, even if she were no longer here.

Ever since she was a child, Penny had been enchanted with tales of the "noble savages," from Hiawatha to The Last of the Mohicans to the Apaches' Geronimo. She had rooted for the Lakotas when she read about Custer's last stand in history class. Eli Parker, prominent Civil War officer, US government official businessma,n and Indian rights activist, became her idol, and she romanticized that, with her Parker surname, she was related to him in some way.

More recently, she devoured the Navajo mystery novels of Tony Hillerman and other Native American works. She adored Native American poetry, and when she learned that Billy Blackhorn was coming to the Rockwell Museum in Corning, she arranged for him to follow with a trip to Buffalo and do a reading in her home.

It would be a fund-raiser for the Erie County Library, of which she was a member of the board. Billy would arrive in a few days and be a guest in her home. Penny could scarcely wait.

But Penny Parker Sandberg, patron of the arts and seeming pillar of the community, had a dark side. Though she had utmost respect for Native Americans, many of her rural properties around New York sat upon the massive Marcellus shale deposits, which extended from New York deep into Pennsylvania. This section of the country *could be* rich in oil and natural gas production beyond anything seen before. That is, if the powers-that-be in New York State agree with Pennsylvania's inclination to go ahead with the actual production mechanisms. So far, Pennsylvania is making it work for them, though at a cost to the environment. New York is chaffing at the bit to do the same.

There are millions and millions to be paid out to people who do nothing more than own the land. Although it is currently illegal to frack in New York, Penny understood that greed would eventually win the day, and Penny wanted in on it. It's the American way, she reckoned. Her propensity to do good would take a back seat to the unimaginable wealth gained from fracking in the State, the shale oil which abounded under her properties, still untapped. This would add to her already huge fortune in stocks, bonds and properties. Altruistic as she might want to be, wealth was more important in the mind of Penelope Parker Sandberg than keeping the land pure.

Thus, she was conflicted regarding Billy Blackhorn. She adored his poetry, but he would have to be kept from participating in anti-fracking activities while on the lecture circuit in New York Penny knew she would have to polish her demeanor for the anticipated deceptions. There would be many required in the coming days. Smiles and greetings would have to be carefully conveyed to keep her image intact. She couldn't afford to get into trouble over the Queen Catherine carving. It was scheduled to be delivered later that evening from the downtown warehouse of Ace and Johnnie Billings, if all went as planned.

Penny had called on the Billings brothers several times in the past when her collecting addiction had required their brawn, guile and particular connections to assure a deal. They had proven reliable, but she couldn't expect them to exercise any real expertise in a pinch, and this might now be pinch time. With a determined detective and a clever reporter giving chase, not to mention the police, things could get tenuous. Penny knew that the Corning detective had been in the Buffalo police department and would have plenty of connections. And a reporter. Hell, that's *all* she needs! With these people nosing around, she was glad to have Phil Jansen, Junior by nickname, as her chauffeur.

Months ago her husband Sam had suffered a mild heart attack. His doctors had suggested that he give up driving. With him temporarily in an assisted care facility, she took comfort in having the stalwart Junior around for her use. He handled the big Lincoln Town Car well and looked great in his uniform, which made Penny decide that he was a necessity. She liked the big car, but if Sam went out of town on business, she could ditch the car and take a wild ride with Junior on his motorcycle. She knew she was a living cliché, but she had too much fun with Junior to care. She was certain of his loyalty. He wanted to keep his job, didn't he?

She had dialed Junior a few days ago and explained the situation. "Phil, could you be a dear and go to Corning? Follow Ace and Johnnie and make sure they aren't being tailed. And don't get into any sort of trouble before they arrive here with the merchandise."

"I'll take care of things, Madame."

"I know you will. Also, look in on Billy Blackhorn at that Elmira church. There has to be a way to intimidate him a little so he won't get the general public on his side about fracking. And don't show your face. I'm going to have him up here later for some poetry readings. I wouldn't want him to recognize you."

"I'll turn the brim down on my hat."

Penny was unaware that Junior, in following her instructions, had mistaken Peter Fenton for Billy Blackhorn and clubbed him on his cranium with a small baseball bat. She would be plenty angry at his strong-armed tactics, especially since he'd gotten the wrong man, but owing to that dark side of her, she would overlook it – so long as he didn't kill anyone. She knew that the family fortune must be maintained at all costs, and the best way to do it, with increase, is to secretly underwrite the effort regarding all of that nice shale oil under her properties. The potential for great wealth, even greater than her family has enjoyed to this point, is to encourage the State to eventually allow fracking. It's really only good business, she figured, and to hell with any alteration in the drinking water and supposed geological vulnerabilities. Billy can write all the poetry he wants. It won't make any difference in the long run.

The Buffalo Skyway is a highway system created many years ago to facilitate drivers who need to go from point A to point B in a city typically cursed with miles of twisting streets. To this day, the Skyway flies over the confusion below with maximum efficiency as it delivers motorists to a number of other highways in the area. High bridges were built to tower over homes and businesses lifting the 4-lane roadways well above the populated confusion of "The Queen City." The nickname for Buffalo was presumably imparted ages ago when the city seemed to be in a commanding position at the confluence of two of the Great Lakes. Some of the luster is gone now, but nickname remains none-the-less, even if currently inappropriate.

Traffic flows well on the elevated Skyway. No one thinks much about what's underneath. Below the many curved bridges lofted five stories into the air, the rough underbelly of the city thrives unabated. Bars and old manufacturing buildings proliferate below the roar of a super-highway din that seems to know no end. The city hums with elevated honks and screeches constantly raining down on the population from a comfortable distance above.

Likewise, drivers on the freeways are generally unaware of the questionable collection of characters down under who may be bent on perpetrating a nightly libretto of dirty deeds and mayhem. It is not a place to be find oneself in the wee hours of morning unless you yourself are one of the numerous malefactors plotting schemes of destruction. Here thefts may be planned, beatings administered, and possibly a murder or two conceived.

Such was the location of a seedy warehouse currently rented by the Billings brothers – Penny Parker Sandberg's two law-benders of dubious integrity. It was a place that Alex Rayburn was presently observing from the deep, shifting shadows in this almost lightless night. He was close enough to hear Ace Billings give orders to his brother.

"Johnnie, put the van in the third bay. I'll raise the door."

Alex had successfully followed them from Corning to Buffalo, despite being shot at and running a motorcycle meanie off the Interstate. He had little sympathy for whoever had been on the bike. What a naughty boy he was to shoot at the great detective. Alex thought hehad probably survived, though somewhat the worse for wear. The scene now playing out in front of him demanded his full attention.

The door mechanism snapped loudly and the bay door rose to full up. Johnnie roared in with the van. His brake lights came on. Ace pushed the switch and lowered the door. The observing detective from Corning itched to get into the building and scout around. He considered that the two might actually live there.

When the brothers left the scene a few minutes later, he breathed a sigh of relief. He noticed Ace secret the key away near a small pipe on a window ledge. Johnnie had come out and climbed in the passenger's side of a parked vehicle. In a moment they passed by him in a car which Alex thought much too grand for them. He quietly wondered about their worth, a notion his brain processed as he melted from one shadow into another, toward the building.

"What luck! They hide their key outside." This was too easy, he thought, smirking as he threw caution to the wind.

A tiny click admitted him to an elevated office within the building. The door snapped loudly behind him. He slipped along farther inside. noticing boxes piled one on another in what looked like a lifetime of scraps, metal pieces and old factory machinery. A hollow darkness hung over everything except in a few spots of welcome streetlight. A pall of airborne dust seemed omnipresent in his viewing frame and the atmosphere had an oily smell. The floor showed muck and mire accumulated in a century of neglect.

Three bays to the right, the van he had followed from the Southern Tier became his focus. The open areas of the warehouse were a symphony of gloom and disarray which caused him to calculate his every step. He moved toward the vehicle with stealth, and saw the object wrapped in a rug through its open rear door. - the statue of Queen Catherine in all its glory,

"Someone must really want this," he said aloud. Just then his instincts conveyed an uncomfortable sense of not being alone. To his left, a voice interrupted his concentration.

"Hey! What are you doing here?" A man the size of a small gorilla stepped out to challenge his presence. The apish figure had a long wooden bar in his grasp. Fear gripped Alex.

"Ah … er …" He struggled for words, but too late. The wooden weapon crashed down on his shoulder faster than a hastily-concocted lie could be uttered. The great detective, now uncovered, could only back up and seek a weapon of his own. He tried to speak.

"Wait! I'm here to inspect the building. I …" A regulation size fire-extinguisher waited on a nearby desk just a bit too far for his touch. He fully realized the inane nature of using it for his defense, and so did the smiling thug.

Within the ape's wicked stare, Alex circled the desk snorting the sounds of chopped breathing. He fumbled with the small cylinder hoping it was charged, but no. It made a weak sound of escaping gas. The moisture on the item was his own.

The big guy flashed an evil grin and came around the desk with determination a-go-go. He swung the bar over the head of the inept detective, who scolded himself for not scouting out the building a little better when he entered. Had Alex looked, he could have seen the lamp and desk in the background where the "watchman" had been reading. It was an overlooked moment he would now regret. Who would have thought the place had an enforcer waiting to dispense trouble? He cursed his naiveté, and prepared to do battle.

The assailant was typically goon – uni-browed and round-faced, short and squat. His movements were strong yet sluggish. He had messy facial hair and ears that had been boxed a time or two. Short pudgy fingers formed a fist that clipped Alex like a freight train, and his kick was that of an angry horse. Alex circled in a boxing pose learned while at camp in the Middle-East, hoping for some kind of advantage. Running away crossed his mind – but how?

After ten long seconds exchanging fist hits, Alex noticed a part of the building which was under construction. It had shaky framing holding up an unfinished second floor. He maneuvered his opponent until he was positioned under most of the bare lumber and slugged the guy hard enough to put a little space between them. He turned around to grab the fire extinguisher, then rushed headlong into the dazed watchman with the item in his hands skewed sideways.

It caused the watchman to fall back and displace some underpinning structures with his back. The entire second floor collapsed on the man and Alex absconded like a terrified schoolboy.

"Mama didn't raise no fools!" he shouted as he ran across the floor and away into the black of night, happy that no guns were needed.

7

THE MOMENT SHE opened the door to her new apartment in the grand old house, Nan felt her spirits lift. She had done all she could – the ball was now in Alex's court. She foraged in the fridge for some supper makings and settled into her favorite chair with a ham, cheese and slaw on rye. All major food groups were represented. She went over her mail, including the latest *New Yorker*, which she believed was essential for maintaining her (hopefully) cosmopolitan image. She spoiled herself with a glass of Merlot, read a few articles, and was almost dozing off when her phone rang. Alex at last!

"Hi!" she answered eagerly, all frustration banished from her tone.

"Hello Nan. It's Billy," the caller announced.

Billy? What could this be about? "How are you, Billy?" she replied, deciding to get right to the point. "I missed seeing you at Park Church after the unfortunate event."

"I had to get back to Corning for an appointment," Billy said. "What happened there?"

"Peter, the anti-fracking guy you met, remember? Well, someone on a motorcycle rode by and bludgeoned him. Hit and run. It put him in the hospital."

"That's really awful," Billy responded. "Is he okay?"

"Yes, but I'm thinking you were the intended target. Peter resembles you in height and coloring. And the guy on the motorcycle was wearing a western hat, cowboy style."

"Cowboys and Indians, I get it," Billy said grimly. "You may be correct. If Peter was hurt because of me, well, this whole affair has gone too far."

"Indeed. I was hoping Alex could be of some assistance resolving your situation."

"Yes, I 'm hoping for that, too. I need to contact him about an upcoming event. Do you know how I can reach him? He doesn't seem to be answering his phone."

Ha! Good luck on that! Nan thought. "Oh, he probably went somewhere without his phone – again! I'm sure we'll hear from him tomorrow. In the meantime, can I help with anything?"

"Perhaps you can. I'm going to Buffalo Sunday to read at a private fund-raiser. I was hoping Alex could accompany me. And you might like to join us. It will be at the Sandberg home on Delaware Avenue. Penny, the wife, professes to be a great admirer of my poetry and a lover of all things Native American. But she and her husband are also big landowners in the Finger Lakes region, and I'm guessing they take a dim view of my environmental activities. It presents me with an interesting challenge, and 'the trouble' may follow me there."

"Yes, I can see that," Nan concurred. Her journalistic instincts were kicking in. "I might be able to get a follow-up to my interview with you. I'm in!" Besides, she thought, a long car trip with a the charming poet would be a treat.

Now all they needed was Alex.

Somewhere on the dark, lonely highway between Buffalo and Corning, Alex Rayburn was grimacing behind the wheel of his sporty Lancia. His head hurt like hell from some of the lucky blows which managed to fall on the side of his temples during the fight under the Skyway. His night vision, usually perfect, was slightly blurred. Corning was still a good distance off as he slowed his forward speed to a steady seventy. Please God, not a concussion, he worried, I'm not as fit as I used to be. A bruised rib, a scraped shin and a profoundly sore shoulder were causing considerable discomfort, as well. Still, he congratulated himself on the ultimate escape. Close encounters like that were not his cup of tea.

The second floor cave-in at the warehouse, however, had precluded his further surveillance of the evil brothers and the precious Queen. Now he knew she was in Buffalo, and he knew who had taken her there. He could give his information to the police, but the possibility of a fatal run-in with the murderous motorcyclist, as well as the warehouse fight, were items he didn't wish to explain. He would have to find out himself where the Smith's great treasure was headed and then retrieve it. No doubt Nan, after talking to her favorite antiques dealer, had some ideas, but being sans phone, he couldn't talk to her just yet. It would have to wait until morning.

Alex spotted the blinking lights of an emergency vehicle ahead, right where he had sent the biker off the road and possibly to heaven.

"Probably not heaven," he corrected under his breath. Perhaps the gun-toting goon had landed softly – or not. He was happily unconcerned. Sometimes Lady Justice peeks out from under her blindfold to help those in need. Pretty audacious to shoot at a person on the highway, he thought.

After the next few miles he arrived at home, glad to be among the living. He parked the Lancia next to the Lamborghini in his garage of dreams. Among the other cars was Todd Everingham's Porsche from his last desperate adventure with Nan. After Todd been taken away, Alex had rescued it from the impound lot, realizing that it was still a remarkable car in its own right. Todd's time in prison will cause him to grind his teeth knowing that Alex bought his car at a reduced rate.

He painfully dragged himself to his top floor apartment and ran a hot shower. A large dose of aspirin followed, dulling the throbbing of his head and the various aching spots on his torso. The cell phone languished on his end table where he had laid it prior to his trip to Buffalo. The large number of messages from Nan caught at his conscience, but only for a moment. He wasn't in the mood for an unleashing of caustic comments from his sweet pain-in-the-neck consort. He fell into the bed with a groan. Such is the glamorous life of the famous Southern Tier detective.

In Western New York, one woman awaiting a phone call was about to receive it, although it was not the one she'd hoped for. Penny Parker Sandberg reached up from the depths of her satin sheets to answer the vintage princess phone on her French Provincial bed table. She was expecting to hear from Phil Jr. that the newest addition to her Native American collection had been safely delivered to the Billings Brothers warehouse downtown, to be brought to her lower vault later on. Instead, it was that slimy Ace Billings on the line.

"Mrs. Sandberg? We have a problem with your item."

"Which is?" she inquired impatiently.

"Well, we have the cigar store item, but we can't bring it to your house like we planned."

"Why ever not?" Penny wanted to know, hoping the thing was at least in Buffalo.

"Junior, I mean Phil, was supposed to let us into your house and the vault."

"Yes, what's the problem? Let me speak to Phil."

"Well, that's the problem. Junior isn't here. We lost him along the way."

"How did that happen?"

"He was following us down around Bath and, I'm not exactly sure how it happened, but there was a shot, sounded like a gun, and then there was a screeching noise. My brother thought someone went off the road behind us, and I figure, it must have been Junior. We couldn't go back to look because of our cargo, and the cops ... well, you know. I'm sorry, ma'am. Maybe he's okay. Junior – Phil - is pretty good on that bike. You know Junior. He'll be fine."

Penny was aghast. "Oh my God! He's probably had an accident! You say this was outside of Bath?"

"Yeah" Ace tried in his Neanderthal way to calm his client. "But if you want your merchandise tonight you'll have to let us in yourself."

"Damn! All right. Bring it in half an hour, Ace. And be sure you're not seen." Penny ended the conversation and called information.

"What city, please."

"Bath, New York. And what's the name of the hospital there?"

"That would be Ira Davenport, ma'am. Do you want the number?"

"That's why I'm calling," she snapped impatiently.

Soon she was speaking to the emergency room doctors regarding the condition of her chief gofer. Sure enough, her chauffeur and confidant, Phil, had been brought to the hospital after tumbling off the road a few hours before. He had myriad contusions and a broken collarbone, all rather light injuries considering his flight off the road at sixty miles an hour. How did it happen? She wouldn't be able to talk to him until morning, when his anesthesia wore off. She would have some probing questions for him then. Did he go off the road himself? Did some car hit him? How does that happen?

Before long she was out of bed and in her lower driveway awaiting the nefarious Billings brothers. She went outside when they came and instructed them to be careful with the precious Queen statue. Under her dusk to dawn lights, they carried it in after inspecting it. Penny was overjoyed to have it in her grasp.

"Phil's in the Bath hospital," she informed the brothers.

"I told you we shoulda gone back there," Johnnie lamented.

THE UNLIKELY ADVENTURES OF ALEX AND NAN

"Dammit, Johnnie! We couldna done anything," Ace shushed him. "Junior's better off where he is. He'll heal up in a few days."

Penny said, "No. I'll have him brought to the house. He'll recover better here. I've got to know what caused him to lose control. It's not like him."

"Another problem," Ace was hesitant to say. "There was someone snooping around in our warehouse to night. An older dude. He got in a fight with our watchman and sped off in a hot car. Our guy got a glimpse of it and said it was a Lancia – they're not seen much around here. But I don't think it has anything to do with our cargo. Really messed up the warehouse, though."

"Can anything else go wrong?" Penny wailed.

Ace assured her, "Don't let it upset you, ma'am. Just let us know whatever you need. G'night, ma'am. We're heading for our house in Corning."

Penny had not yet learned that Phil had bungled his instruction, which was to scare off Billy Blackhorn gently, not in a ham-fisted way. For now, her inquisitive nature refocused on the warehouse intruder's car, the Lancia. Her husband had one in the sixties, so she knew the marque. Oh well, it couldn't be pertinent. Just an old car. But who was the driver?

It bothered her brain like an odd piece of a crossword puzzle. She would have to find out who might have been able to spot the statue at the brothers' downtown compound. He was a potential threat.

And Lydia Esterbrook could be a danger now. Although she had kindly warned Penny about the the Corning detective and his companion, she was well known as a business owner who brooked no nonsense, certainly nothing illegal. She was certainly suspicious of Penny. If pressed, would she throw Penny under the bus? It was possible. She would have to make Lydia understand how much she stood to lose if she crossed Penny.

Her next day's early morning call to Ace wakened him from a deep sleep.

"What the hell ..." he answered angrily. He had driven to the Sunset Drive house in Corning, the one that he and Johnnie called home. They'd stayed up drinking half the night.

"It's Penny Sandberg. I have a task for you."

"Ma'am. It's six o'clock in the morning. Can't this wait? I haven't had much sleep."

"No. It has to be done early this morning before Antiques Unlimited opens in Elmira.

"Elmira? Aw, come on, ma'am."

"I'll double your pay. Again, this has to be done at Lydia Esterbrook's shop when she's the only one there. You know where it is. You've picked up things for me before."

"Yeah, I know where it is." Ace scratched and yawned. "Okay what do you want?"

"She's in a position to cause us a lot of trouble over that Indian statue. She suspects I have it. I want you to warn her off."

"How?"

"I don't care. Just be smart. Use muscle, but don't overdo it, you hear?"

"I got it, Mrs. S."

"And don't tell your idiot brother about it. This is between us."

"Understood. I'm on it."

8

ALEX AWOKE FEELING better than he should have. Pulling in the fresh air of his open-windowed apartment, his lungs were refreshed.

Ahhh! That good Southern Tier air!

Crisp air couldn't compensate for the turbulent happenings yesterday in Buffalo. His achy body was grateful for the night's sleep, but he wasn't topnotch. He asked himself, not for the first time, if there wasn't some way he could pursue his chosen profession utilizing only his "little gray cells" like Hercule Poirot, pouring out his cool logic on some unsuspecting crook, therefore minimizing the damage to his no longer battle-ready body.

After strong coffee caused him to grimace, he called Billy Blackhorn. It was the lesser of two evils, considering the fiery conversation his erstwhile partner Nan was no doubt presently preparing for him.

"Good morning, Billy. I'm sorry I missed your call. What can I do for you?"

"Well, Alex, I called in the hope that you would accompany me to Buffalo tomorrow."

Billy went on to explain his invitation from Penelope Parker Sandberg, and also other concerns regarding the trouble he'd had with people who actually want fracking to occur in New York State.

"I would feel a lot better knowing you were there watching in your special way. You remind me of my own people, holding back, observing until we see through a problem. I'm grateful to you for your involvement."

Hadn't Alex just been thinking of being more cerebral? He was flattered by Billy's confidence in his methods.

"I've also invited Nan Holloway."

Alex snapped back from his self-indulgence and said, "Yes. I'm sure that's a good idea."

He was trying to think things through, Poirot style. He assimilated his own escapade in Buffalo with Billy's request for protection. Of course he would go, if for no other reason than to discover more about Penelope Sandberg. He would have a first-class opportunity to look around her house and see where a certain stature might be hanging out. Yes, this is a good thing to do.

"Sure I'll come," he told Billy. "I'll drive the three of us."

"That will be grand! Thank you Alex."

Billy's business settled, Alex took a deep breath and made his second call – to Nan. He knew she would be furious, and this time, with some reason. But he had a strategy.

"Yes?" she answered, without even a greeting.

"Nan. I have a lot to discuss with you and I need your input. How about breakfast? Shall I pick you up in about 30 minutes?"

"Yes," she said, but not before she had delivered the inevitable scolding, somewhat deserved.

"Look for me in a different car."

"Of course," she sighed.

"The Lancia is too small for the three of us tomorrow. We're taking Billy to Buffalo, right?""

In a short while, Alex pulled into in Nan's parking area with a devastating white Jaguar, straight from England's master automobile craftsmen. It was custom-made for him and had amenities no other Jag possessed. Everything was done for the comfort of the humans who would be passengers, and of course, the driver. It had a backseat refrigerator, not being used at the moment, elegant telephones, warm towels (also not being used), and a cigar humidifier for smoking while riding. A smoke evacuation system made sure no one was offended who was, perhaps, not enjoying the best premium cigars that could be had anywhere in the world. The humidor *was* being used, and was well-stocked. Some special Sobranie Chaliapin cigarettes were in abundance for the ladies. The cigarettes were originally made by the Sobranie company to go easy on the pallet of Feodor Ivanovitch Chaliapin, famous opera star of the nineteen-thirties. They are no longer available, but Alex thought them a nice touch, since he had a number of early boxes. He wasn't a person who paraded his wealth among people, but a guy's gotta live. He just couldn't help being a gear head, with a stable of special automobiles. Cars were his passion, as were cigars. After its run-in with a bullet, the Lancia was resting inside his fourth garage door.

Nan got in the car, bedazzled by its good looks and glove-soft leather.

"Are you sure you don't have more money than God?" she managed.

"Everything I have belongs to God," he replied.

Taken by surprise, Nan choked back her immediate response (I hope God appreciates fast cars).

She recognized that this Episcopalian of many years was sincere in his Christian beliefs and she respected his many charitable contributions and activities. She didn't share his religious views, but they made him even more special to her. Humility in a wealthy man is, well, heavenly. Her mood changed from one of challenge to one of compliance.

"That's a nice thing for you to say." she acknowledged. He was a good guy after all, however uncommunicative. She couldn't hold back any longer.

"For heaven's sake. tell me what happened last night."

Alex launched into the complete story, which, truth be known, nearly overwhelmed her with feeling for him. Here's a guy who doesn't have to help anyone, a guy who could insulate himself with the indulgences others could only dream about and yet, here he is, in the thick of it. A marshmallow herself, she had a new appreciation for a man who was at present, the best guy she'd met since her husband hadn't turned out so well. She was happy to be working with him.

While they were headed for Alex's favorite fast food restaurant, Nan was on the verge of suggesting a more intimate venue, but wisely deferred. Once seated with coffee, orange juice and McMuffins, she began:

"Now let me tell you what happened at Park Church yesterday.."

As she delivered her long, protracted litany, Alex began to put some puzzle pieces together. A cowboy on a motorcycle? I'll bet I know the guy. There was little doubt that it was the same villain who fired a shot straight through the open windows of the Lancia up near Bath. Thank goodness he's out of the equation and would be seen no more.

Alex reached across the table to Nan and brushed some of her errant strands of dark hair off to the side.

"I've been meaning to ask you. Is that white streak in your hair real?"

Nan tossed back her hair back and laughed. Who but Alex could be sweet and insulting at the same time?

"Everything about me is real, Mister Rayburn," she stated emphatically.

"You certainly don't look like the average septuagenarian."

"Why should I," she replied breezily, refusing to take the bait. "Age is just an attitude. Put that in your cigar and smoke it."

"Haha. You amuse me. It's really nice to work with you. A good sense of humor is almost a necessity," he said. "We're a good pair."

Nan was and is always embarrassed when hearing nice things about herself. She quickly got back to talking shop.

"So, the theft of Queen Catherine and the threat to Billy Blackhorn are related?"

"Well, something's going on. Maybe they're not related, just coincidental. We'll have to let this thing play out."

Nan said, "Tell me what Billy had to say when you talked yesterday. Have you learned anything more about the threatening letter?"

"It's complicated," replied Alex, echoing Billy's earlier words to Nan. "Family and money are involved. Did you know Billy Blackhorn had been married?"

"No!" Nan's eyes were now enormous.

"Yes, indeed. A real love match - at first."

Nan insisted that Alex continue with Billy's story.

"It was a college romance. Billy was a football star, with an offer to play for the Green Bay Packers upon graduation. Sieglinde Larson was a cheerleader, a real blond beauty who foresaw a glamorous future as a pro player's wife. They eloped in their senior year. Sieglinde's parents were not amused."

"I can imagine," Nan interjected.

"Well, her father owns a huge Cadillac dealership, a sizable country estate near Milwaukee and a lot of land. Her mother mainly plays bridge and golf. The Larsons are quite wealthy and put a large parcel of land in the young couple's names as a wedding gift. They also financed a short honeymoon, with rock-climbing and white-water rafting in Colorado. Billy says it was paradise."

Nan, who had spent three weeks doing Paris on her honeymoon four decades earlier, shook her head. To each his own, she thought.

"But what did Billy's parents think of the match?"

"Billy's dad was in law enforcement and his mother was a teacher. They still live on the reservation. They gave the couple a piece of rare Asnazi pottery which Sieglinde promptly declared ugly. It soon disappeared."

"I'm beginning to not like her," Nan commented.

"It turned out they had some fundamental differences. They both loved the out-of-doors, but Billy felt a commitment to protect the environment. His wife just wanted to own as much of it as she could. When Billy turned down the Packer's offer and went to work for the National Park Service, his new wife was mortified. Not only had she married below her social class, but she felt her husband had enticed her with false promises of future wealth and fame."

"How unfair, and how sad for Billy."

"He was sad all right, and angry – at himself as much as with Sieglinde. He recognized the marriage had been a blunder and wanted it to end quickly in divorce. Sieglinde had no desire to be the wife of a Native American park ranger, and figured that Billy owed her something tangible for dashing her hopes. Her lawyer pointed out that Billy and his family had nothing to give her materially, so she acquiesced to a paltry alimony agreement which ran out after three years. She went home and took over the management of her father's real estate holdings."

"And Billy?"

"As a ranger stationed at a fire lookout station, he had plenty of time to think and write – time he used well, as you know."

"So are his family problems in the past?"

"Not exactly. Some of the Larson land was leased by the government for the proposed Canadian pipeline, some was slated for fracking by an oil company. Billy became the leader of a group opposing the pipeline, which seriously annoyed his ex-wife and her family. They threatened to disclose the fact that Billy himself was the co-owner of some of the leased land by way of the wedding gift. They decreed that if he didn't cease and desist his protest activities, they would tell the world of his deception."

"Oh, I see. They would make him look two-faced and ruin his reputation. What did Billy do?"

"Nothing. He has a lawyer working on removing his name from the title to the land. He thinks it would only be a minor embarrassment if the story came out and the fact that the Larsons are attacking him would make *them* look bad."

"Or so he hopes."

Alex nodded. "And the note that started this whole mess may have been instigated by the Larsons, not by the oil companies. It was the one thing that puzzled me most – that the oil companies would be foolish – and petty - enough to threaten him by sending a note like that. The note makes more sense as part of an nasty family vendetta."

"Billy was embarrassed, but concerned enough to show me the note," Nan mused. "That started the ball rolling. Perhaps he used it as a fail-safe, I mean, in case the family really meant business."

"Well, someone was serious enough to send a biker to try to crack his head open," Alex said. "I do believe you are correct that the Elmira attack was intended for Billy, not Peter Fenton."

"Poor guy. Thank heavens, he's going to be okay," Nan said.

Alex continued. "Oh, I know exactly who that biker was, not by name yet, but it's only a matter of time, and he's somehow involved with the thieves who took the Queen Catherine statue.

Nan added, "Billy obviously wants someone to watch his back in Buffalo.'

"And I will do so. He also needs a sympathetic person from the media who has a good handle on the back story. We'll be taking another road trip together, my lovely," Alex grinned.

Nan did an eye roll, but she was not displeased with the prospect. Digging out a story was Nirvana for her. So was sharing an adventure with Alex.

"I'm quite looking forward to going to the Buffalo home of one Penny Parker Sandberg," Alex continued. Many questions will be answered when I'm finished giving her the all-seeing eye treatment. Did I tell you – this is another fancy fund-raiser?"

"You didn't have to. I'll have the right dress. Oh, by the way, something I forgot."

"Yes?"

"I want to tell you what I learned from Lydia Esterbrook."

"Shoot."

"Evidently there are all sorts of online directories by which the antiques dealers, and the police, can track lost or stolen antiques. Whoever purloined the Queen Catherine statue from Smith's store will have a hard time unloading it to any reputable auction house or dealer. Lydia suspects that it was taken for a private collection."

"Yes, I'm getting some pretty strong vibes in that direction, and I think the direction is north, somewhere around Delaware Avenue in Buffalo. Why don't you check with Lydia for the names of some antiques collectors up on the Niagara frontier? It could be helpful."

"Okay. After you drop me at my apartment I'll go see Lydia. I'll call you later."

"Be careful with her. She may know more than she lets on."

"I know. I wasn't born yesterday." She added, "I'd like to take another look at that damned expensive mirror she wants to sell me."

9

NAN MADE IT to Antiques Unlimited by ten. She noticed Lydia's car outside behind the building, but the rear door was locked. After trying the front entrance with no success she began to look in the windows.

Peering through a dusty pane in the back, she saw a frightful sight. Lydia was sprawled on the floor, unmoving.

What could havet happened? Did she fall, or pass out? Did someone harm her? Nan rapped loudly on the pane with no response. She remembered the police station just up the street and beat a path to it, glad that she was in good physical shape. Inside the front door, a sleepy desk sergeant was commanded to wake up as Nan did her freak-out scene.

"Something's wrong at the antique store! You need to follow me!"

"What?"

"Come on, officer. It's important! Someone's hurt!" He quickly dropped his recalcitrant attitude.

"All right." What the hell did this woman want?

It was barely five minutes later when two cops used their tools to open the door. Sure enough, Lydia was splayed out on the floor with a little blood coming from her knee and elbow. Nan reckoned that Lydia had very little blood in reserve for such a happening. The cops urged Nan back from the scene, but she was not to be denied. She muscled past them and knelt beside the still form.

"Lydia! What happened?"

Groggy as she was, Lydia managed to raise her head. She said in a desperate little voice, "Some big guy came in the shop as I was opening. He told me not to say anything more about the cigar store statue or he'd come back and kill me."

My God! This is serious. Nan was numb. She almost felt to blame. After all, she was the one who mentioned the statue to Lydia in the first place. How could a cigar store effigy cause so much commotion? And why would anyone strong-arm the little shop owner?

What she needed was a good detective, one who was somewhat familiar with the whole mess, one who could figure out all the unrelated incidents currently confounding everyone involved. Of course she knew such a detective. But would he have his elusive cell phone with him? She punched in his number.

He actually answered.

"Alex! You'll never guess what happened here at Lydia's! She's been beaten and threatened by some bruiser telling her to stop talking about the statue and she thinks he may come back and she looks like hell ..."

"Waaait a minute. Slow down. You say Lydia was accosted?"

"Yes. Somebody wants her to lay off giving information about the Queen Catherine statue."

"Did she get a look at the car he was driving?"

"I don't think so. He left her lying on the floor. But I'll ask her"

Alex could hear some voices in the background – cops and bystanders. A young man heard Nan ask Lydia about the car. He was out for a walk with his dog when the spirited Basenji made its way through the police perimeter and hustled right up to the distraught woman. The youngster quickly stepped into the scene and talked as he marshaled the dog away from her.

"I saw a big car drive away from here in a hurry. I noticed a bumper sticker. It said, 'Boost Buffalo. It's good for you.'"

"Did you hear that? Nan said into the receiver. Both could sense an "Aha!" moment.

She said, slow and measured. "Do you think ..."

"Yes, I think," Alex replied. "A few years ago that bumper sticker was popular in Buffalo. I saw it everywhere, even in the Southern Tier. If I'm correct, we can certainly look forward to an interesting visit at Mrs. Sandberg's evening soiree."

"I really don't think she'd have anything to do with something shady, do you? I mean, she's evidently a pretty prominent person."

"Experience tells me that most people are capable of dirty deeds, no matter who they are."

Nan sighed. "You're a suspicious man, Mr. Rayburn."

"And you're a very trusting woman, Ms. Holloway."

"All right," she finalized. "I'm going to my apartment after this."

"Okay. See you later. I'll collect Billy, then come and get you at about two o'clock. That'll give us plenty of time to get to the event in Buffalo. See you later."

Nan hung up. Lydia was tired of sitting. With a little effort, she got to her feet and insisted that she could carry on without a trip to the emergency room. Nan consoled her for a time and even bought the high-priced mirror, which raised Lydia's spirits. With little else to say or do, Nam departed.

On her way back to her apartment, she reviewed the whole thing in her head: First there was Billy Blackhorn innocently trying to give poetry readings and lead discussions on the dangers of fracking: then the statue of Queen Catherine, stolen in the night. Then Alex got very close to a bullet while tailing the van with the statue in it. After that, there was the fight Alex endured when nosing around the warehouse where the van was found – the whole thing was dizzying to Nan, who at this moment, just wanted to get home and languish in bath water. She was glad she wasn't Alex – running around snooping, getting shot at, and fighting some goon.

Nan referenced her adventuresome friend. "God! How does he do it?" It was a question also asked frequently by the great Corning detective himself. He still felt young enough to find snooping fundamental to his work, but would sometimes sigh and say inanely, "life gets tedious."

Alex was a guy who didn't need to concern himself with those difficult times in life. He had plenty of money, still had his health, and was socially acceptable with women craning their necks to get a look at him. Beyond it all, the fact was he enjoyed helping people who usually couldn't help themselves. Although he considered himself retired, the detective work still held him captive and, lately, thank goodness, a sprite named Nan Holloway had come into his life to have fun with. All was good, he surmised. He would root around and find out about Penelope Parker Sandberg and that business in Buffalo. If the woman was hiding something, as he suspected, she was in trouble. She would soon be under his microscopic scrutiny.

After the intense morning with Alex and then Lydia, midday brought warm air and bird calls through Nan's windows. Coffee brewed in the kitchen for a lazy lunch. Then she prepared herself for the road trip by with a body stretch that Alex had recently told her about, one that would help her avoid any back problems she might encounter. She told herself she'd use the exercise as prescribed by Doctor Rayburn once a day; then, if it didn't work, she would call him out on it – humorously, of course. The stretching movement was very agreeable, just the tonic she needed to begin her afternoon.

Nan checked her image in the new mirror, approving her chosen outfit – a turquoise sheath dress with a turquoise and silver paisley jacket. She also noted that, like the faces in the old family pictures which hung nearby, her features were softening.

Maybe a little more eyeliner…oh, let it be, she shrugged. A sizzle of excitement was at play in her mind. This was going to be a special day. Alex was preparing his Jaguar for the trip and Nan, well, she was ready to operate with all cylinders firing. She couldn't wait for the adventure!

The sumptuous car that Alex seldom drove had been fitted with television and a few sensible accoutrements to keep the traveler refreshed. Nan had gloried in the clean hot towels and the two colognes that Alex had placed in the nearby rack. She adored Tabac and Ambre (both men's colognes) and was pleased to dab some drops on her neck. Billy Blackhorn was also enjoying the luxurious car and its amenities immensely. He tuned in to music from a classical radio service through one of the sets of earphones that were perfectly placed for use by all riders,

This unique combination of friends continued on to the Sandberg mansion on Delaware Avenue, arriving at a prompt 6:30 pm. They were properly impressed by the three-story brick edifice with its mansard roof and elaborate stone trim. "It's magnificent!" Nan enthused. As they disembarked from the Jaguar, the elegantly attired lady of the house emerged to welcome them at the columned entrance.

Penny extended her hand first to Billy. "Mister Blackhorn, welcome. I am such an admirer of your poetry. And I am immensely pleased that you agreed to appear at my little gathering."

"I'm most happy that you invited me," Billy replied.

"And your friends are…?" Penny inquired.

"This is Nan Holloway of Elmira, who hosts a television show," Billy said, "And this is Alex Rayburn, a friend of mine from Corning."

Penny knew who they were, of course. She had made it her business to research the pair after Lydia had mentioned them to her. She smiled sweetly at Nan. "So happy to have you with us, Ms. Holloway."

"Oh, please call me Nan."

"And Mister Rayburn. I look forward to getting to know you." So this was the man who sent her beloved Phil Junior to the hospital. He was not what she was expecting. The Jaguar he left with the valet was in keeping with her information concerning his wealth, but the man seemed older and considerably more urbane than she had anticipated, considering the havoc he had instigated at Ace's warehouse. An interesting adversary!

Penny led the group through the entrance foyer, commenting on the most impressive *objets d'arte* along the way.

"The house was built by my husband Sam's great-grandfather Sidney in 1901. He traveled extensively, collecting French furniture, Italian marbles, Chinese vases ..."

They entered the sumptuous drawing room, where a number of the guests had gathered for drinks and conversation. Crystal chandeliers were suspended from a 12-foot ceiling that was ringed with a deep crown molding. Over-sized paintings in elaborate gold frames lined the richly paneled walls. The myriad palatial adornments, admittedly beautiful, were almost oppressive in Nan's estimation. She mentally compared this house to other fine homes she had visited, such as Amy Huffton's Hill House in Corning which displayed its treasures in a tastefully subdued manner. This place, while impressive, was ostentatious in Nan's estimation, as was Penny herself.

"I've invited forty or so people who are discriminating lovers of poetry," Penny told Billy, indicating five rows of upholstered arm chairs. The chairs faced a raised platform bedecked with flowers and greenery and a strategically spotlighted podium where Billy would read his poetry. In one corner of the room, four string players were setting up their music stands.

"We'll have music and drinks for about a half-hour while people settle in," the hostess explained.

"Now, Nan and Alex, you might like to have a glass of champagne in the foyer while I help Billy prepare for his reading." She took Billy's arm and led him off toward the podium.

A waiter dutifully proffered a tray with flutes of bubbly to the dismissed pair.

"Okay, Nan. Here's the plan," Alex said as they wandered off together. "We'll mingle for a while, but when Billy starts to do his thing, I'm going to discretely disappear."

Before Nan could object, he went on: "You were unhappy with my helping the real Indian while I asked you to find the cigar store Indian. Now we're going to change off. I'd like you to stay close and keep an eye on Billy while I search the premises for Queen Catherine."

"But, what if there's trouble here? Are you carrying your phone so I can reach you? Will you actually answer the damned thing?"

"Yes, I have it. I'll set it on vibrate. I will answer your call."

"You're on, then. I don't mind at all sticking with Billy." Billy was a particularly striking figure thist evening in a black suit with a pale blue shirt that accentuated his dark good looks. Billy favored wing tip cordovans and they were shined to a mirror finish.

According to plan, Alex and Nan were their charming selves, meeting and greeting guests who were, at least, their peers. At the appointed hour Penny ascended the platform to introduce Billy. ting throng. He was greeted with generous applause. Nan moved forward to place herself as close as possible to the speaker while Alex faded toward the kitchen to await his moment.

Billy began by reading one of his best known poems, and within seconds had the audience in the palm of his hand. He's so good at this, Nan thought. She began to lose herself in the enjoyment of the moment, but remembered her assignment and let her eyes scan the room. Everyone seemed totally focused on the speaker.

Nothing dangerous is going to happen here tonight, Nan thought. She wondered if Alex would have any luck in his search.

After 45 minutes, Billy wrapped up his presentation. He had spoken of the Native Americans' reverence for nature but had diplomatically steered away from an mention of fracking or any other controversial subject. After the applause died down, Penny thanked him for the memorable evening.

"Mister Blackhorn has generously agreed to answer any questions you may have for him," she announced to the guests.

As Billy was amiably engaged in give and take with the audience, a commanding presence in vivid violet suddenly entered from the foyer – a tall, handsome, well-built woman with flashing blue eyes and an abundance of hair the color of buckwheat honey. She would have looked perfectly at home dressed as a Valkyrie in a Wagnerian opera. People could only stare as she swept into the drawing room as if driven by a strong wind. Penny hustled to greet or waylay the latecomer, as the occasion might demand.

"Good evening. I don't believe we've met."

"I am Sieglinde Larson," the Valkyrie trumpeted to Penny and the room at large. "Yah, I am Billy Blackhorn's wife." She aimed a brilliant Scandinavian smile at Billy.

Silence fell. All eyes went to the newcomer, and then swung back to gauge the reaction of the recipient of the smile.

Billy's composure broke only for an instant before he replied in a cordial voice, "Sieglinde! What a surprise!" He stepped down from the podium and strode swiftly toward her. He leaned in as if for an embrace, managing to get an arm around her to propel her back into the foyer. Nan, suddenly springing into action, was close at his heels.

Penny addressed her guests. "Let's give them a minute, shall we? I … I'm sure Billy will be back soon." She knew that all in Buffalo would soon be smirking about the untimely arrival of her illustrious guest's wife, whom no one knew existed. What in blazes was the woman doing here? Penny was flustered for one of the few times in her life.

"Why don't we all leave our seats now and enjoy a light supper in the dining room?" She led the way with as much aplomb as she could muster.

Meanwhile, in the foyer, Billy and Sieglinde were engaged in an emotional confrontation that Nan was unable to control, despite her much vaunted people skills.

"Why have you followed me here?" Billy demanded to know. "You're *not* my wife anymore. You have no right ..."

"I have a right to go anywhere I want, when I want," Sieglinde retorted. "Just who do you think you are, to question me?"

"You deliberately came here to embarrass me."

"Now let's remember we're guests in this house, Nan interjected. "Let's not make a scene."

"Making a scene is just what she intended, and she's succeeded," Billy told Nan. Then he turned to Sieglinde.

"You've had your neurotic fun. Now leave."

Sieglinde delivered another one of her broad smiles. "But this is a lovely party. I would like to stay and meet the other guests. I'm sure *they* would like to meet *me*."

Billy groaned and Nan punched her cell phone. She needed Alex now, if for no other reason than to help throw this woman out. She addressed Sieglinde again.

"I don't believe you want to discuss your family business in front of strangers. Why not arrange to meet later, somewhere else."

"Who are you?" Sieglinde interrupted with a frown.

Nan thought fast. Her old ploy might work. "I'm Nan Holloway from WLED-TV of the Southern Tier. I would be interested in interviewing you on my show."

She finally had Sieglinde's attention. "Really? I would like that. Let's set a date."

Billy relaxed visibly. He sent Nan a grateful glance.

"But right now, I would like to have something to eat," said Sieglinde. "I believe I heard the lady invite her guests into the dining room."

10

SINCE PENNY HAD opened the Sandberg residence to anyone who wanted to explore its artifact-crammed nooks and crannies, Alex was happy to know that his quest would be easy. He'd rubbed elbows with some of Buffalo's finer people until he'd had enough. An in-depth tour was definitely on the agenda of Corning's best detective. As Billy got underway with his presentation, Alex noted that the attendees were settling into the chairs closest to him and already listening intently. Good, he thought. When he slipped away, no one would miss him, and the rapt attention the guests afforded Billy would be a further smokescreen for a guy itching to discover the inner workings of Penny and Sam Sandberg's incredible house.

In the kitchen he had spotted a door which didn't seem to go anywhere. After opening it, he'd become aware that this hidden area was where the servants hustled their duties from floor to floor during the heyday of the indolent rich. Now Alex used his opportunity to slip inside and shut the door. Behind him. He found himself in a labyrinthine passage leading in all directions, laced with clever enclaves. The draped openings afforded a cloaked view of the first-floor rooms. Behind scrims, the servants could see the family, but could not be seen themselves.

He also found a stairway with generously wide steps leading to upper and lower floors. This is what he wanted, quick access to the upper floor, and also to the basement for accomplishing his clandestine mission. He quickly ascended to the second floor, passing by any number of elegant anterooms and bedrooms. His movements made no sound, thanks to the solid oak structure of the floor. He glimpsed a room with a messy bed, as though someone were using it. The detective didn't realize that his very passing by the door blinked a shadow into the room from the lighted corridor. In the room a set of eyes found him. He moved back to the stairs and descended to the lower area. Sam Sandberg's gaze followed him.

Meanwhile, at the reading, Penny had become restless despite her appreciation of Billy's poetic words. Scanning the room, she noticed that one particular guest was missing. She motioned for Ace, a minion she didn't really want mingling at the party, to come to her. He was temporarily stationed as a waiter, playing through the crowd with tidbits of finger food for guests, but on call in case she needed him.

"Yes, Missus Sandberg?"

"Ace, have you seen Alex Rayburn? He's the guy who brought Billy and that nosy Nan Holloway up from Elmira."

"Yeah, I remember him. I parked his car. He looked at me kinda funny."

"Well, find him and watch him."

"Yes, Ma'am."

Now, in the lower part of the house, Alex made his way through the basement to a giant metal door. A refrigeration unit? A vault? What is it?

The door mysteriously clicked and opened. Alex jumped aside, expecting someone to come up behind him. When he saw no one, he proceeded beyond the doors into a huge room crammed full of Indian artifacts.

"Whoa!" he said. "So this is ground zero."

He walked gingerly among the treasures within, guessing that Penny had collected them for years. The Queen Catherine statue was plainly visible, indicating if it had been added very recently. Awestruck, he circled around again to take it all in. But why had the door snapped open? Did he trip a device for automatic entry? What's this?

His glance caught the glint of a very shiny object. In fact, there were other glowing objects. He moved closer to discover several pure gold ingots. The bars were small, as ingots go, but there was a very large number of them. Holy crap! He barely had time to think before hearing a voice.

"Yes, Mister Rayburn. Pretty aren't they?"

Shocked, Alex turned 'round to the sight of a 9mm Glock in his face.

"What? Who are you?"

"I warn you. Don't move. I own this place, a place where you are presently trespassing."

"Oh, I, er …" Alex looked at the gun. "So, you're Penelope's husband?"

"Yes. And you were just going for a walk, right."

"In a way, yes."

"Be very careful… Alex, isn't it?"

"Yes… Sam, isn't it?"

"Now that we've met, you should remember your manners."

"I think my manners are no problem when compared to your wife's tendency toward larceny. And why the gold bars?

"You are very curious, Alex, but since you have minutes to live, I'll tell you. The gold is my department. The bars were, shall we say, borrowed from a repository near Fort Knox."

Minutes to live? Borrowed? Alex cogitated.

"I see. That inside job in Kentucky two years ago?"

"Yes," Sam said, with noticeable pride. "No one knows where the ingots are, nor will they ever. These are scheduled to go to the Seychelles tomorrow from your Ithaca airport. You have no idea how nice it is in the islands these days. If you've seen the Seychelles, you'll know why people want to go there. It's a paradise on earth, and there's no extradition treaty. All you need is money in the bank and the Seychellois are glad to have you. My partner and I have lately decided to go there and leave everything behind. Penny and I have raised our kids and I, for one, have no need of Buffalo winters anymore."

"What about your wife's penchant for all things Indian?"

Sam gave a short laugh. "She'll have to deal with that. We'll be divorcing shortly and I will be with my partner halfway 'round the world. She'll be happy here with her Indian trinkets and her boy toy, Phil Junior. She already has him ensconced in one of the bedrooms, but he's still weak after that unfortunate accident you precipitated."

"He shouldn't go around shooting at cars."

"Yes, that was a blunder. The odds were against him."

"You and your wife are quite a couple. You keep larceny in the family."

"We think so, even though we're calling it quits. It's an amicable split."

"What about your properties?"

"You should be more careful in your research, Mister Rayburn. Those properties have been signed over to our children and are ironclad. No one can take anything from them. They will one day be the happy recipients of the fruits of the fracking you and that Indian so thoroughly deplore."

At that moment there was a scuffle in the outer area. It was a man and a woman slipping and stumbling. The woman's chirping sounded familiar. It was Nan kicking and slapping at her assailant.

Ace dragged her in.

"You might want this one too, boss," Ace said, puffing to control the female.

"Well, Ms. Holloway. I might have known you'd be along. Welcome to the vault."

"You must be Sam Sandberg. Your health has certainly improved!" she snarled. Alex glared at her for getting caught.

"Just a ruse. I needed a smokescreen to finish off some other business. My health never was really bad," Sam grinned.

Seeing Ace, Alex said, "What about your lackeys, Ace here, and his brother? And what about that clown on the motorcycle? They might get mad at you for leaving."

Ace was emboldened. "Don't worry about it. We get paid ... a lot."

"My helpers will be well taken care of," Sam said.

"Humph, it looks like everybody's happy," Alex tried.

"Everybody except you two."

Nan looked pitifully at Alex. "Now what?" she whispered.

"Did you ask 'now what' Ms. Holloway?" Sam said menacingly.

Alex kicked himself for not realizing the gravitas of the situation. This guy meant business.

Sam ordered, "Ace. Get back upstairs. And you two interlopers - over here by the gold." He gestured with his gun.

Alex couldn't believe Sam would shoot them. Too messy for his style, yet he seemed ready to do it. Sam backed out of the vault area, outside the big steel doors.

"Tomorrow we will find the two of you in this place where you shouldn't have come. When you are discovered, we will tell the police that you were a victim of your own curiosity. The gold will, of course, be removed after you have suffocated."

At that moment, Sam punched the button on his remote control. The doors activated, Alex made a short lunge. The steel doors came shut with a bang and two well-intentioned citizens from the Southern Tier were left inside to ponder their fate.

Alex said, "Quick, before the lights go out. Look for a flashlight. I saw one somewhere!"

The mad scramble for a torch took a minute or two. At the last moment, Nan found one.

"Here. Oh, God! Now what?"

In semi-darkness, Alex found an electrical box cover and began his search for a screw driver, easy to find on a bench holding many diverse tools. He removed the cover and examined the wads of wiring inside.

"Do you have an idea?" Nan inquired.

"I do. You see, most people don't realize that in airtight chambers, like this vault, industry standards dictate that an escape mechanism has to be in place to prevent people from getting into trouble. I'm surprised that Sam doesn't know this. I'm glad he's not as smart as he thinks."

As Alex spoke, the removal system had begun to evacuate the air from the chamber to preserve Penny's collectibles. For antiques, the less oxygen, the better, and the two of them started to feel the change.

"Now all I have to do is figure out which wire – wait a minute. Well, looky here. This is better than I thought. This unit is equipped with a slide lever. I just have to pull this lever to the side and we should be all right."

"Go ahead. Try it," Nan urged.

"No. We have to wait a little while – let the house go to sleep. When we try it, we'll have to be ready to head out the basement door fast. I'm assuming the car is where Ace parked it. Let's sit here and wait."

Waiting was always difficult for Nan, especially in the dark. Alex put a comforting arm around her and pulled her close. "We'll be fine, cookie."

Nan tried valiantly to make conversation. "I overheard Ace tell his brother that the biker was brought here to recuperate. I'm hoping he's still incapacitated. I imagine the brothers have gone to their warehouse downtown by now. At least, I hope so."

"Me too," Alex agreed.

After a time, they imagined the house was quiet and all occupants might be sleeping. The air was getting hard to breathe as oxygen was being replaced by the carbon dioxide of their exhalations. Nan couldn't believe anyone would purposely kill someone for a few bars of gold and some useless relics. True, Penny seemed willing to keep her treasured pieces and ditch her husband, but what a desperate plan Sam had to leave the country with gold bars – government gold bars, to boot.

"Sam must have been planning this for a long time," Nan offered. "How could his partner and he live in luxury on Seychelles knowing what they'd done to two human beings – us," Nan fumed.

Alex had nothing to say except, "Honey, we're dealing with the human race." He looked at his watch. "It's time. Are you ready?"

"I'm ready. What shall we do about the statue of the Queen?"

"I think I can drag it out, but you should run ahead and get the trunk open. Maybe we can save it ourselves. I think there's enough room for most of it."

"I'm ready and willing to go," Nan stood up, stretched and did a little jog in place.

"You amaze me," Alex said. People think that a person your age shouldn't be able to do the things you do."

"And I was thinking you are rather exceptional for your age too, mister."

"I guess they don't know us, Cookie."

Alex gave the go-ahead. He knew that this spry woman in her seventies was ready to vacate the vault and fling herself out the basement door.

"Glad I took an aspirin. I'd hate to have a stroke halfway to the car," Nan muttered.

"Bite your tongue, sweet cheeks."

Alex took hold of the small lever and hoped he had identified it correctly. He said, "Ready? It's show time."

The air was getting really sparse as he pushed the lever sideways. Nothing happened. He gave Nan a worried look and pushed the lever again. This time it worked.

"I forgot," he admitted. "Sometimes you have to push these things twice."

"Thanks for the heart attack!" she chided.

Alex had given Nan a gold bar to hold as incontestable proof that Sam, putting on the Ritz in Buffalo, was the guilty one who made off with the repository loot in that famous Kentucky robbery. He would grab Nan's cell phone on the way back to Corning and give his cop friends in Buffalo the low down – that way, the two of them would be out of town and not have to answer delicate questions. The hoity-toity Buffalonians in the Delaware mansion would be summarily questioned and found with egg on their collective faces. He knew this whole affair would end well if he and Nan could just get to the car.

As the doors ground open they discovered that Sam had left the lights on in the basement area. Alex was relieved. Escape was better facilitated with light, and the two comrades carefully departed through the lower door with Queen Catherine in tow. Alex's car waited nearby.

As they neared the Jag, a figure uncoiled from the rear seat. Panic gripped Nan for a moment. before she recognized the figure. Billy!

The Indian stepped out. "Where have you two been? I've been asleep in the car waiting for you."

"God! Heart attack number two!" Nan exclaimed. "Boy, have we got a story for you!"

Alex approached. "Billy! Help me get this thing into the trunk."

In the Jaguar, the trunk was big enough to accommodate three-quarters of the statue; the rest could hang out. Nan coaxed Billy into the rear seat and threw the gold bar in beside him. She hopped in. Alex spun the tires in the driveway and squealed away into the very early morning. Soon after Alex's discussion on the phone with his friends at police headquarters, the fancy house would have cops filling the courtyard. But now, the detective aimed the car south on the Skyway and veered off toward the Southern Tier.

"It was a fine escape, Nancy Lou!"

"It got this girl's blood going, I'll say!"

"I'm still in the dark." Billy said. "What happened to you two? I couldn't find you anywhere, yet your car was still here."

"Patience, my Native friend. I'll fill you in," Nan said, as her face luxuriated in a moist, hot towel. "God bless this car!" she added. "Now, tell us what happened with you. And what about your wife, er, I mean, ex-wife."

"Well, after that ugly confrontation in the foyer, I escorted Sieglinde to the dining room and parked her in front of the steamship round at the buffet table. That woman has a prodigious appetite, and I figured that so long as I could keep her occupied with eating, she wouldn't be causing any more trouble."

"Did it work?" Nan remarked.

"Hell, no, it never does. But *your* ploy was brilliant!"

"You mean ..."

"Yes ... suggesting that interview you might do with her. Lord! She is a grandstander. You hit the nail on the head - it was just what she wanted. I went back to the foyer to thank you and couldn't find you. I suspected you'd gone looking for Alex so that we could leave before anything else uncomfortable happened. Then I heard a scuffle and your voice, Nan. I shouted down the hall but you were quite a distance away.

"I hurried toward you and saw the waiter with the mustache manhandling you, pushing you down the stairs and out of sight. Just as I arrived at the stairs, another lug, a big guy, jumped me from behind.

"Well, I'm pretty good in a fight, but it took me some time to subdue him. He got up and ran. By that time you'd been hauled downstairs. I looked around a little but couldn't find you."

"At that moment, my friend, there were steel doors between us. You couldn't have known," Alex interjected.

"I got the hell out of there, took my things and sort of hid in the Jag. When early morning came, I was about to get out of the car and see what I could do at the house when you came running up. Boy, was I glad to see you two!"

Nan filled Billy in on her nightmare in the vault with Alex. The three friends concluded that the best view of the house on Delaware Avenue was the one seen in the rear-view mirror. They were happy to have lived through the night.

"Pretty audacious – trying to suffocate us," she said.

"Yeah," Alex noted. "And it's kind of cold of Sam to vamoose leaving his wife behind. If he's able to get to the Ithaca airport he'll soon be sitting pretty in the Seychelles, leaving Penny to cope with the whole situation. She'll have to explain the questionable acquisitions in her vault, and then try to distance herself from Sam regarding the gold. Old Sam must be closer to crime than anyone knew. It must have taken a lot of moxie to pull off that theft at the Fort Knox gold depository. I think the cops can do their job now."

"The cops have to get on it before Sam gets out of town," Nan offered.

"Maybe we can help in some way. Put on your thinking cap, Nan. Meantime, I could use some coffee. How about you two?"

All were in agreement. Alex pulled in at a roadside 7-Eleven and exited the car. He used his phone to call the police as he walked toward the store. "Humph," Nan had to observe. "At least he has his cell phone. What a miracle!"

"Our gracious hosts will have some uninvited guests shortly," Billy surmised.

11

THE NEXT DAY, back in the comfort and relative safety of the Southern Tier, Nan and Alex sat dining at The Three Birds restaurant.

"What a pleasure to be back in the Crystal City after that ordeal," Nan said.

Corning's trendy eatery blossomed with special bouquets and white tablecloths. Patrons clinked glasses and conversed quietly. It was evening in the city; a cool breeze joined them through open doors and windows. Nan felt wonderful. Alex was glowing with talk about another caper done and gone. Nan raised her glass while asking a question to kill the evening's mood.

"I still wonder where that threatening note came from, the letter to Billy that started the whole thing."

"Let's just enjoy this meal, Mata Hari. Mmmm ..." Alex bit into his delicious rib cut lamb chop.

"Thank goodness that episode is over," Nan said.

"Let's hope, though you do have a point."

"What point?"

"The letter, dear, the letter," he dabbed his lips with his napkin. "Let's get with Billy again and see if anything new has developed. He's around the corner at the Radisson. A few of his friends came into town, so he's safe, at least, with them. Let's see if they want to come over here for a drink. Oh, darn. I left my phone at home."

"No kidding!" Nan gave him a knowing look "I'll call Billy. Somehow, I can't shake the feeling that Sieglinde's family had something to do with that note."

"The Larsons…could be," Alex said.

Nan's own phone suddenly surprised her. She punched the green button.

"Hello."

"Ms. Holloway?"

"Speaking."

"This is Captain Wilson at Buffalo police headquarters."

"Oh?"

"I've been trying to get Alex Rayburn on the phone. Is he anywhere nearby?"

"Yes. We seem to be joined at the hip lately. Hang on."

Nan gave an exasperated sigh. "It's for you, on *my* phone!"

This was a call Alex was expecting. Wilson proceeded to give him a thorough report on happenings after the house raid on Delaware Avenue.

As he suspected, it would be difficult to prosecute Penny, for her collection was all legal now. She could play dumb about the statue. After all, it was simply not there. True, she had to steer through the implications that her husband had illegal gold bars and but she insisted that she had no knowledge of their origin.

As for Penny, she was more concerned about having been married to a man who ditched her when the chips were down, an infuriating development, in her assessment. She was aflutter with reasons, alibis and other lies of convenience which would assure her of one fact: no one could succeed in taking Penny Parker Sandberg down. She would survive and carry on as usual, and probably have a better life enjoying the company of Phil, her biker friend. Maybe she could get on a bike herself, once in a while. Phil Jr. was on the mend, and life could change for the better. No one would ever know that it was Phil who took a shot at that troublesome Alex Rayburn. This overlooked fact could now be forgotten.

Goodbye to Sam, she thought. Her suspicions would continue about the relationship of Sam and Horace Poundworthy, wondering how Sam could fancy a guy so irritating. She had only met him once when Sam had pursued some shady acquisitions of his own. "Well, good riddance," she reiterated, convinced she would never see her husband again. She would retain her social status in Buffalo, truly all she cared about. This entire situation was the fault of a small town detective, his female friend, and an Indian who wrote poetry. To hell with them all!

Sam had quickly moved the gold from the vault and put it in the car for transport. He and the Billings brothers had headed out of town in different vehicles, Ace and Johnnie to the Sunset Drive house in Corning, Sam toward a motel in Ithaca. He was beginning to wonder if he and Horace should use the Ithaca airport at all. He had let that vital piece of information slip while holding Alex and Nan at gunpoint in the vault, never thinking they would escape. Surely they would have told told the cops by now. It might be better to use the second choice. He had other aircraft in other places.

But first he would pick up Horace in Ithaca. After that, the small runway at Costa's airfield, just outside of Corning in Painted Post, would be a better choice for their departure. Sam kept a twin- engine Cessna there for fun getaways, never imagining that he'd be using it to leave the country. It was a strong aircraft, parked in an unsuspecting airport in a small town. No one would put two and two together for quite some time. Meanwhile he and Horace would depart in style – if the plane would hold his chubby friend. Only he and Penny had any knowledge of the small plane. Yes, this was a better idea. Sam would soon meet up with his overweight partner to discuss their change of venue. It had to be done. They would be on their way to the Seychelles, where he had vacationed before and laid the groundwork for life after the United States. Sam's cellphone vibrated.

"Are you there?" said a husky voice.

"Yes, Horace ..."

"Don't say my name on the phone, for God's sake! It's the kind of name people remember."

"Okay, partner."

"Look, I hope you're on your way. Our time to get the hell outta here has come. Make it quick. I'm at the Budget Inn. I'll be watching for you."

"Okay. The cops have been to the house and I assume Penny is beside herself, but we gotta do what we gotta do. I'm on my way. There's a slight change of plans, but you'll like it." He went on explaining the necessity for changing the airport. "I'll be there soon. That punk detective made off with one of the gold bars so he could prove his case, but we'll be long gone before the law can make a move on us."

"Good to know." Horace said.

"We'll stop in Los Angeles to fuel up, then on to Hong Kong. You remember Chun Li – my Chinese contact?"

"Yes. Mister Evil himself."

"He'll change the gold into bank notes, and then it'll be smooth sailing to Seychelles. No one there will care about us – we'll just fade into the population and never come back. There's a restaurant by the ocean I want to buy."

"I hope you know what you're doing. You'll have a high profile. Somebody might want to get back at you – like the U.S. Government."

"I'll chance it," Sam said, with an attitude Horace had seen before. The fat man wanted to be left alone to live easy and eat his fill of island food. Horace recognized that trouble could be brewing between them.

Sam Sandberg looked at his Rolex and hung up. He was relieved that his partner of many years was now on board with the revised plan. No one on earth knew what their itinerary was. He reckoned they'd operate under the radar, literally, until it would be too late to catch them.

Horace Poundworthy sat on the edge of the bed and put down the hotel phone with a frown. He didn't like changes – like this switch to a different airfield, even a different plane! All because his long-time, much-trusted business associate, Sam Sandberg, had been sloppy and revealed too much information to that detective. Horace hated sloppiness. It frustrated him that Sam had overlooked the fact that all airtight vaults had an emergency lever to open the doors. Doesn't everybody know that? It was unforgivable. Subsequently, the detective and that TV woman escaped from their prison. This could be bad. More sloppiness.

Horace bemoaned these two notable loose ends – what were their names? Alex Rayburn and Nan Holloway. A rich detective with nothing to do but chase them, and a TV reporter who could further make his life difficult. Horace considered Alex and Nan to be dangerous to this plan with Sam Sandberg. Who knows what they might do? The sooner they got out of the U.S., the better, before Sam made any more blunders. But those two meddlers would have to be dealt with.

Budget Inn's finest bed was no match for Horace Poundworthy's bulk. The springs creaked and popped as he rose to pour himself a drink from a waiting bottle of Gilbey's. He hefted himself toward his favorite gin, which he always carried, causing even the floor boards to protest his weight. He must be sure to take a case of his gin in the plane with them. He assumed that the airplane could carry his 420 pounds, the gold, and his booze for the good living he was expecting. His custom-made suits would have to go, too, providing him with the slimming effect they were designed for. He wanted to look good in the islands for the many women available to a man of good taste. "A lot of man," he was fond of saying to those who were even slightly interested. The word "fat" was intolerable to him, and hearing it applied to himself utterly enraged him.

He reckoned he would go along with Sam's plan as far as it went. He too, could use a long vacation in the islands. Sam could stay forever running his little restaurant, and would probably have to. Horace would patronize the restaurant as just another big shot American with lots of ready cash. But he was formulating bigger and better plans for his share of the Hong Kong bank notes.

Meantime, he would assure that island idyll was not interrupted by the law. He would tie up those loose ends. He put his half-empty beaker of gin on the bedside table, eased his immense bottom onto the bed and poked a number into his cell phone.

"Ace Billings?"

Ace was cautious. "Yeah. Who're you?"

"This is Horace Poundworthy – you know, Sam Sandberg's partner?"

"Yeah, I know who you are."

"I wonder if you and your brother would be interested in a special job, my friend."

Nan and Alex, satisfied that the Buffalo police now had the situation well in hand – and unaware of any potential threats to themselves - continued to enjoy their evening at The Three Birds eatery. After a time, Billy Blackhorn and two of his anti-fracking colleagues from Pennsylvania joined them in the bar for an after-dinner drink. Nan sipped her Courvoisier cordial, while Alex opted for the Pleasant Valley Sherry Solera from Hammondsport. The Southern Finger Lakes area boasted many prize-winning wines and Alex was determined to promote them. Billy also went for the upstate wines and his two comrades did the same. The conversation was lively, but before long, their talk morphed into a detailed replay of their Buffalo adventure, discreetly editing out the encounter with Billy's ex-wife, Sieglinde Larson. Billy's friends were wide-eyed at the revelations.

After the two friends left to drive home, Billy lingered over his second glass of Taylor's Port.

"I asked them earlier if they had any idea who might have written that note to me." he said. "Unfortunately they had no knowledge of it. But they appointed themselves my bodyguards for my last engagement here – at Mansfield University. They insisted, and will get no flak from me. It will be good to have them along."

"I have a friend who's a newspaper editor near there," Nan piped up. "You remember, Alex – Gina and her friend, the former sheriff?"

"Yes, I remember," Alex said. "They helped us once before."

Nan continued, "I'll put them wise to the situation. Maybe they can be of some use."

"Sounds good," Billy agreed.

Alex said, "Good thinking, Nan."

Billy smiled his gratitude, "You both have taken very good care of me – and it's gotten you in terrible trouble, Peter Fenton too."

"Peter is okay now – not a serious concussion," Nan assured him.

"I'm glad of that! I am truly sorry I ever showed you that damned note, Nan, and got you and Alex so involved. It was cowardly."

"No way!" Nan objected. Alex added, "We're glad to be of service. But at this point, who do you think is responsible for sending it?"

Billy ran a hand through his thick, dark hair.

"At this point? After Sieglinde turned up? It had to be the Larsons. Maybe Sieglinde was in Corning and simply slipped into the Rockwell with it – like any other tourist. I hate to think she could be so vindictive."

"She struck me as being totally capable of it," Nan said. Then she suddenly remembered: "Oh my God! I offered her a spot on my show. Do you think she'd actually come here and take me up on it?"

"You can count on it," Billy declared.

Alex chuckled. "So, I might get to meet the legendary Ms. Larson?"

"You're in for quite a treat," Nan said, with a strong hint of irony.

Billy's eyes got a faraway look. "She is rather magnificent when she's angry, isn't she?"

12

SIEGLINDE LARSON WAS angry but not in the magnificent mode Billy grudgingly admired. She was angry with herself. Urged on by her father, who had checked Billy's website for his speaking itinerary, she had flown first to Corning, to deliver the threat in a plain brown envelope, and then drove a rental car to Buffalo. She checked into a hotel and, as her father had instructed, began preparations to crash the party at Sam and Penny Parker Sandberg's mansion to confront Billy, and let havoc reign.

"I'll stop that crazy Indian in his tracks once and for all," Nils Larsen had predicted. "If the letter doesn't shut him up, the scandal at Sandberg's will. The Buffalo media will pick up on the story and soon Mister Blackhorn will be disgraced and out of our lives forever."

Sieglinde was a dutiful daughter, and furthermore, she was still smarting from the fact that Billy had initiated the divorce with no attempt whatsoever to placate her or patch things up. He had, in a word, dumped her – for no good reason – and all her admittedly girlish dreams were dashed. So she had agreed to the plan. It would be, at least, a modicum of revenge for her and her family.

She had checked into the hotel in Buffalo, and spent the next day preparing for her appearance at Sandbergs. Those preparations included a shopping trip for a dramatic gown, and a visit to a day spa for a mini-makeover. Sieglinde knew she was a good-looking woman, but she wanted to be especially stunning for this event. When the time had come, she took a cab to the Sandberg's house, arranging to arrive late enough to make a grand entrance.

And she had! Her announcement of her identity had been received with shocked silence and all eyes had been on her.

But something happened when she saw Billy. He was as handsome as ever, even more attractive with the added sophistication and confidence of a seasoned performer. He was no longer a football star, but he was definitely a star. When he had called out her name and walked toward her, her heart had skipped a beat.

But she had remembered her mission – to embarrass her ex-husband and ruin his credibility. When finally he'd escorted her into the dining room, she had been proud to take his arm. People had clustered around them, but were less interested in what she had to say than to fawn on Billy. She had comforted herself with a hearty slab of beef until she saw Billy suddenly leave the room. Where was he going? She would find him.

When she reached the doorway and looked down the hall, she spotted Billy in what looked like a fistfight with some big bruiser. Billy knocked him down and the two men rushed off in different directions. What in the world was going on? Sieglinde sought out her hostess and related what she had seen. Mrs. Sandberg looked worried but told her that it was probably just "boys being boys." and not to worry.

Sieglinde returned to the buffet table, but the naughty fun of bad-mouthing Billy was over. She was surprised to find herself concerned about him. She loaded a plate with shrimp and settled onto a small settee to wait for Billy's return. The party drew to a close and Billy never reappeared.

Penny approached her. "Are you still here? May I call a cab for you? Billy evidently left without even saying goodbye – rude of him, I must say."

"Billy is never rude," Sieglinde responded. "I think something is wrong here."

"If there is, it's none of your business. You weren't even invited. You may wait in the vestibule for the taxi. Ace here will see to you." A tough-looking character with a big moustache pressured her out and into a cab

It was a bitter pill for Sieglinde to swallow. She'd gone to the party to insult Billy, but had ended up being insulted herself. Back in her hotel room, Sieglinde discarded her purple finery and stepped into the shower. She'd done all her father had asked of her, but she did not feel triumphant. She felt ashamed. Billy had made a great success of his life, if not in the way she had expected. And she had allowed her family, with their overwhelming desire for wealth and power, to influence her too greatly. She had read some of Billy's editorials, listened to his speeches, and had to admit that he made valid points about preserving the land. It was not all "tree-hugging crap" as her father called it. And heaven knows, the Larsons had enough money already without squabbling over a few pieces of land in North Dakota.

Sieglinde pulled on her satin pajamas and sighed deeply as she eased under the covers of the king-size bed. Seeing Billy again reminded her of their honeymoon – it had been heavenly. She and Billy had been so young when they married, with very different expectations for their life together. Had they given up too soon? Given another chance, she would try to be the sort of wife she should have been all along – kind, supportive and unselfish.

Now she lamented that she had delivered that threatening letter to Billy and gone on to confront him at Sandbergs. Why had she allowed her father to convince her to do such mean and stupid things! How could she ever make amends?

As she replayed the events of the evening in her mind, she remembered the TV woman in the foyer. Of course! She sat up and reached into her evening bag on the nightstand. There was the card! "Nan Holloway, WLED-TV." Yes! She would call Nan and get herself down to that TV station for an interview. She would say what needed to be said to get back in Billy's good graces, say whatever was necessary to rekindle their romance.

And she would give her father a big, fat piece of her mind about that letter. Yes!

In returning Queen Catherine to her proper pedestal at Smith's Cigar Store, Alex Rayburn instantly became hero of the hour, not only at the cigar store, but in the minds of the entire clientele, and then some. All the people of Market Street, merchants, visitors and even children raved about the big homecoming. As current owners, the Browns decided to throw a welcome home party at the store for the Queen which would be hosted by Barry Brown himself, with Alex and Nan as guests of honor. Most of the downtown bars and restaurants wanted to join in by providing food and drink; the mayor issued a proclamation declaring it Queen Catherine Day. Amy Huffton, Alex's ideal of beauteous womanhood and VP of Huffton Glass Company, naturally arranged a generous corporate contribution to help fund the festivities, which had burgeoned far beyond Barry's initial idea of a store party. Probably never in history had a cigar store Indian occasioned such a celebration.

Billy Blackhorn decided to extend his stay in Corning so he could attend the event. He offered to pen a poem in Queen Catherine's honor and read it in Centerway Square, just across from the tobacco store.

Nan did her part by lining up copious media coverage. She also made sure to invite Lydia Esterbrook. At first, Lydia wanted nothing more to do with the whole cigar store Indian fiasco – she still bore the bruises inflicted at her store by Ace Billings, delivered on behalf of Penelope Parker Sandberg. Penny had conveyed copious apologies to Lydia, but Lydia wasn't feeling receptive. Nan pointed out that Lydia would be given recognition for her role in tracking down the statue, and that it would be good publicity for Antiques Unlimited. Lydia acquiesced.

Nan also checked with Alice Fenton to see how her husband Peter was doing after that near concussion in front of Elmira's Park Church. He was out of the hospital and was left with only a colorful bruise to keep the injury vivid in his mind. Nan invited the Fentons to the Corning event, as well. She knew they would like to see Billy again.

It was promising to be a grand conclusion to the Queen Catherine caper, with thoughts swirling in Nan's head about writing a book about the story – if Alex didn't beat her to it. She had nothing to worry about. Alex couldn't care less. To him, the episode was over and good riddance to it.

Alex extended a special invitation to his street informant, Tommy Barber, to thank him for his information on some pretty desperate characters (of course, Tommy would have shown up anyway). He also asked Tommy to reprise his vigilance regarding the house on Sunset Drive. Something told Alex that the Billings boys were still around and had momentarily escaped scrutiny by the police.

Indeed, the Billings brothers were not entirely out of the picture. Horace Poundworthy had a plan to cover up what he always called "loose ends." He had managed to talk to Ace on the phone and ply him with money. Ace agreed, and things would get hot again for Alex and Nan.

When Nan Holloway has news, she likes to share it with her best friend, Gina De Vito. Gina had been a newspaper reporter for years and then, briefly, Nan's partner in a PR firm. She was now the editor of a small Pennsylvania weekly. Although Nan's recent adventure in Buffalo wasn't really fodder for Gina's paper, which concentrated on local happenings, she was bursting to tell her friend all about it.

The women met in their usual lunch spot, The Hand of Man in Owego, a gift shop *cum* cafe on the banks of the Susquehanna River. Over cocktails and quiche, Nan filled Gina in on recent events – Billy Blackhorn's disclosure of the letter warning him not to talk, the theft of the cigar store Indian, the attacks on Peter Fenton and Lydia Esterbrook.

"Good Lord! So many unrelated incidents!" Gina exclaimed. "Are they connected in *any* way?"

"It came together in Buffalo," said Nan. "At one of those elegant Delaware Avenue homes." She went on to relate all that occurred at the Sandberg mansion, including the terrifying prospect of suffocating in the airtight vault.

"My God! You were almost murdered!"

"You said it!" Nan agreed.

"So the ingenious Alex found a way out of your dilemma and has the bad guys on the run?" Gina summarized.

"Of course," Nan confirmed. "Although, who knows how it will end. We're wondering if the Buffalo police will be able to stop Sam Sandberg and his business partner before they take off with their loot."

Gina was astonished. "At least you two and your friend Billy are out of danger now."

"Yes. But Billy might still have some problems so long as he's speaking out about fracking. That's one reason I wanted to talk to you."

"Me? Why?" Gina asked.

"Well, it's Al we really need," Nan explained, referring to Gina's long-time gentleman friend and former county sheriff. "Billy will be visiting Mansfield University tomorrow to read his poetry, and he always includes a plea to preserve the environment. I don't suppose there will be any trouble on the campus, but maybe Al could put out the word ..."

"Consider it done!" Gina assured her. "You know Al likes to keep his hand in the law enforcement biz."

"That's great! I'll relax now," Nan replied. "Billy is going to stay around Corning till Saturday, when the Smiths, and practically the whole town, will be having a 'welcome back' celebration for the Queen Catherine statue. I hope you and Al will come."

"We wouldn't miss it!" Gina replied. "You can finally introduce me to the famous detective, I hope."

"Of course."

"I've been meaning to ask you, Nan. You and the area's most eligible bachelor have been seeing a lot of each other in rather dramatic circumstances. What's the story?"

"The story is, we're just friends."

"Earth to Holloway!" Gina chided. "Don't be coy with me, girl. I'm your best buddy. You can tell me. I won't print anything … yet."

"Well, Alex and I are *good* friends," Nan stated.

Gina backed up. "Well, all right. But inquiring minds want to know."

"Know what," Nan said.

Gina grinned mischievously. "Is Alex a good lover?"

Nan gulped and blushed furiously. "I have no idea."

Gina shook her head. "Deny, but I'm not convinced."

Nan had had enough. "Okay then. Alex is an incredible lover. Now, change the subject."

Gina looked at her old friend through narrowed eyes. "I can always tell when you're lying. You really *don't* know do you?"

Nan laughed. "You're incorrigible! Now, shall we split a slice of key lime pie?"

"Heck, no. I want my own slice!"

Nan wasn't seriously upset with Gina's teasing. She wondered herself about her relationship with Alex. She knew he enjoyed her company and valued their collaboration, but was there more?

Nan knew of Alex's devotion to Amy Huffton. The Rayburns and the Hufftons had been friendly since the Hufftons first introduced their glass company to the area decades ago. But Amy was at least 30 years younger than Alex. It might be a sort of father-daughter thing, she thought. There were any number of other women closer to his age who might be candidates for romantic affairs, and then there were Alex's occasional "dates" with men. Who knows? Was he just being clever? Elusive? Nan was undeniably attracted to him, but remained skeptical. She simply didn't know where his passions lay.

Perhaps it's better this way, she sighed. No complications.

13

TOMMY BARBER WASTED no time that evening reprising his role as informant for Alex. At the Sunset Drive house, trees and darkness hid the fact that Tommy was on the job. He wanted to do his best for his friend the detective, who relied on him for occasional information. For him it was fun to be watching and reporting around the Corning area. He also knew how much Alex paid.

Behind the Sunset Drive property he slithered here and there and successfully distracted the dog with tasty biscuits, which he knew beforehand would eliminate the barking problem. At times he looked squarely through the window into the face of Ace, who sat across from his brother at the kitchen table. They talked, he listened.

"Ace, who was that you talked to on the phone yesterday?" Johnnie inquired.

"It was Sam's partner, Horace Poundworthy. You know, the slob? We only saw him a couple of times in Buffalo. Since Sam and him ran off, I thought we wouldn't hear from them again."

"I remember. Boy, is he fat!"

"Smelly, too," Ace added.

Ace never wanted to tell Johnnie too much because he sometimes blabbed it at inopportune times. Johnnie wasn't going to like it, but Ace needed him for the job Poundworthy had discussed. Ace suddenly spoke in low tones making it impossible for Billy outside, to hear plainly. What he said shocked his younger brother.

"What!?" Johnnie was incredulous. "The fat guy wants us to …"

"Johnnie!" Ace warned. "Keep your voice down! You know this neighborhood! Sound travels! The windows are open."

"Oh, uh, yeah." Johnnie lowered his voice. "This is big," he whispered. "Are you gonna do it?"

Ace hesitated, but finally said, "Yeah. I'm gonna."

"Oh man! You sure, Ace?" Johnnie was scared.

"It'll be okay, little brother. It's only a matter of finding out when Rayburn and Holloway are alone. If they're in a crowd, we'll wait until they step away, or somethin'. It won't be hard. We just have to watch and fit into their life – they like to go places together. Holloway will slip up and say something on her dumb TV show."

"How do you know she'll slip?"

"She's a woman, ain't she?"

"Heh, heh! You're right, Ace."

Their low voices were starting to bug Tommie. He wanted to get everything they said, especially after hearing that part of the conversation which involved Alex and Nan. This was very important. It seemed the two of them were plotting some kind of revenge against two people he liked. He would try harder. He would stand closer.

Ace appeared at the window and slammed it shut. He turned the kitchen lights off and left Billy in the dark. Alex's slick informant got on his way quickly and called his boss. Naturally, he had to leave a message. Exasperated, Tommy lamented "He never answers his damn phone!"

Nan had hoped she wouldn't hear from Billy Blackhorn's drama queen of an ex-wife, but sure enough, a message from her was waiting for Nan at the station. Sieglinde was in Corning and eager to appear on her show "as soon as possible."

"Damn! Better get it over with." Nan checked her schedule of guests, did some fancy footwork, and made a spot for the big blonde. She returned the call.

"Miss Larson, I can fit you in tomorrow, but it will have to be brief at such short notice. I can give you ten minutes. Will that work for you?"

"Yes. I can say what I need to say in that time. Thank you very much."

"You understand that I will be interviewing you, asking questions – you won't be making a speech."

"Yes. But you must ask me the right questions."

The talk show host rolled her eyes. "We'll talk about it when you get to the station."

Nan was surprised when Sieglinde arrived for the show early the next morning. She wore little make-up and was dressed casually in a cornflower blue turtleneck sweater and black jeans. She looked … wholesome.

Sieglinde shook Nan's hand vigorously. "I'm so happy to have this opportunity," she said.

"My pleasure," Nan returned automatically. She ushered Sieglinde into the home-like set where the interview would take place: "Just like we're two friends having coffee," she explained. "Now let's sit down and chat about the topics we should cover. Perhaps you should tell me how you first met Billy."

"Yes, that would be a good place to start," Sieglinde agreed. "I want to talk about my family, too. My father. He has been bad, and he has involved me. I want to say I'm sorry to Billy in front of the camera."

Now Nan's attention was riveted on her subject.

"You're sorry? For what?"

"For threats my father has made against Billy over our land in North Dakota. Especially for the letter he told me to deliver, and the big fuss at the fancy house in Buffalo. I think I made a fool of myself, yes?"

"You were very – impressive," Nan hedged. "But are you saying it was you who left the letter for Billy at the Rockwell Museum?"

"I left the letter, but my father wrote it. And there is much more I will tell you when we talk … on the air."

And she did, ending with a sad-eyed plea for Billy to forgive her. "I would like us to be friends again, Billy, like we first were. Remember?"

Great theater! Nan had informed Billy that Sieglinde would be on the show, and knew that he would be watching. Would he accept Sieglinde's apology at face value? Or was it just a farce to entangle him in further trouble? Nan wondered. Sieglinde certainly seemed contrite.

Anyway, it was a good note on which to close the show.

"That concludes the excitement for this week. Tomorrow I'll be hiking in the beautiful Watkins Glen gorge with Corning's great detective, Alex Rayburn, to unwind from those recent hijinks in Buffalo And then I'll be attending a fabulous party in Corning's Centerway Square to celebrate the return of the Queen Catherine statue to Smith's Cigar Store. Try to make it to this historic event! Next week my special guest will be Barry Brown, owner of the statue. Be sure to join us. Till then, take care of yourself and be happy."

Nan hoped Alex had watched the show. She would love to know what he thought of Sieglinde's surprise apology and admission that she had planted the letter days ago at the Rockwell. She picked up her phone to call him, but quickly thought better of it. Why frustrate herself with a man who never answers his calls? They would talk tomorrow on their Watkins Glen outing.

14

UNBEKNOWN TO ALEX and Nan, Sam Sandberg and Horace Poundworthy were just finalizing their plan to make a clean getaway using Costa's small airport in Painted Post. The two crooks had run from the law before, so they knew that timing was everything. As yet, no one, including Penny Sandberg, knew where they were. Good thing, Sam reckoned. Penny would be busy in Buffalo repairing her social circle after she explained her actions to the police. She'll be all right, Sam thought. She can contrive a line of BS appropriate to any situation. Perhaps he'd get together with the old girl again some day.

The two aviators would show their flight plan to the ground controller at Costa's and be on their way. They would state that their intended destination as San Francisco, with a turn-around in a day or two. Only they knew that they would not be returning anytime soon. The alternate plan using this small airfield would confuse any entity of law enforcement that might become interested in their whereabouts.

After a fuel stop in San Francisco, their trek would become a blur as they crossed the Pacific, cloaked from the law, for points far away. They would dispense with the gold in Macao, outside of Hong Kong harbor, to a waiting Chun Li, the infamous Hong Kong banker whom Sam knew from past dealings. For a price, Chun Li would take care of the gold and make everything appear normal. The banker would have no trouble changing the raw gold for an electronic transfer to his bank in Kowloon. Sam and Horace would also be given papers that would give them *carte blanche* funding wherever they went. The bank in the Seychelles would already have the money in their account as they pulled in after their long flight. Things were going well. Sam was happy.

But best-laid plans do so often go awry.

The first part of their journey went smoothly, to San Francisco to refuel, and to refresh themselves for the night in the airport Sheraton Hotel. They had good food and good drink at a nearby steakhouse and laughed it up at the bar with two women. The women were ready for more, but Sam advised Horace that they must be fresh for their trip to Hawaii several long hours away. They were getting the idea that they had really made it this time, that nothing could stop them now. Morning would find them quickly out across the sea, hoping to make their next fueling stop brief. Satisfied smiles lit their faces as bedtime approached. Sam lay comfortably and pondered for a while. Horace slept.

When they took off the next day, the weather was bright and no storms were evident on the forecast screen. For miles and miles they continued to congratulate themselves for foiling the cops just by moving fast.

"Remember, Horace. Timing is everything," Sam remarked.

"You are so right, partner."

Unfortunately for Sam and Horace, when they stopped later in Honolulu for fueling, one of the airport workers noticed a gold bar lying on the ground near their damaged cargo compartment. Because of the weight of the gold, several bars had been bumping at the hatch near the plane's tail, and had, alas, bent the cargo door just enough to allow one bar to slip out into the open. Airport workers around the world had been alerted about the gold theft in last year's assault at the Fort Knox receiving area, so the classic law enforcement criteria was fresh in their minds – observe, observe, observe. Would the coincidence dash the plans of two nefarious characters who had only to clear the Honolulu fuel depot to affect a perfect getaway? The two malefactors watched helplessly from the cockpit windows when surprise registered on the face of a transportation agent standing nearby. He saw the gold, then looked at them. The serial numbers were examined by another agent standing by with his computer. It was over. The jig was up.

The numbers in the computer proved to be the same as those on the pilfered bars, and the two malefactors were ordered off the plane. Guns were drawn, additional agents came running. Sam and Horace were summarily arrested, their situation indefensible. All that was left for the two clever criminals was the gnashing of teeth and the summoning of Sam's lawyers to try to mitigate the undeniable. No more easy life for them. In the pleasant state of Hawaii, the road had suddenly ended.

Likewise, events back in The Southern Tier were going to change for Alex and Nan. It was unfortunate that Horace had succeeded in siccing the two Billings brothers on them as a consequence of their earlier meddling in Buffalo. Now, the piper must be paid. With a simple plan conjured up by Ace, the Billings brother's evil task would now move on inexorably toward a final chapter in the lives of a snoopy detective and nosy woman reporter.

As it happened, the brothers had tuned in to Nan's TV show to find out where she might be, and what she might do in the near future. They heard her say that she and Alex would take a day trip to the gorge in Watkins Glen to relax after a week of so much excitement. Still believing they would be well-paid by Horace, Ace and Johnnie quickly formulated their vengeful plan. The Watkins Glen gorge would do nicely to get Alex and Nan isolated and vulnerable and out in the open, Where the water has tumbled, and rock faces have been carved deep by a small unassuming stream of water splashing to and fro, downward through bedrock since before time began. The brothers would wait at the upper reaches of the rock walls, some spots three stories high, and use their best rifles to end this vexing problem once and for all. Johnnie would be high above on the southern side and Ace would be on the opposite side near the down-sloping Indian Trail. Surely, one of them would succeed in placing some bullet holes in their hapless victims with no one the wiser. Their getaway car would be at the restroom area at the top of the park, and after the shots, Ace would scurry across the highest bridge to join Johnnie. They would then abscond quickly on little-used back roads.

Yes, the gorge would be a good place to erase the detective and his woman from the earth as ordered by the fat man. Though this new *modus operandi* was not something they had ever anticipated, the promise of a big payment justified their desire to proceed. Ace's notion to retire in Mexico would now be possible with all of that beautiful American money to play with. South of the border, the brothers could live it up for years and years – no more petty deals in Buffalo, no more frigid winters and no more Penny Sandberg. This was serious business and they intended to make their mark for bragging rights later in the Mexican cantinas. It would be high-swagger for couple of two-bit hoodlums who, at this moment couldn't wait to get over to Watkins Glen, nestled in the hills surrounding Seneca Lake. To their minds, the placid lake would later belie the fact that a couple of gruesome murders had upset the pastoral tumbling of water through the rock face gorge.

In the morning of the appointed day, at the kitchen table on Sunset Drive, they got their rifles ready and talked. Through an open window, Tommy Barber watched and listened.

That same day Alex Rayburn awoke from a recurring dream. First he was running up to Buffalo and got shot at, and then he was battling the caretaker at the Billings Brothers' garage. Next came the dark, suffocating vault at Sandberg's house and their last-minute escape. It was a mental mixture of circumstances served up in his head, with a kinetic sense of urgency. However, upon finally opening his eyes, he felt the relief of knowing that it was all past history.

"Damn," he uttered, as he yawned himself awake. The clock face read 9:40 am.

He quickly rose from his bed and stretched. Nan was expecting him to arrive in a scant twenty minutes, so no shower today. Didn't matter. His nice hot shower last night would suffice.

He didn't need breakfast. They would visit McDonald's on the way out of town toward "the Glen" and be happy about it. One of his passions in life was fast food, despite its artery-closing properties. Though his morning "date" was more sensible regarding her diet, Nan would cave in to whatever Alex served up. Fast food, it is.

Alex wanted to show Nan what a true luxury car looked like. He brought out one of his favorites, a 1956 Lincoln Premier convertible, for the trip to Nan's apartment and a short spin north on route 14 to unwind at the Glen. Owing to the fact that Alex loved flashy colors, the paint was coral and white, magnificently trimmed with chrome. He knew that this archetypical Detroit masterpiece would blow Nan away, and would be just plain fun. The car's leather interior was also coral and white, and roomy enough to accommodate four people in the back seat. Gas mileage was no problem for Alex, even rated at 12 miles to the gallon. The soft ride bordered on obscene, with the usual accouterments added later by Alex himself.

His Lincoln was the epitome of a "boulevard car" with plenty of acceleration. When cruising through town, the vehicle always turned heads, being almost laughably long by today's standards. His mother once remarked, "It's wider than a dance hall." Modern parking spaces could not contain its length. He'd often joked that the car was longer than two Toyotas and a BMW. Alex thought that in a day or two, he would drive it to Centerway Square for the celebration of Queen Catherine's return to her pedestal in

Smith's Cigar Store where she could be properly admired instead of languishing in some dusty corner of Penny's vault.

Nan had no difficulty jumping out of bed. It was wonderful going around with a guy who could show her some fun and adventure, and she was pleased that Alex would be chauffeuring her today. He would probably bring a comfortable automobile from his stable of vintage cars. What a guy, she thought. Thinking about how settled she had become with her cozy apartment and the routine of her TV show. her situation began to show in great contrast to that of the detective, whose life careened along at a much faster pace. So of course it was stimulating to be romanced by a handsome rogue like Alex, and. she should count her blessings, she thought. Hmmm … romanced? Really?

She opened the door to her closet and chose her day's ensemble. Jeans, sneakers (that pretty pair with the pink soles), an appropriate shirt and a ditty hat, as she called it, to keep harmful rays off skin that seldom saw harsh sunlight. Also, a little SPF50 for her face. She didn't want to appear on her show looking like a lobster. People are too quick to let themselves get toasted, she knew. A TV host shouldn't go on the air with a bad sunburn.

Nan was always thinking. To her, a couple of things didn't add up, or maybe it was her imagination. Anyway, she would bring them up to Alex over breakfast. It was he who suggested a trip up north on Route 14 out of Horseheads for a relaxing day at the Watkins gorge, and she was grateful. It had been years since she had walked the gorge trail and the Indian trail above it. And the swimming pool at the top? If a person wanted to refresh themselves, and especially their kids, the pool beckoned. After the exhausting trip to the upper part of the park, one might stopl the Seneca Lodge for cocktails before taking the bus back down to the parking lot. Yes, this day would be enjoyable and relaxing – a distinct contrast to their Buffalo excursion.

The down-side of trekking up through the twisting trail was that people have been killed stepping off the trails and being otherwise foolhardy with their lives. Sometimes careless college kids would regret horsing around, turning their ankles or falling to their deaths in any number of places. Nan knew the danger because her friend Gina had taken a misstep once and slid off the upper Indian trail. She had to be rescued by none other than her significant other, Al, the former cop. Sometimes the scene that a person wants to photograph isn't worth stepping out on a precarious ledge or a steep rock face. Much less a selfie shot that no one really cares about receiving. Nan remembered some of the places were always wet and slippery; sneakers or tennis shoes were in order. She would be careful and not tempt fate.

Yes, it would be good to relax and enjoy the company of Alex Rayburn, the desire of all local womanhood. Who knows what that cool air circulating down through the gorge might bring on a warm early autumn day? Romantics come from all over the world to experience this natural wonder, carved out of the terrain by millennia of nothing more than running water. It would be a great day!

Alex picked Nan up at 10:00 am sharp. She floated out to meet him awestruck by the sight of the antique auto.

"Oh, my God! I've never seen anything like it," she stammered.

"It's just an old Lincoln," Alex offered with a modest smile.

Nan satisfied herself by deciding that Alex's Lincoln wasn't pink – it was "coral," thank goodness She was pretty sure she couldn't abide pink cars, though this color variation was close. She plopped into the generously proportioned seat. "This is like sitting at home in an overstuffed chair."

"It's got everything you need for creature comfort," the detective said.

"I'll say," Nan remarked as she glanced into the glove compartment mirror. "How many cars do you have?"

"As many as the garage will hold – about 22 I think."

Nan was pondering the rent of her apartment, quietly comparing her funding with Alex's. How nice to be so wealthy.

Yes, it was "old money" but Alex had made a lot of it on his own. He also had a philanthropist's heart, being well-known for giving sums away to good causes. He even conjured up reasons to give his informant, Tommy Barber, cash from time to time. At this comfortable moment, Alex and Nan were not aware that Tommy was calling Alex's phone again.

"Oh, hell! Why do I try?"

Tommy's desperation was real. Alex and Nan were in danger; he could be holding the key to life or death. He had tried to walk quickly up to Alex's house in the early hours, but no dice. The man had already left the scene in Tommy's idea of a ridiculous car, akin to a giant bottle of Pepto Bismal. He watched helplessly while the Lincoln moved out of sight down the hill. What now? He quickly raced downhill thinking Alex would go to his office/apartment on Market Street, but again, no luck. Where had he gone? How could he let Alex know what the brothers talked about in their kitchen? He could only hope that Alex was keen sighted enough to anticipate trouble, which, as a detective of some repute, he should certainly be expecting anyway.

"Why does that man even have a phone?" Tommy moaned aloud.

But now on the road, trouble was the farthest thing from Alex's mind. The buffeting breezes swirled around him and Nan, with an old original-equipment VCR tape deck playing a sonorous group of opera arias. They added magical moments to a journey in a car more like an apartment living room than a moving vehicle. The day was bright and mild, though a trifle cool for top-down traveling.

"Are you comfortable, sweetness?" Alex inquired.

"Are you kidding? I need more of this, much more."

"I've been thinking."

"Oh? Nan wondered. "Not too hard, I trust."

"Let us remain on guard, for a while." His old detective instincts had kicked in, even on this happy excursion.

"Why's that?" Nan said, practically cooing, face to the sun. "The Queen Catherine case might be considered resolved by now."

"Well, remember, Ace and his brother escaped from the police. They could be up to something. Maybe I'm just being paranoid, but that's how I think."

"I would imagine they're lying low somewhere," Nan said, reassuringly.

"Loose ends always bug me. Just stay on guard for a few days, okay?"

"Whatever you say, detective."

The sun was now behind them as they turned north. Indeed, it was a perfect day for motoring through New York State. The Southern Tier had become a destination for retired persons, despite the fact that winters are sometimes harsh. Retirees who choose to be in this part of the state say that this area beats places that have crocodiles on the lawn, insufferable heat, wilting humidity and roaches the size of small birds – and they fly! Palmetto bugs, mosquitoes and termites are never seen, (well, termites once in a while), however, in general, the warm summers and sparkling autumns seem to outweigh the intolerable deep snows, sometimes experienced here, in a locale which is well able to cope with it.

Nan put her head back and closed her eyes. It seemed like heaven to her.

15

SPLASHES OF SUNLIGHT from between groves of trees intermittently lighted the car in fine pastel as they descended from the last traffic light at the top of the hill to the one in the village at the bottom. All the way down the hill, the grand vision of Seneca Lake stretched toward the horizon and appeared to go upward, a celebrated illusion known well to the local citizenry. The long hill downward provided a view, not only of where the lake was bounded now, but also of where its edge had been thousands of years before. Off to the right toward Montour Falls, Nan noticed the long area of reeds and bulrushes showing where the lake boundary was located back when ancient glaciers dug out the original lake bed. She noticed a farm with a white house and silos a distance up the hill on the other side of the waters, looking like it had been purposely placed there for viewing. Just another agreeable piece of the welcoming scene, Nan pondered. So far, there was absolutely nothing wrong with this splendid day.

Once in the valley, about a mile forward on the main drag, a glance to the left showed the entrance to a magnificent cathedral of rock walls and pedestrian walkways. A driveway led into the parking area and onto the smooth, time-worn stone of the gorge trail.

"Oh. What a wonderful sight," she repeated, having said it many times before.

"I'm with you – a perfect place to relax for the day," Alex returned.

"After the gorge walk, I'd like go to Famous Brands and check out the latest deals."

"Sure, Cookie. This is our day to take it easy," Alex replied. "I'll pick up some jeans, too."

Before long they pulled into the lower parking lot to exit the car. The staging area for walking tours was located just before the arched opening of the cave-like entrance. Alex put the car near the creek wall, built to support the parking level. Nan popped out and stretched her legs. "Look at those rock walls! They seem to go upward vertically, and then curve out over us. Another illusion?"

"Yes. I believe they are straight up. But they do seem to bend forward," he agreed.

"They won't drop rocks on us, will they," Nan worried (she really knew better).

"No. The rangers keep a close watch on the walls. A few rocks may fall in spring, but they are constantly observed for public safety."

To visitors who frequent the town, Watkins Glen had never seen a more perfect day. Warm in the sun, cool in the shade, with low humidity. Nan was already feeling her vitality quotient increase. She wanted to get started into the gorge – to hike up the bedrock walkways as they ascended beside the creek about two miles to the top. She was eager to reach the place where the water from the creek caused a small waterfall to tumble over the trail. Standing behind the waterfall gave one a feeling of wholesome cleanliness, and would cool a visitor with a gentle mist on hot summer days.

"Oh, Alex, thanks for coming up with this wonderful idea. Each time I've been here in the past seems to be eclipsed by the next time. It's a great way to forget all that's happened."

"I couldn't agree more, Nan. It's been rough."

Alex delighted in seeing her comfortable and happy. She had been through a lot for an elegant, modern woman unaccustomed to the dangerous pursuits involved in the detective's life. In future days he would see to it that she did more exercising – maybe with him at a fitness club in Corning. No one can deny the value in that, he thought, as he used his trained eye to admire her curves and general good looks. This was a fine woman.

"People have tried to climb these walls and some have actually made it to the Indian trail, just over the top," Alex told her. "Of course, some have *not* made it. Usually some college kids with more brawn than brains find a way to misstep and skid down the rocks with painful results."

He continued. "When I've come here in times past, I favored going all the way to the headwaters of the creek and climbing the steps to the upper trail. Then I could join the Indian trail, which bought me back to the beginning, but high above the gorge along the northern face. From up there, I could glance down at the deepness of the gorge and be amazed by it all. The trail runs along the top of the north edge, and will bring us back to where we started."

"Yes, I remember it well," she said, not needing the explanation.

"It's a gentler way to descend to the parking lot at the bottom. Are you game to try the entire walk?"

"Are you kidding? Of course!"

Alex offered his arm, and away they went. As they entered the dark of the cave opening, he pulled her off to one side.

"Here. Take this. I'm glad you didn't leave your shoulder bag in the car. I want you to stash this away."

She saw the small gun he kept in his ankle holster. She stared in disbelief, but, trusting him always, she reluctantly took it in hand. The derringer was his buffer against unexpected emergencies, and he reckoned that it might show under his cuff. It would be hard to explain.

"What if the rangers find out about it?"

"It's okay, Nan. Would I lead you astray?" he smiled impishly. "It's totally harmless with the safety lever in the on position. See here? Just snap this off and the weapon becomes ready to use." Hidden temporarily in the cave entrance, he gave her a quick tutorial on the gun's operation and had her point it a time or two. "See? Harmless, with the safety on."

"I'll take your word for it! So it can't go off?"

"Not if the safety lever remains on."

Nan fretted. "I don't think this is a good idea."

"Take it easy. You'll never know it's there, Nan."

Her face maintained an uneasy look of disapproval as they emerged from the entrance cave to the first bridge. She experienced a slight wobble looking off the deep side, which had a stunning view of the valley beyond the parking lot. It only added to her concern about the gun. She continued to look disapprovingly at Alex.

The high stone bridge transported them across the creek to the south side of the bubbling waters. Beside the trail, the rock walls went up dizzyingly, with the top edges hardly visible.

"I hope no one saw me pointing that thing."

"Don't worry, I checked the other hikers. No one saw you."

Occasionally the path narrowed, so that visitors had to travel single file. The creek's altitude increased imperceptibly with the accompanying walkway hugging its waters. Bedrock sculpted since time began spun the water to and fro in a maelstrom of whirlpools and falls. Anyone losing his balance and falling would surely regret hitting the hard rock surface in the disorienting slosh. The view became more spectacular by the moment, and mildly frightening.

The Billings brothers were also in attendance today. The wayward siblings were already high along the upper edges of the gorge stationed on opposite sides, signaling across the space to each other. Ace was on the Indian trail on the north face and Johnny was across from him along a rough trail used mainly by workers and rangers. The terrain was more difficult for Johnny, shifting carefully among the leaning pine trees. He was along the ragged edge and shimmied himself into a perfect spot for a downward shot.

The brothers had excellent rifles – very accurate, with long-range scopes. They were able to observe both sides of the creek as visitors shifted from one side to the other. This way, the two rascals were sure to see their quarry plainly, no matter where they were or when they crossed. Either one of the brothers would be able to take them out easily.

The stage was set for the undoing of Alex Rayburn and Nan Holloway, two intrepid individuals currently a thorn in the side of Horace Poundworthy and Sam Sandberg. The brothers were eager to get their shots off, hurry to the upper parking lot near the swimming pool, and get the hell out of there. They looked forward to the big payoff Horace had promised. They hunkered down on either side just beyond the small waterfall currently splashing over their two potential victims below.

Alex had coaxed Nan under the little waterfall until she cleared the other side. He usually got the heebie-jeebies, as he called it, when there were too many people on the gorge trail. It made him feel as if someone – him – might possibly be brushed off the traveled surface and deposited in the swirling waters of the creek, especially where the trail narrowed under this misty waterfall. Today was exceptional in that the usual crowds were not bothersome, and actually rather sparse.

A moment later they had come into range of the brothers and their high-powered rifles. Nan stopped to lean on the wall and study the rock strata. Alex admired her curiosity as she tried to name the wildflowers. A shot split the day.

"Holy crap!" Alex shouted, watching a bullet ping off the rocks very close to Nan.

"What …?" Nan squeaked.

"Nan! Move it! Come towards me!" Alex yelled.

She did just that, as another bullet hit the wall close to him. He judged from the angle of impact that the shots had come from somewhere above. He scanned the wall and saw the glint off a rifle's chrome trim on the opposite side.

"We're under attack!" he told her. "Some madman's shooting at us!"

Overhearing Alex's panicked tone, nearby hikers began to fill the air with screams and shouts. Though there were not a lot of people on the trail this day, there were enough to cause a mini-stampede. Everyone had suddenly realized that they were out in the open.

"Get yourself under cover!" Alex ordered.

All who were near enough to hear him shuffled quickly toward the next grotto, where safety seemed attainable. A young couple rushed dangerously close to the edge, while another hiker lost her footing and fell into Alex's arms. One elderly man hurried as best he could with his walking stick and made it. All arrived safely within the grotto, still wondering if the gunshots were real.

Alex, in predictable fashion, prepared to rush headlong into the problem. He knew that a person running side to side could usually avoid getting shot by a long-range rifle. The distance would be too great for fast refocusing. He spotted a slope under the gunman's position on the opposite wall and told Nan to hang tight. She was now in the grotto with the others and was, for the moment, safe.

"What are you going to do?" she asked apprehensively.

"I'm going to cross the stream and scale that spot over there, to the right. I'll come up under the shooter," he huffed. "I'll be close to the wall on his side. He won't be able to see me."

"No, for God's sake! Are you mad? There may be a shooter on this side, too. He'll see you going up the hill."

"I have to take that chance!" Alex asserted.

He rudely dismissed Nan's concern. "I doubt there's two."

"Damn you, Alex! Listen to reason for a change!" she spouted.

"No! Gotta go!" He surprised her with a fat kiss and stalked off. At this moment, she was dazzled and mystified. Alex? Kissed her?

He could see the opposite-side shooter. But could he get there? He hoped someone with a cell phone had tipped off the ranger station down at the parking lot. Surely they would come on like gangbusters.

He wasn't convinced, but Nan's theory might be right – a shooter on this side, too? Didn't matter. He was going, and that was that.

"No!" Nan exclaimed helplessly, as he moved away, toward a narrow part of the creek.

Everyone watched when he crossed to the other side. Johnny was ready to pick off anyone who tried to help, though they wouldn't be the main target. He kept his rifle trained on Alex who had suddenly appeared beyond the creek's racing waters. "Heh, heh. Rayburn, you're toast." he muttered. Johnny was almost giddy when he realized that Alex would easily be in his sights when he started his climb. Alex was out in the open now, and couldn't zigzag on the hillside as he had been doing. Johnny knew that if he allowed Alex to get to the top of the opposite side, his brother would be in danger. He carefully lined up his sight with Alex's back. This was going to work. They would soon be rich and in another country. He changed positions and smiled as he began to squeeze the trigger.

"Men!" Nan muttered in disgust to a woman beside her. "Why do they never listen?"

She fumbled around in her bag for her cell phone. She was sure she had it with her. Where was it? She turned her bag upside down and watched as Alex's gun fell out.

Mouth open, she finally felt the gravity of the situation. "Oh, God, no! How's he going to …?"

The past few months with Alex had made a different woman of her. No more Miss Priss, no more caution when the chips were down. She looked at Alex beginning his journey up the hill and made a decision. He needed his gun.

Meanwhile Johnny pulled his trigger with disappointing results. His gun sights were set too far to the right, making his aim slightly off. He had pumped off a shot toward Alex but it went wide left. It struck a rock near the climber, who gnashed his teeth in defiance.

"Dammit!" he muttered. "She was right! Gotta climb faster."

Ace looked at Johnny and wondered what he was shooting at. He glanced below, but couldn't see his side of the ravine very well. That damned kid – shooting at anybody! He re-cocked his gun and waited to see if anyone ran out of the grotto. Fortuitous for Alex, Ace was reloading his rifle and missed his athletic leap over the stream. Ace was not yet aware of his own jeopardy, and the inescapable force named Alex Rayburn moving up the hill under him.

On the other side, Johnny reckoned he could compensate for his badly sighted muzzle by moving his body a little to the left. He shuffled around again to make himself comfortable and heard an ominous cracking sound. He thought nothing of it as he again got ready to fire.

In a moment, there was shudder under him. The slant of the trees on the rim increased, imperceptibly at first, then steepened their angle, leaning more and more ominously as the ground moved under Johnny.

"Oh, no! Oh, no!" Johnny screamed, as the edge of the rock wall tilted precipitously. The shifting earth relaxed under Johnny and began a slow, inexorable slide forward. He reached for the root of a tree but missed it by a fraction. He slipped over the edge of the cliff just forward of the loosened rocks and debris. From behind, irreversible destruction chased him to the bottom trail.

"No, no! Ace! Ace!"

Ace looked across the chasm and saw the terrain shifting under his brother. The walls in this part of the gorge were roughly a hundred feet high on both sides, but were soon to be slightly lower in one spot. Johnny had crawled too far out to execute his last shot at Alex. His face showed terror as he fell downward to his doom, in front of a massive segment of the upper cliff coming on like a freight train. He hit the walking trail with a vengeance, followed by tons of rock and debris crushing him brutally into the surface. The group ducking out of the way in the grotto coughed and hacked amid dust and falling trees, but again considered themselves lucky. The thundering roar was heard in echo, all the way to the ranger station at the base of the hill. The mass of rock, earth and trees drove Johnny's body into the rock trail without pity.

"No, Johnnie!" Ace bellowed. Nan heard him.

"I knew it!" she thought. "I knew there was a second shooter!"

She quickly ran through massive amounts of debris and water to reach the other side of the creek, wondering if there was anything she could do to help Alex, about halfway up the slope. From above, his "Good crap!" had echoed after the calamity and gave her a wry moment.

Ace stared mournfully at the catastrophe and sat down. There was his brother, buried under the tons of earth and rock. He felt a great sadness for Johnny, a kid he had belittled and laughed at all through high school. Now he was gone. Ace hung his head. His eyes filled with tears.

But as he was looking into the maw, he spotted Alex Rayburn on his way up the hill below him. Ace's sorrow turned to fury. He blamed Rayburn and that woman for all the troubles that had befallen him and his brother since those few days in Buffalo. He made himself ready to watch until Rayburn poked his head over the edge of the ridge. He would sit and wait. Soon there would be no Rayburn, and the woman could go to hell.

Nan looked up at Alex and wished him luck. She said a prayer to God, a personage she didn't usually acknowledge. Alex was near the top. What could she do but pray? She tried to think of what could be done this late in the game. In a gesture of support, she started up the hill, knowing she couldn't make it.

Alex, meanwhile, had reached the top. He cautiously peered over the edge.

"Good afternoon, Mister Rayburn," Ace spat angrily. "Come on up and meet your end."

Alex was puffing for breath as he hoisted himself over the ridge and rose shakily to a standing position. Exhaustion claimed him, and he lowered himself to sit on a fallen tree. Breathing in fits and starts, he spoke.

"Come on, Ace. Give it up. There's no place you can go."

Ace was grimly amused. "Oh, I think I can make it to the car before anyone gets here, old man. First I'm going to kill you for messing up my life and Johnny's."

"It wasn't me. You did it to yourself."

Ace brought the butt of his rifle across Alex's face. The detective, with all energy spent, rolled off the tree dangerously near the cliff edge and stayed down.

"Don't tell me what I did! You shouldn't have meddled!"

Alex recovered a bit. "Still, you could have done better – with your brother."

"Shut up! Don't say that!"

"Look Ace. I'm sorry about Johnny. But it was nature that took his life."

"I said shut up, damn you!" Ace stared and went quiet.

A great foreboding struck Alex. He couldn't see any way out of this. He felt oddly happy that he'd split the family fortune up with his lawyers, in case he might finally find himself in some inescapable situation: The Orchestra of the Southern Finger Lakes; Smile Train, to change the lives of children born with problems; the Cancer Society, in honor of his dad; and Nan, who could now take it easy and stay away from guys like him. At least she was safe on the trail below. It had been a good life, he thought, and the Christian in him said, "You'll be all right." He prepared himself for the worst.

Ace raised his weapon to do it quickly. He had to get moving. Further conversation with this Rayburn guy would only make him feel his own pain more. He cocked and pointed his rifle.

"Good-bye, Rayburn. I hope you go to hell!"

Alex closed his eyes tightly. No going back now, he thought. He wished to heaven he could pull his one-shot ankle gun from Nan's bag and save his life one more time. He remembered Duce, his special Seneca friend, whose justification for eminent demise was: "It's a nice day to die." Typical Indian wisdom, he reckoned, as he sighed, looked down and relaxed. He gave it up, and suddenly felt his age.

Behind him, a gunshot split the air.

"Holy mackerel!" he shouted.

A bullet whizzed over him and passed cleanly through Ace's right deltoid muscle. Blood splattered a tree adjacent to Ace's shoulder and the pain was apparent on his face. His rifle flew out of his hands and dropped close to Alex, who quickly scrambled to retrieve it.

"Oh! Damn! Son of a bitch!" Ace said, falling back.

Nan stood up from her crouching position off the edge of the hill having clawed her way up the slope behind him and said, "Take that, you rat!" Her trembling hands now held Alex's smoking gun.

He spun around and saw the woman who had tried very much to nail Ace in the heart.

"Nan! What … how?"

"That's all the climbing I'm going to do for the rest of my life!" she said, breathless. "Hey, he's getting away!"

"It's okay. We have no need to shoot him again. He won't get far. By now the rangers are all over the park. They'll get him, I guarantee." Then, with a catch in his voice, Alex said, "I've never been so happy to see you."

She righted herself after the climb, threw the pistol down and went to his side.

"Are you all right?" she panted. "Your face is bleeding!"

"Yeah, I'm okay. You saved my life!" Alex breathed

"Whew! That was close. I've never shot a gun in my life."

"For this, you'll get a Girl Scout merit badge!"

She pulled the kerchief from her neck, wiped the blood from his right temple and helped him stand. A light rain began to tap against the leaves underfoot and the day went suddenly dark.

"We should find shelter. Let's get you up to the ranger station beside the snack bar," she ordered. "Can you walk?"

"Yes, Nancy Lou. I can walk," he replied, still dazzled by this woman of many surprises. He wouldn't have dreamed this in a million years. She wouldn't have either.

They could see Ace a distance away crossing the upper bridge and running hard for his car. In a moment, he disappeared.

16

AS A NORMALLY optimistic person, and a strong one, Penelope Parker Sandberg had been certain she could survive the Queen Catherine debacle and her husband's "disappearance" with her reputation and social position intact. But mere hours after the news that Sam Sandberg and Horace Poundworthy had been apprehended in Honolulu with the Fort Knox loot, everything changed.

First there was a phone call from the president of the library board, assuring Penny that they appreciated all her contributions over the years, but under the circumstances, he must ask for her resignation from the board "just for appearances' sake." Two similar calls followed. Penny terminated the last call without even waiting for the caller to finish. What good would it do? She quickly assessed that her life as a pillar of the Buffalo cultural community was over. Now what?

She would still be a wealthy woman: the house and other properties had been put in her name. But she would be living on Delaware Avenue in splendid isolation. The important people of the city would no longer flock to her parties nor invite her to theirs. And there would never be a Penelope Parker Sandberg wing of the Buffalo Museum. The carefully collected treasures were now nothing more than tawdry evidence of a rich woman's whim.

Penny resisted the impulse to break down and sob. She was totally devastated, but she was tough. She would somehow find a way to enjoy the rest of her life. A plan began to take form.

Phil Junior was malingering. His injuries, less serious than they had first appeared, were healing nicely, but he was in no hurry to leave the sanctuary of the luxurious bedroom in the Sandberg mansion. He liked having his meals brought to his bedside by the cute maid, and the great selection of videos he could watch and games he could play. Why give all this up to resume his duties?

He also rather enjoyed being fussed over by Penny. She would visit him through the day to arrange his pillows and brush the hair off his forehead, and even give him a back rub with that nice-smelling oil. So when she suddenly burst into his room, he welcomed her with a big goofy smile.

"Vacation's over!" she announced, and yanked his covers off. "Get up! Get out of bed. You're fine."

Phil was aghast. "What's wrong? What's going on?"

"Move! Take a shower and get dressed. We're going shopping," she barked.

"Shopping? What for? Why the hurry?" Phil, clad only in his skivvies, cowered as he mde his way toward the bathroom.

Penny softened and called after him. "Don't worry, Junior. You're going to love this shopping spree!"

It was the day of the "Welcome Back, Queen Catherine" celebration in Corning's Centerway Square. Purveyors of food and drink, and vendors of hastily devised Queen Catherine souvenirs, circled the town's main meeting place. Centerway Square is a brick-lined plaza right in the middle of the Gaffer District – the main merchandising section of town - an appropriate title, "gaffer" meaning "gather," and a title given to a glass gatherer in the industry. Throughout the summer, entertainment emanated nightly from the bandstand, which was off to the side of the public area. A community band or some rock group might be wailing away most any weekend. Numerous tables and chairs were available for amblers who wanted to sit and linger. The now-famous wooden queen had been gently spruced up and carried across the street from Smith's Cigar Store to the bandstand in the square, where a spotlight bathed her in a golden glow. A Seneca troupe had traveled from Salamanca to perform some appropriate native dances in her honor. The Senecas had never approved of such effigies used in cigar stores, but as Alex's late friend Duce would say, "That was then, this is now."

A crowd had gathered around the bandstand as Billy Blackhorn began to read his special tribute poem:

"... *Catherine, loyal daughter of her people,*
Strong and loving sister, honored mother,
Whose wise hand forever guides us,
legendary leader ..."

Close at Billy's side was his once and future wife, the radiant Sieglinde. The couple had reconciled and were acting like infatuated teenagers, Alex noted with some cynicism. Granted, Sieglinde was a stunner and seemed truly contrite for her part in her family's malignant machinations, but could two such strong personalities possibly coexist in the long run?

Nan, so skeptical about her own personal relationships, was a sentimentalist to the end when it came to other people's situations. "They make the most beautiful couple, don't you think? I'm so glad they got back together. It's a really good ending to their story."

Alex observed sagely, "It's hardly over. There will have to be a lot of compromising along the way if their future is to be a happy one."

"Well, of course," Nan conceded with a pout. "But I still think it's wonderful the way things turned out." She was beaming with the excitement of the celebration, the exhilaration of their recent adventures, and the fact that Alex had his arm around her – in public!

"What's next on the agenda?" she inquired.

"Don't know," Alex said, smiling "We'll think of something."

"Things do seem to come up!" she laughed.

Nan seated Alex at one of the tables on the bricked tarmac beside the bandstand and drifted off to find her camera crew. People were passing by, eating and laughing in this small upstate city that makes any excuse to get downtown and have fun. Cited in travel magazines, the Crystal City is known as a place to "get your groove on." Today's festivities would be repeated on the "News at Ten" on WLED-TV, with many visuals featuring the effervescent Nan Holloway narrating the action for eager audiences. Friends from the cigar store popped by and sat with Alex to get the lowdown on his Buffalo hijinks. Of course he faked embarrassment. He was just relieved to know that all of the characters recently paraded through his life were finally safe from that Buffalo madness. It was indeed a day for celebration.

After a time, Nan reappeared at his table and plopped herself down. "Whew! What fun! Top Brass is going to play – they usually perform the big band sounds you like."

"Wonderful! I'm really *in the mood*," he quipped.

In a moment, the band opened with "String of Pearls," followed by "Stella By Starlight." Although they were both a bit stiff from climbing the slope after Ace Billings, Alex was on the verge of asking Nan to dance. The roar of exhaust pipes suddenly interrupted the music.

Alex's hair stood on end when two motorcycles rumbled into the square and pulled up at the bandstand right beside him. The riders pumped the engines deafeningly to gain everyone's attention. On the seats of the two new glossy red and silver machines, two figures in matching outfits commanded the scene. They killed their engines and parked the vehicles. One of the riders rushed onto the bandstand and grabbed the microphone from the startled vocalist. Everyone wondered if this might be part of the entertainment. The interloper pulled her helmet off and introduced herself.

"Hello everyone! I'm Penny Parker Sandberg. I've come from Buffalo to help you celebrate!" The puzzled audience fell silent. Alex and Nan were open-mouthed with astonishment.

"I can't believe my eyes – or ears," Nan croaked. "The nerve of that woman!"

"I am here on a special mission," Penny continued. The people began murmuring – most of them had read the account of the Catherine theft in *The Leader*, or watched the story on WLED-TV. They knew the details of the past weekend, and that the statue had been found in the Sandberg mansion. Penny raised her hand to silence them.

"I had no knowledge that the thieves had hidden the statue among the other Native American artifacts in my collection. My friend and yours, Lydia Esterbrook of Antiques Unlimited is here ... I see you, Lydia." Penny waved gaily to a white-faced Lydia, who responded by choking on her green tea smoothie.

"Lydia can vouch for my absolute insistence on proper provenance. And now Queen Catherine is on display here where she belongs. No harm done." Penny smiled broadly at the confused crowd.

"No one's buying this, are they?" Nan fumed.

Alex guffawed. "This beats all!"

He turned his attention to the other rider as he removed his helmet. Could this be the Neanderthal who had taken a shot at him on the way to Buffalo – the one whom Sam Sandberg had referred to as Penny's "boy toy?" Alex, fresh from three near-death experiences, felt a rush of fury. He couldn't prove it, but he'd still like to give that shooter a good going-over.

Penny announced triumphantly, "Now to make amends to this community and to the Browns, I wish to say that I'm donating my entire collection, my *priceless* collection, to your Rockwell Museum, right here in Corning."

This brought a gasp and a hush from onlookers. All who heard it were bewildered, including Alex and Nan.

"Wow. She certainly has chutzpah," Alex said.

"*That* is hardly the word!" Nan steamed.

Penny continued. "And I do this in honor of Mr. Billy Blackhorn, the great Native American poet. I hope the museum will consider naming my donation, "The Blackhorn Collection." Penny gestured toward the thoroughly outraged Billy, who could only cave in and smile.

Sieglinde, who didn't know the whole story, began to clap and cheer as only a former college cheerleader might do. Others joined in, and soon there was an eruption of raucous applause.

"Penny can't do that!" Nan objected. "There's a protocol to follow. The museum might not want to accept the stuff."

She was drowned out by the crowd and the roar of the motorcycles preparing to depart.

"Alex! You're not going to let them get away!" Nan tugged frantically at his sleeve.

Alex, who just minutes ago had considered beating Phil Jr. to a pulp, laughed.

"Yes. Yes I am. If Junior is willing to live out his life as Penny's lap dog, I figure that's punishment enough for both of them!"

Nan raised her hands in a gesture of defeat and joined his laughter. "You're right!"

Alex's phone rang. Nan was amazed. "Again my ears hear the impossible. You've actually got your phone with you."

"I always have it with me," he lied, with a grin. "I just now turned it on."

Alex said hello.

"Mr. Rayburn! I finally got you. Tommy Barber here."

"Tommy, my man. How are you?"

"Better'n you, if you don't get outta there quick!"

"What? What do you mean?"

"I was trying to get you!"

"Sorry. My phone was off."

Tommy was breathless. "I was just up to that house on Sunset. That Ace guy was talkin' to somebody on the phone in his kitchen. He's comin' after you down in the Square. He's got a rifle!"

"No, I've got his rifle. I took it away from him ..." Tommy cut him off.

"I'm tellin' you, damn it! He's got a rifle!"

"Another rifle? Good crap! Where are you, Tommy?"

Nan's ears perked up.

"I'll be down at the square in about a half an hour," Tommy said.

"Okay. See you then."

"I'm not kiddin'. Get outta there, Mr. Rayburn!"

Alex hung up. Nan saw something in his face she didn't usually see – fear.

"Everything all right?" she inquired.

"No. Not really." A number of things were bothering him. First, why would Ace, who so fortunately had evaded capture for a second time, still be hanging around the area? And then, why would Ace keep coming at him? Thirdly, what about his wound?

"Come on, tell me," Nan prodded.

"It's nothing. Tommy was just telling me he'd be here shortly."

"For now, I'll believe you," she chided.

"Don't worry."

How could Ace come after him in the heart of town? And with a rifle. A handgun would be more easily cloaked. What was he planning? Did Tommy hear it correctly?

The eastern and western sides of the square have old, ornate buildings five stories high, brick, with terra cotta insets. At the top of the western building, the old Baron Steuben hotel displays a fifth story deck, a leftover from the now defunct Starlight Room. The building also has a bunker in the basement used as a regional office for the FBI. Alex had this in mind and decided to tell Tommy to tip them off should there be trouble. He would return to his keen-eyed vigilance and tell Nan as little as possible. He was sure Ace wanted to settle the score with him, not Nan. Ominous thoughts ran amok through his head. He was all eyes, mentally checking everything in the immediate surroundings. He purposely stepped off to the side of the crowd to let Ace see him easily, and to protect the public if Ace fired at him.

Ace, not up to date on the news, was still hopeful of reaping the reward from Horace Poundworthy, and the thought of Alex Rayburn escaping from him made him crazy. He would snuff him out one way or another for killing his brother Johnny, ignoring the fact that Johnny had brought it on himself by crawling a bit too far out while stalking Alex in the Watkins Glen gorge. He would get him this time with a new plan. Even if he got caught, Rayburn would be gone. But he would make a clever escape after assaulting the detective. He had his rifle in a guitar case, just like in the old days of prohibition. He was pleased with himself. This was going to work.

Ace was a bit bolder than he should have been. He planned to get lunch just like anybody else in the ground floor restaurant across from the cigar store, and just observe the crowd through the windows. He was unaware of the lower level offices of the FBI in the same building, but sometimes being blissfully ignorant gets the job done. He was relaxed in the Old World Cafe, knowing that all he had to do now was get to the top of the building near the roof and fire from the deck. The fifth floor patio wasn't hard to get to – he'd explored it before and knew that the elevator went straight to it. It was an area not in use anymore after the Starlight had gone bust. The place would suit him well for hastening Alex Rayburn's final moments.

Ace also relied on the fact that nothing desperate ever happens in Corning – everyone has a casual attitude toward life in general, and, when there is an event in the square, the cops are often nowhere to be seen. There are no beat cops anymore to worry about.

He took lunch with his violin case at his feet. The soup was beef Stroganoff – something to warm his insides before he did his work. Besides, he liked looking at the waitresses. Cute girls from the Corning Community College. Always a pleasure.

Patrons talked in low tones throughout the quaint eatery. Outside the leaded windows, an occasional flash of Nan Holloway or Alex Rayburn would pass in the crowd. He sat sipping his soup and thought again of his brother. Too bad about Johnny. Had he ever really been the kind of brother Johnny could look up to? Not really. He punished himself in reminiscing about their fractious childhood, but kept a vigil at the windows. He stole another look out through the crowd, growing in number and realized he'd have to be dead-on with his aim, lest he waste ammo on pedestrians. Anyhow, he would get Rayburn this time without fail. After the attempt, before anyone could react to his presence, he'd be off. He'd use the stairs instead of the elevator, then head out the back door, into the parking garage. Once in his car, he would be too difficult to find in traffic.

Ace finished his soup and paid the girl he thought was cutest. In a moment, he walked around the elevator tower inside the building and pushed the up button. His shoulder still hurt where Nan's bullet had gone cleanly through his muscle, but determination filled his mind. He would tell Horace Poundworthy what it took to eliminate this detective. And maybe he could lobby for a few more bucks, now that Johnny was dead.

17

THE CELEBRATION IN Centerway Square was in full swing. The community band was playing John Phillip Sousa's patriotic marches, and the general public was in great abundance. Food vendors had set up beyond the clock tower to accommodate visitors from the glass museum who had learned of the event and were spilling off the walking bridge from the city's north side. A couple of bicycle cops came by and chatted up tourists who mostly needed the rest rooms. Billy Blackhorn and Sieglinde were facing a small crowd growing by the minute, which seemed to want Billy to continue with some more of his poetic creations. Alex had been sitting, but was up walking around, and Nan was busily giving orders to TV camera crews.

It was indeed a proper gathering for an icon displayed in the cigar store for many, many years. The Browns kept their cigar store open, but came to the door many times to observe the lively happenings across Market Street. The Square was today's big destination. Everyone had a smile. Alex hoped it would stay that way.

High above, where no one was looking, Ace attached the sight to his rifle. Alex, at the same time, was carefully looking through every facet of the event's layout and as yet, had seen nothing. He took the optimistic route. Surely Tommy had heard wrong when he was outside the house on Sunset.

Tommy Barber finally arrived. He moved cautiously alongside the bank building opposite the old hotel. He, too, was watching keenly for any sign of Ace. There were no really good places for Ace to be skulking, he thought. He spotted Alex and circled around to his location.

"Mister Rayburn!"

"Oh, hello Tommy. Thanks for your message, but I haven't seen Ace yet. Are you sure you heard it correctly?"

"Yes! There is no doubt he plans to do something. Maybe you should announce that you had to leave for some reason. Maybe he'd go away. After all, it's you he wants."

"That's why I'm standing over here by the clock tower. I might be able to use it as a shield and still be away from the crowd a bit."

"Well, okay. But I think you should get outta here."

As they talked, a large man lumbered near him. He bumped Alex causing him to move sharply sideways. At that propitious moment, a bullet cracked deafeningly through the square and landed next to his feet. "Yikes!"

"I told you!" Tommy cried out. Alex again used his accustomed expletive, "Good crap!"

At first, no one could tell where the shot came from. One of the cops looked up and saw the shooter pull back.

"Up there!" he directed.

Ace cursed himself at having missed his nemesis again. Nobody heard him when he shouted into the air. "What does it take to kill this guy?" He took two more shots, then wiped the rifle clean of fingerprints and dropped it on the floor boards. He leaped towards the patio door and flew down the stairs two at a time, figuring he could always get another weapon. His new mission was to get downstairs to the side door utility closet before the cops could plot their course through the building. He knew they would try to use the stairs, as well as the elevator, to trap him. After his sizzling run downward, Ace found the small closet near the ground floor exit. When the city cops rumbled past him, he heard the FBI agents join them from the basement. They formulated a plan as they hurried by him. "Oh God! The FBI, too?" Ace lamented, overhearing the men talk.

Tommy had been given orders to roust out the FBI men and was on his way, without knowing that the agents were already climbing the stairs. Mayhem was everywhere. Each of the cops who had decided to use the elevator yanked open his holster and grabbed his police special at virtually the same moment. The cops who had taken the stairs had already made it to the third floor landing and were heading upward.

In seconds, the elevator doors popped open at the fifth floor level and all agents reconvened at the old restaurant. With stealth, they swept the area outside on the deck to no avail, then turned inward.

They moved near the stairwell realizing that precious time was favoring the escaping shooter.

The rifle was found. The search continued inside the former hotel.

Below, Ace became giddy with escape fever when he heard the stairwell go quiet. Things were sufficiently calm; he peeked out. He suddenly darted from the side exit, across the alley to the parking garage and into his vehicle, poised for takeoff. In a moment, he exited the garage gate in his car and pulled away from the scene slowly, so as not to draw attention. His shoulder wound was killing him. He motored carefully, easing himself along Tioga Avenue toward the east end of town.

"Ha! Damned fools," he sneered, making his way beyond the melee. But his arrogance was short-lived when he spied Alex Rayburn watching him. He pushed desperate words through his teeth.

"Dammit, dammit!"

Confusion continued in the square. The crowd ran in every direction, some across the street to the cigar store.

"What the hell happened?" proprietor Barry Brown demanded.

A patron spoke in short breaths. "A shooter! Someone was shooting!"

"Wow!" he said, excitedly, rubbernecking from his doorway. "Glad I'm not over there."

Alex called on his quick wits to come up a solution, as the city cops and the FBI were clearing the upper floors in sad ignorance of the facts. Like gangbusters they continued their sweep of nooks and crannies and restrooms, convinced that the shooter was still in the building, but Alex knew better. Of course Ace would have a good plan of escape once he got to his car. Alex kept adjusting his own options. What now? He thought.

In his car, Ace was angered to know he'd failed again to pick off his sworn enemy. But there would be other times, he reckoned. "I'll get that guy if it's the last thing I do." He would return someday to finish the job, he thought. But for now it was time to get away.

Alex was standing near Nan, who was cowering behind a patrol car.

"Get in," he ordered the surprised woman.

"What?"

"Get the hell in, Nan!"

"Oh God!" she said, following the command.

Alex hit the ignition switch and the prowl car roared to life.

"What are you going to do?" Nan stammered.

"Hang on, Nancy Lou!" he barked. "This might be fun!"

Nearby, two cops standing by their car saw what was happening and jumped into the chase. Alex was known to them so they weren't exactly upset. But they figured they ought to know where he was going with the car. Must be important.

Alex tore off after Ace who was driving a vehicle not really up to the task. He rattled and banged on the omnipresent potholes on Tioga Avenue but managed to pull away from Alex. Knowing the police vehicle had a superior motor, Alex pushed the accelerator to the floor.

"Oh, no! Not again!" Nan howled, recalling an earlier chase.

By the time Ace made it to the Denison Parkway interchange, the traffic light favored him. He crossed the parkway and split off to the left, charging down Park Avenue with a vengeance. He ignored the dangerous speed; Alex, behind him slowed to consider the other traffic in the area. Ace crept away from him and shot down a side alley, which led into Denison Park.

Alex had seen Ace turn left up ahead. He turned left himself on another entrance to the park, drove in and looked to his right. He connected with Ace momentarily, coming up right beside him on his immediate left. Ace showed his teeth to Nan through the side glass as they ended up about a foot from each other. The accompanying police charged up from the rear. Ace was frantic.

The escapee then turned near the reflecting pool to go around it. Alex raced with Ace directly beside him as they tore down the park's curving road surface until Alex forced Ace to bear sideways across the lawn.

They both missed a giant willow tree. Alex bumped Ace abruptly with his car's right side. Nan winced as Ace went immediately to the right and plunged headlong into the spring-fed pool with exceptional speed. The water blasted fifty feet into the air before the hapless Ace finally slowed to a stop in the water. Nan had watched the reflecting pool come closer in a hurry, and put her hands over her eyes. Alex pulled up before hitting the water in a brakes-locked, four-wheel skid.

"Oh, my God!" Nan managed to squeak.

Alex caught his breath and said, "It's okay, now. He's not going anywhere."

After a minute, Ace dragged himself out of the water and the cops read him his rights. Alex was told to take the squad car back to Centerway Square with the order: "And go straight there!"

Frazzled, Nan tried to compose herself and wondered what she'd say on camera for WLED.

"Damn! Alex, what an afternoon!"

"As usual, Cookie," he smiled.

18

THE GUNSHOTS AND subsequent arrival of police, followed by the frantic search for the shooter and flurried departure of official vehicles, had drawn even more people into Centerway Square. By the time Alex returned with the car he'd purloined, the mayor had already announced from the stage that the danger was past and festivities should resume. Top Brass had taken to the bandstand again and was playing their popular repertoire.

While Alex was debriefed by the authorities, Nan rounded up her crew and delivered her first-hand report on the chase and apprehension of one Ace Billings, the villain who had been involved in the theft of the Queen Catherine effigy and two attempts on the life of local detective, Alex Rayburn. She tried to find Alex for comment, but he had retreated to the depths of Smith's Cigar Store. Barry Brown presented him with his favorite Fuente, Opus X cigar and insisted he stay and burn it to a nub. After twenty minutes of serious puffing, and banter with some specific cronies, Alex finally relaxed.

In a while, the setting sun flashed red hues in great profusion off the western side of the Centerway walking bridge. Street lamps twinkled on. Alex figured Nan would have wrapped up her on-camera reporting by now. He could easily find her across the street in the waning crowd. A few people wanted to hurry home in time for the six o'clock news and see themselves on TV. The remaining crowd seemed to want to stay forever.

Nan had called the station to get her story cued up for broadcast and considered her work finished for the day. She was wearing a bright yellow jacket, easy enough for Alex to spot, and was standing near the band stand, moving slightly to the beat of the music, head upraised. Looking for me, no doubt, Alex thought. He could see the adrenaline was wearing off and she appeared just a bit weary. Well, no wonder. Why had he pulled her into the police car with him - hadn't she been through enough at the Watkins gorge? He realized it had become a reflex for him to include her in the action, whether it made sense or not.

"Hey, beautiful. How about a dance?" he asked.

"Oh, Alex! Where did you disappear to? I was hoping to interview you."

"And I was hoping not to be interviewed," he replied smoothly. He held out his arms. "Dance?"

"I'd love to," she glowed.

Her spirits seemed to revive as they moved in sync to a few measures of Cole Porter's "Night and Day."

"Of course, you're a marvelous dancer," she observed. Was there anything this man didn't do well?

"I try," said Alex, and spun her around with precision. She laughed and settled into his arms, her head resting on his shoulder.

"I like this," she cooed "This is the safest I've felt since getting dragged down to the vault in Buffalo."

"I've put you in a lot of danger," Alex acknowledged. "Perhaps it's too much ..."

"Oh, no!" Nan pulled away and looked up at him. "You know I hate being left behind!"

"So you do, bless you. And I like having you with me." They resumed the dance. Alex held her close. Yes, he liked having her with him. He liked the fact that she followed him, trusted him, through all their adventures and misadventures. And she had saved his life.

He pulled her closer and whispered in her ear. "Nan."

"Hmm?"

"Have you ever thought of taking our partnership to the next level?"

Nan froze. She couldn't believe it. Was this Alex? Actually wanting a commitment? And what sort of commitment? Each of them had lived alone too long to be interested in marriage. An affair? That would be much more in keeping with Alex Rayburn's reputation as the consummate bachelor and man-about-town. Her heart was fluttering wildly.

"Yes, I've thought about it," she admitted.

"And ..."

"I think it's a bad idea."

Alex pulled back. He was stunned, but was loathe to show it. In his many past associations with women, he had never met with refusal. And this was Nan, *his* Nan.

"Why?" he wanted to know. He was aware that she cared about him - he couldn't be mistaken about that.

"Well, Alex, as it is, we have a very special...relationship. I don't fancy being just another scalp on your belt."

Alex opened his jacket and glanced down at his ostrich leather belt. "Look. No scalps. That would be your friend Billy Blackhorn. No notches, either."

"That bit of ethnic humor isn't worthy of you, Alex," Nan said. "But you know what I mean. I don't want to be known as just the latest in your long line of conquests."

He slowed their dance to a halt. "Come on, Nan. It's not like that. *I'm* not like that."

"People already think ..."

"What do you care what people think? And what people?" Alex was getting annoyed.

"Well, Gina ..."

"What does Gina think?"

"She asked me if you were good in bed," Nan blurted out.

"And what did you say?"

"I said you were incredible." Nan blushed furiously.

Alex laughed, breaking the tension. "Well, you were right!"

Nan shook her head. "You're incorrigible!"

"That, too." Alex took her hand. "Forget it. I took you by surprise. Let's just dance."

Nan resumed her place in his arms, although less comfortably. What was he thinking? What did he really want? Had she jumped to conclusions, made a fool of herself, ruined everything?

Alex held her carefully. What had possessed him? He had embarrassed Nan and himself. Next time, if there were a next time, he would... she would ... He stopped dancing.

"Nan. After all the excitement this afternoon, I think we could use a drink."

"Yes, please." She was relieved. "And dinner?"

"Of course. The Three Birds?"

"Lead on. I'll follow you anywhere," she assured him.

Some day, you will, Alex decided. Someday you will..